ADVANCE PRAISE

Sleuth Slayer is a sly and witty mystery that's populated with memorable characters. The book is entertaining, intelligent, and a fun read.

-Barbara Quinn
Publisher & Managing Editor
The Rose & Thorn Ezine

The Burtons have a real gift for storytelling and this book is compelling and engrossing. It's kind of like they used a time travel machine to go back and create an alternate reality. It's also a hell of a lot of fun. If you want to spend a really nice afternoon, kick back with this book. I hope to see more of Davitt and more from the Burtons. Seek this book out, you won't be sorry.

-Jon Jordan, *Crimespree* magazine

This is an interesting concept and formed an excellent basis for the well-developed plot with characters who are skillfully portrayed. It is an involving story, well-written with an unusually different perpetrator with a motive that one would never guess. RECOMMENDED.

-*I Love A Mystery* newsletter

Someone is murdering mystery writers on the West Coast. You'd expect mystery authors, steeped in arcane and unusual ways to off their enemies would solve this mighty quick. Not so; turns out crime authors panic just like ordinary citizens. "Good God, Guy, this is absolute murder!"

-Carl Brookins, author of *Bloody Halls,*
wherein murder stalks the halls of
academe

Sleuth Slayer does its own game of grip, release, grip, release, on and on until you think you'll scream. Or did you scream? It gives readers a Gordian knot, a rat's nest, that is *today!* Witty and wild it squeezes us by the throat – but just enough to keep us breathing - in this masterful tale of death and corruption. Bouquets of cilantro give enough heat to burn your insides, as Burton and Burton twirl to their own "My Fair Google" and pollute with words as games that infuse your mind. I love to read and write about murderous murder; right now I cannot decide which is best in *Sleuth Slayer*, the evil within, or the word play that tickles the reader to *death.* Perhaps it's the artful combination of the two? Tell me! oh yes, please *do* tell me and keep me from my own murderous discontent!

-Babs Lakey, suspense writer and founder of
Futures Mystery Magazine

Sleuth Slayer

Jeffrey B. Burton
Bruce W. Burton

Pocol Press

POCOL PRESS
Published in the United States of America
by Pocol Press
6023 Pocol Drive
Clifton, VA 20124
www.pocolpress.com

Publisher's Cataloguing-in-Publication

Burton, Jeffrey B.

   Sleuth slayer / Jeffrey B. Burton, Bruce W. Burton.
   – 1st ed. – Clifton, VA : Pocol Press, 2008.

      p. ; cm.

      ISBN: 978-1-929763-32-0

      1. Authors--Fiction. 2. Detective and mystery
   stories--American authors--Fiction. 3. Mystery fiction.
   I. Bruce W. Burton. II. Title.

   PS3602.U786 S54 2008
   813.6–dc22   0805

ACKNOWLEDGEMENTS

Jeff would like to acknowledge his wife, Cindy (for her unconditional belief in him); his daughter, Maddie Rose (for letting him know—in no uncertain terms—exactly how square he truly is); Eric Braun Photography (for making him look less frumpy); and the wait staff at Moose Country (for generously over-serving him whenever he suffers from writer's block).

Bruce acknowledges Marlyse Ferguson Burton.

DEDICATION

Wilhelmina (Minnie) Burton, 1908—1992.

"I have always had an idea that I would have made a
highly efficient criminal."

-Sir Arthur Conan Doyle

Prologue

The woman's voice was silken. Her soothing tones carried images of soft summer nights spent drifting absently on lazy porch swings. "You've had an extraordinary rock climb today, Dr. Janikowski, all the way up here on the Eiger's North Face, all by yourself. You're simply parched, aren't you? Perhaps I can get you a big glass of water, Dr. Janikowski."

Her tapered fingers lovingly stroked Janikowski's brow as he drained the large tumblerful. "It's going down smooth and clear, isn't it? The best water you've ever had. It soothes, Dr. Janikowski, soothes every pore in your body. So refreshing, so very refreshing.

"So you don't believe in hypnotism, Dr. Janikowski? A 'dark art' you mumbled. You may be right, Dr. Janikowski. In fact, I know you're right. My gracious, you've just completed a full hour on the Stairmaster, Doctor, and now you're very, very thirsty aren't you. Dying of thirst I believe the cliché goes. Why don't you let me pour you a big glass of cool water? Here you are. Down the hatch, Doctor."

When he'd finished she took the glass and said softly while slowly refilling it, "Heavens, Dr. Janikowski, you look flushed today. You put in such long hours here in the surgery, so much pressure. So much tension. Perhaps you could use a big glass of water? Yes, take a moment to relax, and have some cooling water. See, I've poured you one. Here we go. Bottoms up. That's the way, Doctor.

"The power of suggestion is a mighty tool, Dr. Janikowski, you'd agree with me on that wouldn't you, knowing how dearly the two of us now love, and trust each other? You know what I heard, Doctor? I once heard a person would never carry out under hypnotic suggestion that which they would not normally do. But speaking rhetorically, Dr. Janikowski, don't you think hypnosis can accelerate what a person normally does—longs to do—wishes to do all the time? Dream-fulfillment in a sense?

"My gracious it's so hot, I've never known the Mojave to be so scorching this time of year. Isn't the heat terrible? Is the awful dryness of this place getting to you, too, Dr. Janikowski? You're totally parched...I know what, a big glass of water would really hit the spot, Doctor. Here you are, now don't sip it too slowly to enjoy. And we've plenty more where that came from.

"An excellent example of hypnosis, Dr. Janikowski, might be that of...well, say for instance...an alcoholic. A person already disposed to imbibing if you will. Someone whose friends and family and even his medical colleagues would never suspect a thing if, say an accident, or something untoward were to occur from his drinking. I

1

imagine they'd all shake their heads in pity, maybe even blame themselves as much as the deceased. And why not? They should have seen it coming shouldn't they—should have headed off the tragedy? Wouldn't you agree, Dr. Janikowski?"

Excerpt from *Lady Mesmer's List*
By Edgar-winning writer Frances Whiting
Published by Avis & Crowle

Chapter 1

"Jesus, Jax, what time is it?" I rubbed the back of my neck, squinted hard waiting for the orange numbers on the digital clock of my CD player to come into focus, wondering if I'd be able to fall back to sleep once he'd gone. "Have you been drinking the bong water again, kid?"

"We gotta talk, Guy. It's serious. Big time serious."

Diminutive, Yoda-faced P. Jax Thornton III sat on my sagging couch, nursed the tepid root beer I'd poured him, from what was maybe a halfway rinsed coffee mug with a busted handle that'd been turning into a Petri dish in my sink. Which is all the hospitality you can expect when you bang on my door at 2:30 a.m. and drag me out of deep hibernation.

I'd first met Jax at a writer's convention at the L.A. Hilton a handful of years ago. He'd insisted on buying me a chain of Bloody Marys made with Luksusowa—I love Polish potato vodka almost as much as I once loved my ex—and I'd insisted on drinking every ounce. Jax had flattered me with praise, said my Conner Alba series were amongst his all-time favorite whodunits. Cultivated me with his view on how the network bungled the TV movie—I knew that humorless sad sack from ER was embarrassingly miscast, but had no say beyond the bank at which I cashed the network's check—and Jax figured a younger Tommy Lee Jones would've been the perfect Connor Alba. And we'd spoken of Jax's *Corpse* series.

Perhaps you've been lucky enough to read one of Jax Thornton's mystery novels….if you're even luckier, perhaps you haven't. Jax waddled onto the literary scene half a decade back with his instantly forgettable *The Dancing Corpse*. It was a vanity press piece and he spent a million dead presidents to sell 200,000 copies. I'd even heard from a colleague that to spike his sales numbers Jax had one of the Thornton family foundations donate an autographed copy to every library in the country…but I think the colleague may have been joking. Mystery hacks have a cruel sense of humor.

A small time publisher followed up with Jax's indifferently awaited sequel, *The Singing Corpse*. I'd never heard of Jax's publisher before—and I read everything in the mystery genre and know of every American or British publisher, big and small, all the way from *Alpha Press* to *Zumwalt Books*—but this new one's Web site certainly went first class after Jax's corpse began its song. Jax followed that up with last summer's smaller slice of tedium, *The Smiling Corpse's Mona Lisa*. I'm not sure if book sales gave his publisher much to smile about, but Jax was on a personal roll for as long as he didn't run out of participles to describe the cadavers populating his titles—I once seriously insisted he use *The Masturbating Corpse*, but you know how things can get at dawn in a Tijuana cantina.

As you may've figured already, Jax is from very big bucks. His grandfather, P. Jax Thornton I, made megaloot in tiled swimming pools starting in the early 50s, which bucks paled by comparison as Jax's parents quintupled the family fortune selling pool liners. With his elfin face, plumpish and balding Jax III was at the ass end of his twenties and would be passing into the toupee side of 30 any day now. He was possibly five-five in his cowboy boots, and a buck fifty soaking wet. Most importantly, Jax III had enjoyed a bottomless checking account since he was in diapers. Prior to undertaking his literary career he'd only lived for four things: tooling around L.A. in his Porsche 911 Turbo-S ragtop, reading mystery novels, playing The Grateful Dead, and smoking reefer. After the shock of Jerry Garcia's death, he'd dedicated himself to writing mysteries, although he'd kept current with the weed to honor Jerry.

I'm a democrat when it comes to bending elbows with anyone. So I was one of the few in the mystery writer's clique that didn't mind Jax buying his way into the club with Luksusowa or single malt Scotch and thick tenderloins and prime controlled substances for any of us who'd speak to him. I figured what the hell—if I'd inherited Jax III's kinda scratch, I'd be pitching for a ball club that I owned and trying to hobnob with Barry Bonds—steroids and all. As his semi-mentor and faithful friend I'd even managed to read all of Jax's books…well, that's not literally true, I only flipped through the latest installments. If you've read one *Corpse* you've read 'em all, believe me. Although I don't imagine his constantly recycled plotline was as bad as, say, a virulent case of herpes, I didn't have the heart to be blunt with Jax. So when he'd ask me for my assessment of his stuff, I clichéd him with "you got a great starting point" and "catchy title" and "interesting concept" and "what time's the Dodgers' game start?"

Jax sat across from me, took a trembling sip of the questionable root beer, put the cup on the table and began that thing with his eyes. Jax almost never made direct eye contact. Drove folks nuts with the way his elusive gaze kept darting hither and thither. He looked at his cup of root beer, his shoes, the lamp, my bare feet, the doorway, the kitchen stove, and finally back to his root beer cup before he spoke.

"Angus MacDougall died of alcohol poisoning in Toronto last month."

"I'd heard. Hardly a pre-dawn news flash, Jax."

"But alcohol poisoning, Guy? Gimme a break. Except those drink-till-comatose parties of the Colorado frat boys, no one dies of alcohol poisoning. No one."

"Come on, Jax...MacDoogs was never *not* drunk. I had to pour him into a cab after the Edgars last year."

Jax was so deadly earnest his eyes actually settled into mine for a spell. "Alcohol poisoning's for homeless rummies, burnouts sleeping under freeway bridges who snarf down sterno, Freon, and lighter fluid. And inexperienced college kids. Never seasoned, die-hard drunks, which is what Angus MacDougall was. Never."

"Jax, after four decades of a quart a day, MacDoogs' liver was Swiss cheese."

"Of course his liver was in shreds, but MacDougall didn't die from cirrhosis. His brain stopped doing all the autonomic stuff like breathing and heartbeat because his acute blood alcohol level sent him straight into a coma and he died as a result."

"How do you know all this?" I was becoming faintly interested, mainly because Jax's sustained eye contact reached more'n ten seconds. Quick, call the Guinness Book of Records.

"I spent all afternoon in the UCLA Medical library, Guy. Mostly researching the stats on alcohol poisoning. You know how many seasoned lushes over forty years old checked out that way in the past ten years? I mean normal affluent guys who weren't hobos sucking antifreeze, but guys who drink real booze they bought at retail in sealed bottles bearing tax stamps and bar codes?"

"Haven't the foggiest."

"Here in America in the past ten years, a grand total of one reported case. One! Some depressed 80 year-old widow lady from Tacoma who was never known to imbibe and who suddenly zonked herself on a litre of Gordon's Gin. The Tacoma M.E. said maybe it was her first real blast, maybe she got lit like those inexperienced frat-house chugglers." Jax's eyes began darting again.

"Yeah, but you know MacDougall was Canadian so your American stats don't apply," I took another peek at my clock, "probably he got to the point where Scotch goes down like Kool-Aid and lost count of how many quarts he'd emptied. Besides, Jax, I'm sure MacDoogs had a string of other health issues that sped things along."

"What about Alexandra Case?" Jax spit out.

I was stunned for several seconds before I could assemble my thoughts into words. "Alexandra Case? Dead too? Alcohol poisoning?"

"No, not from alcohol. From smoke inhalation, plugged up chimney in her fireplace or something. Ugly huh?"

"Jesus. When was this?"

"Today. Well, as of now its yesterday—don't you ever catch the news, Guy?"

I assimilated this latest information. The great Alexandra Case—San Francisco's Octogenarian of Homicide—mystery's Grand Dame who'd ushered in the gay detective genre in the mid 1960s with the introduction of Monsieur Pointer, hair salon entrepreneur turned sleuth when a series of murders devastates the Bay area's homosexual community. Alexandra continued the Monsieur Pointer series even after Hollywood cranked out a couple of absurdly stereotyped, campish Pointer movies in the mid-seventies. Alexandra disowned the movies which have, ironically, these many decades later achieved cult status.

Still, it's not as though old Alexandra or MacDoogs were my closest friends. Case wouldn't know me from Adam if I sat on her lap during one of her frequent 'Booknotes' interviews and, apart from polite cocktail party chit-chat at a few publishers' events, we'd never been in the same room together. As for MacDoogs, Angus MacDougall wasn't my lifelong personal bud, although he often drank me under the table at conventions. "Well, Jax, life can be a funny bird all right," I stretched and displayed a noisy closure yawn as I spoke, announcing it was too late or too early to think about such stuff.

"Don't pooh-pooh this thing, Guy. It's freaking real."

Yawning again I spoke softly to my guest, hoping to get him gone so I could at least stare at my bedroom ceiling tiles until the alarm went off. "Jax, I'm sorry we lost two colleagues. And I really hate to break this to you, buddy, but everyone checks out sooner or later—even founding members of the Edgar Award's Pantheon like MacDougall and Alexandra Case. Hell, even hacks like us. Human fate, man."

"But they're both *dead*. Truly dead."

"Along with every other name in the obits, Jax," I said, "you can check it out, every paper has a daily section."

"It's too damned coincidental, Guy. First Angus MacDougall. Then Alexandra Case. I've been rolling this thing around in my brain all night. Finally I jumped in the Porsche and rushed over."

I stretched and stifled my third yawn. "Oh hell, Jax, you're sounding more paranoid than all three Brontë sisters."

"It's clear you aren't with it, Guy. I expected more." With a glare of reproval, Jax rose to leave, his eyes darted from floor to root beer to clock, "I'm very sorry I woke you."

"Don't worry about it, Jax. It's an interesting concept, but needs a few rewrites. Besides," I chuckled as I walked him to the door, "don't celebrities always go in threes—meaning a third one'll go tits up any day now, huh?"

The turnout at the Episcopal Cathedral proved very large—probably family acquaintances, and I knew absolutely none of them. The post-services fare in the Cathedral dining hall was bland. Ham sandwiches sans crusts, two kinds of church ladies' potato salad, chips and homemade chocolate cake—all washed down with funereal cappuccino, my least favorite blend. I yearned for a cigarette but these devout Anglicans had mounted P.C. signs on every wall prohibiting the mortal sin of smoking in God's temple.

It had been a closed casket affair—violent car wrecks'll do that. But I visualized if I slipped out of the dining hall, crept back upstairs, snuck over to the church's adjacent burial grounds before the diggers finished their work, and quietly pried up the lid on the polished oaken box I'd find that, very unlike his fictional corpses, P. Jax Thornton III would definitely not be dancing or singing or smiling.

Chapter 2

Following the post-funeral reception, plus a double Bloody Mary and a couple smokes at O'Gara's Pub, I drove my rusting midlife crisis, my sputtering '98 Mustang convertible, up West Canyon Road. The road's narrow mountain corkscrew that eventually leads to the Thornton family's enclave in Sequoia Canyon.

As one of Jax's few semi-close pals—probably the only one—I figured I should maybe stop by with a couple private words of comfort for Jax's parents who'd spent the reception huddled in grief with the rectors and their wives. Assuming they were now back home from the burial and felt up to it.

West Canyon was the only access to the Thornton's three-story villa with a couple dozen bedrooms, twenty acres high on the Canyon's crest, built in Citizen Kane-style architecture. At Southern California's bloated land prices running about two million per acre, well go figure.

I'd been up there many times when Jax threw lush parties for his friends and fellow scribblers in honor of his own scribblings, every time one of his dancing-singing-smiling corpses tumbled into publication. Also in honor of other monumental items—a New Year, a full moon, a Pacific wind shift. He'd lay in a huge supply of Chopin and Bock—no, not the music, Chopin Vodka with Shiner Bock chasers. Thus, Jax's parties were always sleepovers, black tie events with live jazz of the first rank, geysers of free hooch, caviar canapés, plus enough Maine lobster and rib eye au jus to feed the Philippines. Did I mention the free grog included magnums of Chopin?

By comparison, my own crib—a two-bedroom duplex of faded pink stucco in a faceless L.A. suburb—fell several lifestyles short of the opulence that Jax III had grown up accustomed to. But at least I'd always lived independently of my parents, praise God on High! Jax, however, hadn't minded living in the Sequoia Canyon compound with his parents—occupying his own poolside bungalow with half a dozen rooms plus a couple connected guest cottages—where Jax did his writing surrounded by tennis courts, stabled horses, and a squad of servants to pick up his stray laundry. But as Jax once explained to me, the senior Thorntons also owned and greatly preferred their sprawling place in Key West. Accordingly, as the family's only child, Jax III had the run of the Sequoia Canyon estate for most months of the year. So why should he ever leave home? Why would anyone?

In his daily routine, Jax was nocturnal. He'd stay up till three or four in the morning listening to his CD collection, watching classic mysteries on his giant HDTV screen, eating pickled crawdaddie and smoking maryjane. But, Jax swore on Holy Writ he never touched grass

8

when he was in writing mode…he'd laughed up the perfect storm when I suggested maybe he should...he thought I was joking, or pretended to.

Downshifting my transmission-challenged Mustang I ground my way slowly up West Canyon Road. Winding uphill, around a wicked hairpin turn, I spotted a small mountain of fresh purple and yellow roses arranged on the roadside. I figured this spot in the narrow switchback had to be the site of Jax's fatal accident. I drove slowly on the shoulder as I confessed to myself this was the real reason I'd come up here. Call it curiosity, compulsion, morbidity or whatever, I'd felt drawn here. I simply had to inspect the death site where Jax'd smashed himself and his beloved crimson ragtop—a year-old Porsche 911 Turbo-S Cabriolet with over four hundred horse muscle under the lid—into the next life.

I parked my asthmatic Mustang on a small turnaround embankment some yards upgrade and hiked back down to the floral display beside the torn guardrail. There were several orange construction markers and orange arrows written in ground spray. L.A. County D.O.T. had already begun the layout on widening the curve and reinforcing the rail. The speed of the repairs gave testimony to the triumph of wealth over bureaucracy. This part of West Canyon Road is mostly used by the Thorntons and some gray-haired pair Jax had once told me were living on rerun annuities from a popular Saturday morning cartoon show. I paused by the mound of flowers and carefully studied the site.

General impression: The road snaked upward to the sharp curve where Jax's Porsche Turbo had hit the barrier, skidded along it, then vaulted from the road and into eternity. Beyond the edge of the road was far more than a gentle downslope, more like a plunging canyon at least a thousand feet through dense strands of Jackpine and Aspen. So what had happened?...Jax must have been hot-assing it home around 2:00 a.m., took the curve too fast, launched his Porsche Turbo off the road, the muscle car going airborne for a long, heart-pounding moment, then smashed its way a couple hundred yards down the steep hillside. Before coming to a stop, upside down, next to a row of towering pines. One report said both driver and car had been folded into an accordion. The sad, ingratiating little poseur never had a chance once he left the road.

But general impressions and news reports are only the starting point for obsessive cops and anal-retentive writers like me. I made mental notes as I methodically checked four of the five classic indicia of the crash site—T-S-S-M-VD—an investigative trick I'd learned from my main police source, Lieutenant Madeleine Neff of LAPD's West Robbery-Homicide branch.

9

T-S-S-M-VD, the acronym Lieutenant Neff had told me is sometimes used as off-color limerick humor by some of her cop colleagues. The limerick stresses toilet and sexually transmitted diseases. However, in the acronym's sanitized, scientific version, the "T" is for "Topography." The other letters stand for "Skid" marks, "Surrounding" foliage, "Man-made" structures and the "Vehicle of Death."

As far as Topography, the road was at least a 7% grade, all treacherous switchbacks and hairpin curves, of which Jax's crash site was the worst. Starting with "S," I looked over the residue of the black skid marks. Jax's Turbo had burned five yards of Michelin, the trajectory being a radically sharp swerve from the right lane, across the left lane, and slamming the guardrail above the drop.

I thought through the lightening sequence of events. First, Jax had to have been doing 60, not the posted 20, as he banked into this hairpin. Then suddenly he'd swerved hard left. Why? To avoid something? Or maybe he was drunk? Or on a drug trip? Or simply over-steered, lost control due to the car's speed? At that point, according to the skids, he'd hooked his Turbo onto the rail. I turned my attention to what remained of the low, man-made barrier.

The car's impact on this structure of steel and cable was revealing. Luckily the D.O.T. workers hadn't yet fully removed the low-cut railing's radically twisted metal edge. The rail was not completely torqued asunder. From the film clips of the Porsche Turbo being winched up from the chasm, which I'd caught several times on cable news, it was clear something had peeled open the driver's side of the rocketing Turbo, opened her like an overripe orange rind. Studying the site I could visualize this metal ripping violence as Jax's car skidded sideways along the railing. The upper edge of the steel guard rail had acted like a serrated paring knife as it dug deep all along the Turbo's skin.

I'd forgotten whatever I'd learned, if anything, in freshman physics at UCLA twenty years ago. All those equations concerning energy and speed and mass and momentum, I could no longer even begin to set up the dissipation formulas. But I knew enough about driving to feel the shuddering force of what'd played out here. A 911 Turbo-S rockets in at fifty-sixty per. Suddenly swerving at the steel and cable, sideswiping the barrier, then tearing along the low guardrail a couple yards up to the place where it curved along the snaky road. But Jax's headlong trajectory didn't curve with it...Jax ripped through and once past the barrier, the Turbo launched into the blackness. Then what?

Another letter in LAPD's acronym, I checked out the "S" for Surrounding foliage. There were some bark-skinned trees, stout Aspens, a few yards down the steep bank. The first couple, a pair of thick old beasts, had been stripped of their bark at a spot where their thick trunks stood well above ground. A third tree, an enormously thick Aspen a bit further down, had a very large, very fresh, very curved gouge in the side of its trunk. The gouge was the size of a steamer chest, like some Jurassic Park monster had chomped out a hunk of the Aspen at a point about seven feet up from the tree's base. Hmm.

This indicated what? Jax's hooking the rail must have done two things. Obviously, it threw the Turbo out of control, peeling open the side metal of the car. But even more fascinating, it had helped levitate the wounded vehicle. Jax had left terra firma like a space shuttle at liftoff. While airborne the Turbo had ripped past the two closer Aspens. Then plummeting further down, the German-built fender or maybe a bumper, had chomped a three foot hunk of cellulose out of a third. But that didn't stop the Turbo as it skidded Jax to his rendezvous with the afterlife still further down the steep slope. Ironically, only half a mile from the main gates of the Thornton estate.

The guardrail was "M."

I'd now accounted for four-fifths of T-S-S-M-VD—but not the death vehicle itself—when I sensed an approaching car. It was a black limousine, an overstretched Lincoln that was slowly winding up the hill toward me, obviously Jax's parents returning from the funeral. Would my stopping here, my exploring the accident scene, appear a little sick to the Thorntons? Morbid even? I hadn't thought of that earlier and now I felt awkward, embarrassed about being here on the day of their son's burial.

The limo slowed. The uniformed driver had obviously been ordered to pull over next to me. I couldn't run, couldn't hide. So, awkward and embarrassed or not, I'd have to face them. I hoped I wouldn't give off guilt vibes, like they'd caught me red-handed in some ghoulish ritual.

The limo stopped beside me and the nearest back window purred down. Pool-liner magnate Mr. Jax Thornton II, ashen gray, gaunt, and redeyed was fading fast, more haggard than he'd seemed at the services some hours earlier. But his black suit was still crisp and spotless, his white walrus moustache still immaculately combed; he hadn't even loosened his tie since the reception. His haggardness was not on the surface but in the eyes, more like a soul-deep pain was crushing the breath out of him.

From rheumy pools, his bloodshot eyes studied me. Unsmiling, he nodded in recognition, then opened the door and very slowly, wearily, climbed out of the limo, moving like he was 60 going on 90. "Thanks, Guy, for being my son's friend."

Mr. Thornton's cold, clammy palm shook my hand and held on for several beats longer than needed. I became very uneasy but Mr. Thornton's gaze finally left me and traveled over to the guardrail. He released his grip and choked down a shudder.

"I'm so very sorry, Mr. Thornton." I shook my head slowly, side to side, then to fill the silence I awkwardly blurted, "I'm really going to miss Jax." Which was true, I'd miss how he'd always pick up the bar tabs. Most especially I'd miss those overnight suck-up parties the little wannabe gave for us minor fixtures of the writing establishment.

"There's a lot of papers up at the pool house, Guy. Lots of Jax's...I don't know what all...writer's papers. Looks like piles of plot outlines, drafts, character notes. That sort of thing. Literally boxfuls. I believe he'd want you to have them."

"That's awfully nice of you, Mr. Thornton, but I'd feel uncomfortable poaching on Jax's..." I scrambled for a polite word, "...Jax's creativity."

"Creativity? This is no time for gilding the lily, Guy. Let's face it, his books were horseshit."

My jaw dropped. I started to protest, but Mr. Thornton cut me off.

"I loved my son, but I'm a blunt businessman. Always have been. If you're uncomfortable with horseshit, I can say his stuff had...um...limited literary merit. But I'll bet you'd agree with my first choice of words except you're too polite. Y'know, Jax thought the world of you, Guy. You were the big brother he always wanted but never had. He even gave me one of your Connor Melba mysteries you'd autographed."

"Alba."

"What?"

"Nothing."

I cringed at having corrected a grieving father's misnaming of my fictional character.

"Anyway, I read your most recent book and found it," our eyes connected, "better'n horseshit, almost good."

I smiled at the man's blunt honesty, "That's pretty much what the *New York Times* had to say."

"Anyway, Guy, I'd like you to stop by. Not right now, but in a couple days. Soon. Come up to the house and go through Jax's files and his story ideas and whatever other crap he had in those cabinets and cartons."

"Well…"

"Please come by. What in hell else will I do with it all?"

"Sure. I'll phone ahead, of course."

Thornton stared here and there about at the death site. "This goddamned road should've been widened years ago. Those pricks at the road department…" With a bitter snarl, he vowed to install higher, sturdier guard rails that would completely wind around every curve on the snaky canyon road as it slithered upward, from the Pacific Coast Highway's dogleg to Santa Monica. "Those bureaucratic pricks," he muttered again.

I guess in times like these, after the loss of a loved one, you need to find something of purpose, something to hang onto. Even rage at the road department.

We mumbled a few platitudes at each other. After shaking hands again, he reminded me to phone soon, then slowly climbed back into the rear of the town car, but left the window down. As they pulled away, I noticed Mrs. Thornton sprawled on the seat next to him, her eyes vacantly staring into space. She looked sedated, nearly comatose. Probably washed down too many valium with gin from the limo's rear bar, whatever it took to get her through the day's ordeal.

For awhile I stood next to the small mountain of roses. Didn't they say DiMaggio, for decades, kept fresh roses at Marilyn Monroe's burial plot? I was sure this floral homage to Jax III would be refreshed daily far into the foreseeable future.

I peeked over the edge again, this time leaning as far out as I dared. I peered down into the chasm. Though I'm not normally scared of heights, I felt a wave of vertigo wash over me. I eased back slightly from the lip.

"Aw, Jax, you poor dope," I muttered to myself. My thoughts turned from pity to questioning. What in hell were you doing? Speeding up this road in the dead of night. You knew better than that. You weren't some teenager freaked on his own hormones. How in hell could this happen? You knew these roads like the back of your hand— you'd driven this stretch your whole life.

I examined the core issue—what had caused him to swerve from the right lane and across the left towards the rim? I glanced around and wondered if a coyote or jackrabbit had jumped out in front of him at the worse possible time? Or humans, who then fled the scene? Possibly. I looked up and down the road, could some kids out necking in a moving car come downhill straight at him? Some fluke of sexual timing— maybe some form of lap play was going on and caused the pimply teenage driver to wander into Jax's lane—at precisely the fatal moment?

13

Spooked by what they'd done, the neckers would then have fled the scene.

I sighed again and began walking toward my rusty Mustang when a glint of sunlight caught my eye from off the road. I was uphill from where Jax swerved out of his own lane, at a spot where the road was less steep. I squinted over the railing at the glint. It was probably from a piece of broken glass from the wreckage reflecting the sun. No, that's not right. There'd be no wreckage up here as Jax's Turbo never reached this point, it flew off the guard rail many yards further down.

The flash came from a spot off the side of the road and a bit down the slope. I studied the place. The bright object rested at a ski hill angle. I decided to fetch it. I cautiously climbed over the rail. Leaning into the hill, I worked my way down, grabbed the sharp shard of glass with the wad of my handkerchief. Then crawled back up to the safety of the road. The whole effort took me under four minutes, but I was breathing hard and damp with perspiration.

The glass turned out to be a ragged shard of mirror the size of a Kleenex box. No wonder it caught my eye. The hunk was too big to have come from any rearview or side mirror of Jax's Porsche. Could it have come from the big side mirror of a truck? Or maybe a trailer? No, it was too heavy, too thick, to belong to a vehicle. How would a broken hunk of mirror find its way down there? The issue gnawed at me. Several possibilities galloped around the track in my brain, Litterbug taking first place by a nose. I lay the shard in the Mustang's cluttered glove box, did a turnabout, and headed back to town.

Chapter 3

Some day I'll write an epic love sonnet and title it "My Fair Google."

Like being with a hot lover in bed, everything's right there at your fingertips. No longer do I linger about public libraries, struggling to Dewey Decimal my way through book research for cars, guns, history, people, locations, medical procedures, sports, industries, clothing fashions, banking schemes, et al., etc., ad infinitum. Now—if you can slap a name on it, it can be Googled, exponentially. And if you're too cheap to pay ten bucks a month for basic Internet service you can use freebies—every branch library's now equipped with computers, ditto every university. Dashiell Hammett, eat your heart out.

My current trek through Googleland netted three deaths…not the mere twosome Jax had turned up and not including Jax's own recent departure from planet Earth. Yes, Angus MacDougall had liquored himself into the grave. Yes, mystery's Grand Dame Alexandra Case had choked on noxious fumes from her own fireplace, both in recent weeks. But earlier in the year there was the tragic demise of Beck Quinn outside her country house in Grosvenor Dale, Connecticut.

Late that afternoon when I unsurfed from Googling the recent deaths of mystery writers, the hairs on the back of my neck felt the prickly urge to check out every inch of my duplex, every shadowy nook and cranny, draw the shades, deadbolt the doors, and sit up all night with a 4.10 shotgun in my lap. If I'd owned a 4.10. But I did own a Lady Smith. After a moment's hesitation, I climbed the stairs to the attic crawl space and retrieved my Lady Smith from the gun safe I'd bolted there years before. When I say "Lady Smith" I mean as in Smith and Wesson, as in a 9 mm eight-round stainless steel piece graced by a three and a half inch barrel. Lady Smith and a chipped front tooth are all I have to remember my ex-wife.

I'd first acquired Lady Smith for Karla, my once beloved bedmate, as protection against those lurid California headlines where gangs of unholy Visigoths ride supercharged Harleys into one's parlor, wielding chains and machetes, bent on rape and homicide. You read of such grisly stuff every morning in the *Los Angeles Times,* compounded each evening by local newscasts—if it bleeds it leads, they say. Plus, both Karla and I had often drifted off evenings into nightmarish sleep glued to reruns of *Cops.* Buying Karla a Lady Smith seemed like a good idea at the time and Karla and I even made it to the gun range once or twice to train ourselves for the onslaught by a horde of Rutger Hauers some dark and clammy night.

During our third month of making the beast with two backs, on an ill-considered lark, Karla and I drove I-15 northeast to Vegas for some quick nuptials presided over by an aging Elvis and his notary-organist. Instantly thereafter, Sweetly Passive Karla introduced me to her theretofore unknown doppelganger, Angry Aggressive Karla, who our marital vows had somehow unleashed from the dark recesses of her bi-polar dungeon of dysfunction. And eventually—after some peculiar episodes that I'll be more than happy to continue blocking for my remaining days—I came to realize that Karla was seriously truth-challenged much of the time. If he'd ever met her, Raymond Chandler would've described Karla as a *sharp kick to the teeth sideways*. We bickered our way through two years of what could never be mistaken for wedded bliss and then barked at each other from separate cribs for another year before officially screaming *No Mas! No Mas!*

I hear Karla's remarried to a guy who owns a used car dealership in Pasadena. Good for her. I wish her all the best. But, periodically, late at night in a lonely bed, I miss her lying smile, her lying blue eyes, and even her lying purrs of ecstasy at the moment of climax. But enough of Karla and me.

The daisy chain of deaths I'd Googled had set me on edge, particularly my discovering the modus-extinctus in the death of Beck Quinn. The late Connecticut writer had successfully penned cozy detectives since the late eighties. Beck Quinn's formula featured a blue collar sleuth, a rural mailman named Hodgers. In one predictable volume after another, Hodgers kept tripping into diabolical plots involving murder most foul, always situated along his rural Connecticut delivery route and always demanding Beck Quinn's fans read on in a strained state of suspended disbelief. I never quite finished reading any of Quinn's sagas, laden with hicks-from-the-sticks shtick, despite striving as I always do to keep abreast of the competition.

According to the online news articles, Beck Quinn had died in a tragic home accident. She had apparently been fixing something near the roofline of her Connecticut farmhouse, had misstepped on the extension ladder, plummeted 40-odd feet to her reward in the rock bed below. The poor girl might've lived if she'd had immediate attention, but her husband, an investment banker, didn't find her until many hours later, after he'd come home late from his office in Hartford. Assuming Beck was out hiking in the woods, as she was wont to do, the hubby began making his own dinner. Eventually he peeked out the kitchen window to wonder why the extension ladder lay cattywampus in the backyard. Looking closer, he spotted a dark form in the rock garden. Although she was always tinkering with house projects, Allan Quinn wasn't exactly sure what she'd been attempting to repair this tragic time, perhaps exterior siding or some window trim.

I felt as though I'd just walked over Jax's grave. Mine too as I reread the Connecticut news reports a second and a third time. In Jax's final book, Jax had come to me for help. He needed to stage a mundane accident where a sociopath personality eliminates a rich spouse—shades of *Double Indemnity*—and Jax wanted something that would play. Over pizza and beer, we'd concocted a yarn. A hired killer comes over to the house while the killer's employer—in Jax's book the hubby—is conspicuously working late in his office. At gunpoint the killer, posing as a garden-variety thief, forces the wealthy wife—who was known as a can-do fixer-upper—to set the ladder in place above a rock garden. The killer explains to the too-trusting wife that he doesn't want to hurt anyone, just make his thievery look like a second-story-man burglary to throw off suspicion, but can't set up the ladder himself because of a rotator cuff injury. So, at gunpoint, she sets the stage for him.

The rich wife is confused, but she goes along with the ladder gambit because the killer provides a ray of hope for her not being shot, so the naïve woman figures the best thing to do is obey. Which makes no sense when you think on it. The killer tells her to climb up the ladder, ostensibly to remove the screen from the back window, but when the rich spouse is at the top of the ladder, the killer kicks it out from under her. The rich woman plummets to the rockscape below. Exactly where the homicidal hubby has spent the last couple months arranging a violent array of jagged boulders and stones.

I giggled, couldn't help it, when I recognized the plot. Beck Quinn's "accident" was a case of life imitating art—if you could call Jax's work art. Naturally the fatal fall part was plausible. Pick any weekend all across America, thousands of ERs are jammed with a stream of fractured limbs, severed fingers, crushed toes, burned flesh, and broken necks as amateur home repairers tumble from roofs, ladders, and staircases or otherwise inflict mayhem on themselves. A medical comedy of errors, the most severe of which fills 10% of the weekly obits. If you doubt this, merely walk through your local Home Depot and you'll see dozens of booby traps waiting to happen for every under-experienced do-it-yourselfer, male or female, with visions of home improvement projects dancing in their wee little heads.

More in point, one article revealed that the Connecticut coroner's hearing had concluded that poor Beck Quinn was probably trying to pop back into place a dislocated piece of house siding. Beck'd lost her balance—found herself on an intimate basis with Newton's law of apple trees—and plunged to her tragic doom, smashing ribs, fracturing multiple bones, and traumatically cracking her head on the unyielding rock bed. Her shocked and saddened hubby, hardworking and with an airtight alibi—although he wasn't exactly Johnny-on-the-spot at phoning 911—received the total supply of heartfelt sympathy from the villagers of Grosvenor Dale. My exhaustive Google search about Beck's death revealed nothing concrete to tie my suspicions to. The story had quickly settled into a sad blurb of history.

Jax's prime suspicion had been far more recent. The shuffling off this mortal coil of Toronto's hard-drinking Angus MacDougall. As I mentioned earlier, I knew MacDoogs semi-well. The Canadian sot was a damned good journeyman writer. If your John Sandfords, Alexandra Cases, James Pattersons, and Lawrence Blocks are first tier, MacDoogs was consistently second. I qualify as an expert on the pecking order among mystery yarnspinners, myself having once been acknowledged, however briefly, as a member of the second tier. Compulsive me, I follow such stuff almost daily.

Over the past decade MacDoogs and I had bumped into each other in hotel bars throughout the country at a wide variety of writer conferences or award events. Uniquely, MacDoogs' books didn't follow a series, had no common characters, that is to say each of his novels was invented anew, peopled anew, each and every one. No borrowed interest, no ongoing structures, a totally freestanding universe of characters and situations with each writing—a truly Herculean feat even the Blessed Saint Agatha had never attempted. You really gotta respect that kind of effort.

The *Toronto Star* had been kind to my old friend. After all, MacDoogs had been a colorful local character, so they euphemized that he'd "finally succumbed after a long health decline aggravated by his struggles with alcoholism." *Struggles* with alcoholism? What in the name of George Orwell's Newspeak was that crappola about? The Angus MacDougall I knew wasn't struggling with alcoholism, he joyously embraced it, courted it, bought it roses, and drank to the hooch not only with his eyes but enthusiastically with esophagus, bladder, liver, and kidneys.

As I'd told Jax, I don't think I ever saw Angus MacDougall dry. At conventions, he outpaced my Bloody Marys four-to-one. As with most mega-drinkers, MacDoogs didn't appear to have the shut off valve in his head to tell him when, dammit, enough was enough. In every single one of our tippling trysts I'd leave the bar first, stumble back to my room, often make an offering to the porcelain god, and then pass out atop my hotel bed. Next morning, I'd struggle down for the networking breakfast, my hands visibly shaking as I clutched the traditional cups of free caffeine, and then I'd spot a sunny MacDoogs—all aglow, shaved and dapper, suit nicely pressed. He'd serenely sip tea with his morning

Danish and work the *New York Times* crossword. A truly Homeric liver and kidneys, a metabolism to be mythologized post mortem. With MacDoogs dead, I figured I'd blow off the upcoming Agatha awards, they just wouldn't be the same without him.

Because of his history, on the surface it was easy to accept that he passed away last month from alcohol poisoning as noted in the final paragraph of the follow-up news story. Was there any other way to look at it? Decades ago MacDoogs' liver and kidneys had long since taken a number, waited in line to check out, and the number had finally been called. Still and all, MacDoogs was bright enough not to own a car and took cabs everywhere. And the watering holes he chose for his nightly binges were high-end pubs, never dives with questionable brew, never risky juicestands with the kind of clientele who'd kill you for your tasseled Ferragamo's.

I'd felt bad about not flying up to Toronto for the funeral last month, but it would've been on my dime. I'd already burned through the entire advance for Connor Alba's next adventure—and all I had as yet were empty pages. Feeling guilty, I sent his family a modest flower arrangement and an eloquent sympathy note instead.

Pondering MacDoogs' departure, I more and more considered Jax's central point. Alcohol poisoning? I surfed an on-line medical site sponsored by Substance Abuse Anonymous and found Jax had been right on the money. Alcohol poisoning is a novice's risk—a risk to teen tipplers, freshman frat boys, addled octogenarians, and a homeless delegation of sterno-swigging derelicts tossed in. Not affluent, upscale sots like Angus MacDougall—when that seasoned sort of boozer dies of grog-related disease it's from cirrhosis, coronaries, kidney failure, stroke, or diabetes. It would be informative if I could somehow unearth the actual M.E. report about MacDoogs.

I turned my attention to the Grande Dame of Mysteries: Alexandra Case. According to the Googled articles, the San Francisco coroner classified the demise of the aged scribbler as a tragic household accident. Case had lit a monster fire in her downstairs fireplace, forgotten to open the chimney flue and, evidently, failed to close the metal screen to blocks sparks. Then she'd toddled upstairs to the kitchen to pop herself some corn, returned downstairs to an unbreatheable blanket of smoke from the burning logs, compounded by the fact some of her carpet was also smoldering. The elderly Alexandra had been able to fetch a fire extinguisher and successfully foam down the carpet. Then the aging Grand Duchess of Whodunnits had tripped over something that was not identified in the newspaper, bumped her head, and passed out on the floor in front of the flickering fireplace, which ultimately asphyxiated her.

This was the death that pushed me across the line. This was why I retrieved Lady Smith from the attic gun safe, checked behind every door, under the beds and larger furniture, and double-bolted my doors. Why my sudden panic? Not because I don't know that smoke inhalation kills more people than any actual blaze. Not because I didn't know that freak accidents involving fireplaces happen every single day, from sea to shining sea. And certainly not because I couldn't fathom why aged Alexandra didn't simply run outside and phone the fire department from a neighbor's.

What sent me rushing to lock down the duplex and then to my gun safe for the comfort of Lady Smith was when I recalled there was something frighteningly familiar about the Alexandra Case death saga. I'd read something like this, a few years back, in some damned potboiler or another, whose author and title, try as I might, I just couldn't remember.

Good Christ, Jax my little chum, what have you done? Have you unearthed some serial murder chain? And not just any ordinary chain of potential murders. Nooo, that'd be too straightforward by half, but something nefariously closer to home. Could we have here the possibility of a very special chain, a chain of deaths regarding mystery writers? What motive to go about killing off mystery writers? What madness is this, Jax?

Did you have any glimmer of the hellish scope of this lunacy? What in the green muck of utter uncertainty have you left me with, Jax? I'm drowning here and you're rolling around on the other bank of the River Styx laughing your demented ass off at me, you goddamn Yoda-faced dwarf!

Chill out, Guy, chill out, I ordered myself. Potential murders ain't necessarily actual murders. Suspicions ain't necessarily reality. Despite appearances, it ain't necessarily so...thank you, George Gershwin.

First things first, Guy, you need to sort through this. First and foremost. Then figure what to do about it if the worst-case scenario turns out to be true. Which, praise God, I assured myself, was not high on the probability curve.

But still...

Chapter 4

Every sleuth needs a real-life guru. Let me explain. There's an array of approaches within the mystery genre…you've got your police procedural, your hardboiled private dicks, or your cozy detectives who often are simply gifted amateurs. As sleuths you've got classic archetypes, such as your Auguste Dupins, your Sherlock Holmes, Blessed Saint Agatha's contrasting tandem of Hercule Poirot and Miss Marple, to say nothing of the Sam Spades, Philip Marlowes, Perry Masons, Ellery Queens, Lew Archers, Lucas Davenports, Jack Reachers, Charlie Parkers, V.I. Warshawskies, Harry Boschs. And, of course, my own two-fisted creation, the inimitable Connor Alba.

Ah, placing Alba up with the first tier was fantastically pleasing, nearly as good as sex on the beach with my ex-wife. Let me explain further. *Night of the Wind Chimes*, the first full-length Connor Alba mystery, opens with Detective Alba working Narcotics at LAPD. He stumbles over a series of homicides, at first thought to be drug-related but there's far more than meets the eye. By the time the dust settles, the sitting female mayor of L.A. has been indicted, a California real estate magnate has fled to Algeria, and a Federal Reserve official is being tried on three counts of murder as well as conspiracy to murder. That is, if the Fed official survives the two hollow points in his left kidney administered by Connor Alba his own self.

As for my two-fisted detective, well, former LAPD Lieutenant Alba got personally muddied while cracking the big case and was forced to resign from the police force rather than face some rather freedom-limiting restrictions. But fear not, dear reader, as that's only the beginning, Connor Alba returns tougher than nails and running his own P.I. agency in *Dead Times*, the follow up whodunit that, according to *Writer's Digest*, 'crackles on the iron.' Whatever in hell that means.

Through them all, from Poirot to Alba to Charlie Parker, there is one common thread. From first tier to bottom feeders, all of them share this: The main sleuth invariably must have guidance from an off-stage someone. An all-purpose person—adviser-friend-partner-confidante-assistant-consultant-helpmate-resource-sounding board-colleague-resource-collaborating rival—take your pick. As a mystery writer I too have an all-purpose person, in my instance the resource type. A keen-minded member of the Federal judiciary, thus enjoying lifetime tenure and though well into his seventies having no intention of ever retiring, to say nothing of dying. I figure God, like everybody else who knows The Judge, is too cowed by the son of a bitch to suggest either.

The Judge had been my invaluable resource over the years when it came to legal insights. The ins and outs of criminal procedure, unlawful evidence scenarios, and the rest. I'd ask him could the suspect plead this? Would the perp get bail? Is this a logical case for appeal? Would a killer walk away on this procedural point? If convicted, how many years would he get? What really goes down in The Joint?

But for all these technical points with which I'd peppered Connor Alba's world, there was always a price. It takes a singular act of courage on my part to seek The Judge's thoughts. Each encounter is an exhausting ordeal, but more often than not I come away from such ordeals with useful information or insights. Tonight I sucked it up and made the late drive down to his condo in Newport Beach.

The silver-haired Judge sat quietly for thirty minutes while I laid out everything I knew about the demises of Beck Quinn, Angus MacDougall, Alexandra Case and, of course, P. Jax Thornton III. It was a test of nerve for me each time we spoke, always had been as far back as memory goes. But the old guy had a brain, a formidable one, I have to give him that. And I wanted his thoughts on my snarl of hunches and suspicions.

As I spoke, his customary gaze—a bemusal-on-steroids expression—penetrated through me. Years ago I dubbed it The Gaze. As ever The Gaze made me feel as if I should apologize to the man for being so mentally challenged in fumbling to express myself. At length I finished my exhaustive catalog of items Jax had brought me plus my own Googlizing. "So what do you make of all this?" I asked, nervously short of breath.

Silently, The Judge studied me with those 70-year-old pale gray eyes I'd feared since our first conversation. I'm nearly forty and been around every track twice, so you wouldn't expect any other human's look of cold skepticism would still cut and intimidate me when focused in my direction. You'd be wrong. The Gaze could still unnerve me in a microsecond. He'd once said acidly my chosen career was a waste of time and effort, something his now-deceased wife told me was typical of him. She'd confided The Judge hadn't one supportive gene anywhere in the six trillion snippets of DNA making up his austere genome helix.

"You're asking me what do I make of this frothy heap of non-facts you've presented me with, Timothy?" he asked slowly in his archly superior tone, the same tone of voice, coupled with The Gaze, which freezes solid the souls of experienced trial lawyers who appear before his bench. "Is that your question, Timothy?"

"Yes sir, but please call me Guy like the whole world does."

The Judge sniffed, said nothing, and "The Gaze" continued. He impatiently tapped his forefinger on his desk pad.

"I don't know what you expect me to add, sir." I was uneasy. Although The Judge had proved a cornucopia of technical information and insights into the court system over the years, this was already shaping up as one of those especially hyper-tense encounters.

No response. The continuing silence generated pressure behind my temples, like when I'd gone too deep during my first scuba trip beneath the Great Barrier Reef.

At length he asked blithely, "Am I to take all you've said seriously? Or are you simply wasting my time while bouncing a plot idea around?"

"Take it very seriously."

"Then the villain must be Conan Doyle's criminal mastermind Doctor Moriarty...I understand Doctor Moriarty has escaped from the asylum for the criminally insane and is out gunning for third rate authors," The Judge softly chuckled with his patented mockery.

I'd already begun regretting this visit. Well, two can play the sarcasm game I thought as I corrected him, "It's *Professor* Moriarty, Judge. Watson was the doctor." I'd known driving down we'd waste a certain amount of time in verbal fencing. If I didn't hope he may have some insights for me, I'd have skipped the trip.

"You mystery writers are an obsessive breed to begin with. One of you gets a hangnail and the others run around clucking hither and yon like Chicken Little."

"Judge, can we get to the..."

"If not Moriarity, maybe it was the infamous one-armed man who forced your friend off the road? Did you ever think of that, Timothy?" For the first time this evening, the old man flashed his snaggly-toothed smile that always erased 40 stern years from his face.

"Can we do without the sarcasm for a moment, Judge?"

"For a moment, perhaps, but you so invite it. Maybe your deceased friend was simply a case of DUI?"

"He wasn't drunk, Judge. The guy smoked marijuana, but rarely drank."

"Marijuana's a gateway drug to all of the others. In their infinite wisdom, OSHA's even determined that people shouldn't operate farm equipment while doing crystal meth."

"Jax didn't do crystal meth."

"I'm sure the toxicology report will show whatever it was he'd been taking...and that will be that."

The Judge had seemed the logical guy to take my facts to, but he was sounding exactly as I must have sounded to Jax that last time we spoke. Dismissive and sarcastic. And he was right, Jax might've crashed his Porsche while he was high on something. I gave a concessional grunt.

"Look here, your friend died in a freak car accident. I'm sorry for that. But death happens—so deal with it. Somewhere, right now as we speak, some poor...what is it the college kids say...some poor *dickweed* who may be as sober as a Methodist deacon is tooling down a freeway, a cup of hot coffee clenched between his thighs. Suddenly our dickweed hits an unexpected bump or swerves or brakes to avoid another driver. Result? Scalding hot coffee drenches his dangling participle and both of his parentheses, causing him to swerve into oncoming traffic canceling three or four magazine subscriptions in the process. Film at eleven."

"Scalding coffee didn't take out Jax Thornton, Judge. Nor Angus MacDougall in Toronto, nor Alexandra Case in San Fran. That's my point."

"Connecting the dots from Toronto to Santa Monica to San Francisco and tying them into a harebrained conspiracy theory about serial killings of writing hacks? Amusing, but I'm not laughing with you, I'm laughing at..."

"That's damned near exactly what I told Jax, Judge. When he came to see me in the wee hours, carrying on about Angus MacDougall's death. Nearly word for word. And a couple days later Jax died in a freakish car crash. Too ironic to be mere coincidence, wouldn't you say?"

"Utter rubbish! Mankind's most foolish false assumption. Two things happen closely in time, ergo, they must be products of the same cause. That's the parenthood of every conspiracy theory since Philip of Macedonia's syphilis killed him but the whispers blamed his widow and his warrior kid. All utter rubbish. Look here, Timothy," his tone had a molecule of human warmth for the first time, "you're in denial right now over the death of someone near and dear—and you're looking for somebody or something to blame—it's painful to lose a friend, human nature to try and escape. So your brain seizes on this theory that your friend's suspicions were valid. You persuade yourself it must be so because why else, with utmost literary irony and a novelist's too-perfect timing, would your friend die so unexpectedly right after confiding his suspicions to you? But it is no more than synchronicity—tragic synchronicity to be sure—but irony is only a literary device, not some portal to the truth. Hell, the older I get, the more I see that the actual events of life play out with seemingly less and less chaos, seemingly more and more coincidence, than I ever dreamt possible when I was young. But the coincidences are merely the necessary products of synchronicity—random chance. No, before I can buy into linking such stuff into a pattern of conspiracy I'd have to see some hard facts.

24

Something truly compelling. And, Timothy, as a hardheaded writer, so should you."

"Don't keep calling me Timothy." I corrected him for what felt like the ten-thousandth time on this matter. "You're the one who Knighted me 'Guy' darn near four decades ago cause you kept getting me confused with the older kids and the dog. I was ten before I realized that 'Guy' wasn't my real name."

"Well, I had quite the caseload back then. And you did look a lot like your four brothers. Even your mother thought so."

"Whatever…." I sighed. "About those hard facts—what kind? And where would I go to find hard facts, Judge?"

The pale gray eyes stared out the window towards the ocean as he pondered, "Something scientific would be nice—your friend's blood content would be sensible. And at least the police reports on the others, preferably the autopsy findings. Those things are real and testable. Hard evidence. Not just probabilities and speculations and, with all due respect, escapist fantasies."

"Naturally, I…"

"You've written enough potboilers, you know I'm correct, don't you?"

"Hard evidence would be nice, Judge."

With a mysterious smirk the old man paused for effect and added with a scoffing laugh, "But, then again, it could turn out to be Jesse James."

"Wrong genre, Judge."

"You know, Timothy, you should write a western. Did I ever tell you that you should write a western?"

"Only all the time."

"I love old Louis L'Amour. Fall to sleep with one every night."

Chapter 5

Hard facts, not speculation and probabilities, The Judge had said. I needed hard information, even scientific evidence, to test Jax's theory and either prove or destroy it. I sit at my writing desk and ask myself the WWCD question—What Would Connor Do? But that's easy; he'd have a shot of Bourbon. Needless to say, next paragraph someone would phone him or drop by or send a letter that would eventually lead Connor to a keen insight or two…or if my writing was blocked that day, maybe Connor'd simply begin pistol-whipping clues out of the usual suspects. Also needless to say, WWCD failed me.

So I logged into "Watson Chatroom"—known to its users as WatChat. WatChat was one of the privileges of being a member of the Mystery Writers Association. To become a member a scribbler of mysteries needs to have at least gotten a handful of stories published, at least in marginally paying markets. I often surf WatChat for advice on publishers, markets, agents, rumors, the inside poop on what's coming down the pike. But mostly I drink Guinness and bullshit with whom I very loosely call my colleagues. At its core, WatChat is the 21st Century equivalent of the Citizen Band radio. Uh breaker, breaker, come in writer buddy, that's a big 10-4.

I intended to bounce Jax's idea off the rest of my brethren. WatChat was chockfull of the usual clutch of arrogant wannabes, smart asses, poseurs, and gate crashers. You usually don't find many of the A Team whiling away their hours in WatChat, but once several years back I brushed cyber-elbows with Thomas Harris, pre-*Hannibal*. Another time in virtual reality Valhalla, Robert Crais referred to me as *numbnuts*. All rational inferences to the contrary, I prefer to think if it really was Crais he meant it as playful camaraderie, a locker room towel snap from an esteemed colleague.

Since mystery writers are an acerbically flippant lot—takes one to know one—I'm not exactly certain what I hoped to accomplish by logging on. I guess I wanted to bounce my thoughts around the room and see what bounced back. Using my chatroom name of CAlba, I typed in an abbreviated version of the recent daisy chain of deaths—Angus MacDougall-Alexandra Case-Jax Thornton III, plus the slightly older news about Beck Quinn. I added that shortly before his death Jax had begun making a connection.

The WatChat responses were immediate.

Ripper: Claptrap! Paranoid claptrap!
CAlba: I clap thee not, Rip, and I'm not a conspiracy moonbat, but these *coincidences* are stacking up like fire logs.

26

Ripper: Paranoia squared, Guy, and everyone knows you're nuttier than squirrel poo.

CAlba: Now that's not very netiquette of you, Rip. Did you misplace your Viagra again?

Ags: I'd heard about MacDougall, but not the others. I'm in Miami, though.

CAlba: Google the names, you'll find 'em all.

Ags: I hope I'm not in MacDougall's will—the old swiller probably left me his bar tab.

SkinnyMan: If what you posit is correct, Guy, what could possibly be the motivation for such a harebrained plot?

Ripper: It's very simple, Skinny, Guy's a nutflake who hasn't sold in six figures for a decade now, so he's gone Dealey Plaza on us looking for sinister forces to blame for his cratered career.

Sleuth: Screw off, Rip. Guy's onto an interesting plot concept—question is how do you sustain disbelief for 300 pages?

CAlba: I'm not floating a story idea, Sleuth, I'm dead earnest.

Ags: Wrong-O, Guy, I and only I am "Dead Earnest"—don't anybody even think of flitching my latest title—I've already copyrighted the piece and it's scheduled to hit Barnes & Noble for the Holidays.

Ripper: Guy wouldn't recognize a story idea if it walked up and bit his foreskin.

CAlba: Still miffed about your Amazon ranking are you, Rip?

Ags: Motive, Guy, you gotta start there. Sex? Money? Revenge? Sex? Power? Jealousy? Sex? Whew—I'm getting a little turned on here.

Sleuth: Betrayal? Blackmail?

SkinnyMan: You know if any Flatfoots are investigating this stuff?

CAlba: "Flatfoots?" Did you enjoy your 40 years in cryogenic saran wrap?

SkinnyMan: You know—Gumshoes.

CAlba: No, Skinny Man, not that I can find. No Gumshoes and no Fuzz, Goon Squad, Shamus, Smokey, Badges, Kojaks, or G-men packing gats.

Sheesh, I thought. What century's this guy coming from? I didn't know SkinnyMan—his logon name likely a rift on *The Thin Man* so maybe this guy sees himself as the literary heir to Dashiell Hammett. I'd give SkinnyMan half a brownie point for the moniker, but he should not pass Go or collect his 200 dollars for the Flatfoot and Gumshoe uses.

On WatChat you can set up your profile so your user name can be anything you make it, as noted by the incredibly ingenious one I chose for myself. Perhaps Robert Crais was on to something, maybe I should've taken *Numbnuts* as my nom-d'-online. Double-clicking a user name displays the writer's self-written profile. Mine displays my true name, a dashingly good picture of myself with a bushel of curly hair taken about the time I squeezed out of UCLA—hey, let's keep the myth of eternal youth alive—and a paragraph or two about my Connor Alba series.

A possibility flitted dimly into my consciousness. Inspired, I returned to my keyboard.

> **CAlba:** I grant this is probably a Hail Mary, but do any of you know of books where fire is used as the primary weapon?
> **SkinnyMan:** How 'bout every novel?
> **Ags:** Insurance schemes up the ying-yang.
> **Sleuth:** Murders, timed explosions, covering up crimes, destroying evidence, you name it. Used in every TV movie, too.
> **CAlba:** Okay, what about books where hypnotism is used against someone?
> **SkinnyMan:** How about every other novel?
> **CAlba:** Name two.
> **Sleuth:** Ripper's right about you, CAlba.
> **Ags:** I caught a Basil Rathbone on Nick-At-Night last weekend where they dinked with hypnotism.
> **SkinnyMan:** How 'bout Dickie Condon's *The Manchurian Candidate*?
> **Sleuth:** Connelly's *The Poet*?
> **Ags:** One of Lee Child's Reacher novels has it.
> **Ripper:** Guy, why don't you do your own thinking like a good parasite?
> **CAlba:** Numbnuts.
> **Ripper:** Who're you calling numbnuts?
> **CAlba:** Using it collegially, Rip ol' chum.
> **Ags:** How about Whiting's *Lady Mesmer's List*?
> **Sleuth:** Who?
> **Ags:** Frances Whiting. She writes yachting mysteries.
> **Ripper:** Yachting mysteries, O Holy Jesus!, be still my heart.
> **Scythe:** *Dead Man Typing* by Justin Way.
> **SkinnyMan:** Hey Ripper, don't let Whiting's yachting genre offput you. Just check out the Frances Whiting Web site. The woman's really worth a gander.

Sleuth: I'm googling for her, I'm googling. Oh lord, Babe-O-Licious!

SkinnyMan: Prime Cut, huh?

Ags: Why'd you ask about hypnotism, Guy? What you thinking of?

CAlba: Probably nothing, an impulsive hunch. Scythe, did you say *Dead Man Typing* by Justin Way?

SkinnyMan: All of you with X-chromosomes should take a look at this Whiting hottie.

CAlba: Scythe, are you still out there? Answer please.

Sleuth: Whiting's gorgeous in that nothing bikini. I'm thinking of buying a yacht.

Ripper: Trouble with women that sexy-looking…D.O.A. between the sheets!

CAlba: Scythe…you out there? Scythe, please answer me!

SkinnyMan: You ever had anyone between the sheets who didn't charge by the hour, Rip?

Sleuth: Hey, Guy, what's with the hypnotism kick?

Ags: Yeah, Guy, you started this thread.

Ripper: Earth to Guy Davitt. Come in Davitt.

I was still online—but my skin crawled with goose bumps as I sat there paralyzed with shock at Scythe's words. It took a full minute before I began breathing again. Focusing my thoughts, I opened a new window, brought up Google, and searched for *Dead Man Typing* by someone named Justin Way. Mostly, the search results were pages of Cyrillic gibberish. I tossed some quote marks around the title to refine the search. Nothing. I followed suit with Yahoo! Nada. I spent another minute at Amazon before throwing in the towel and returned to WatChat.

The chatroom had moved on. I scrolled back up to the unanswering Scythe's singular comment. I double-clicked Scythe to display the corresponding profile and find out the joker's true name. No name given. No picture or background information, either. Chatwise speaking, Scythe was an empty cybershell. How had Scythe entered WatChat?

CAlba: Scythe, are you still there?

Ags: Look who's back from the dead.

CAlba: Anyone know Scythe?

Ripper: I'm not tracking.

Sleuth: I think he's new. Never heard of him before.

Ags: Me neither. Since I don't have a life, I hang here 24-7 and this is the first I've ever heard of him.
CAlba: Hey Scythe, I know you're there. Tell us about that book—*Dead Man Typing*.
Sleuth: *Dead Man Typing*—??? I've never heard of it.
CAlba: Scythe, c'mon, what'd you mean by that?

Scythe didn't respond to my repeated pleas. My anxiety slowly turned into anger, and then anger turned to another burst of fear. I logged off. Although I could find no book titled *Dead Man Typing*, nor any author named Justin Way, I certainly recognized the name Scythe had dropped. It would be hard for me not to…Justin Way is the street where I live.

Chapter 6

My desk phone jangled away my dark musings about Scythe's lethal comment, the brevity of human existence, and the bitter injustice of life. The phone jangled again.

The Caller ID read Sandra Kearns, my book agent at MACA, and although I'd rather place my tongue on frozen sheet metal, I knew I had to answer. I'd been playing phone tag with her for almost a month—one-sided phone tag, actually, since I'd tactically ignored all of Kearns' calls to me made during business hours, and then returned her calls to her MACA answering service at midnight, each time fearing to the core of my deceiving, writer's-blocked heart that some night Sandra Kearns might actually be working late and pick up her phone.

"Where's the manuscript, Davitt?" Kearns demanded.

Sandra Kearns was ruthlessly razor sharp in negotiations—the reason I'd switched to her eight years and four books ago—but, as I've come to realize, the woman was a double-edged sword if you ever cross her. And I'd crossed her months back when half the manuscript became overdue. Truthfully, I simply couldn't get rolling on the project...the ennui virus had me firmly in its grip. My sole creative achievement in months—assigning names to my newest cast of clichés, most of which I stole from the phone book without an erg of inspiration or even interest.

"Sandra, how great to hear from you. How're you doing?"

"How am I doing? Sweet of you to ask. I just endured a 40-minute harangue from Graham Steyn at Barnstorm Press—so please, let's cut the shit."

Normally Sandra Kearns could always be counted on to have me weed out the gratuitous profanity from my novels, so if Sandra Kearns was cursing in that grim tone of voice it was damn certain I'd sunk beneath the deepest level of doo-doo. Problem was, I'd flim-flammed a sizeable advance late last year on my song and her dance to Barnstorm for my working title *Return of the B-T-M Killer.* Our pitch was brilliant—a cabal of Washington power brokers, you know, a senior senator, an NSA advisor, and someone near the top of the FBI totem pole, have hatched a nefarious scheme—their goal's some McGuffin or other, doesn't matter what. In order to complete their dastardly deed, these villains need some higher ups eliminated. To throw suspicion elsewhere, they rig the murders to look like the work of a once infamous and uncaught serial killer who went dormant several years back—the self-baptized messiah of "Bondage-Torture-Murder." The media had dubbed their darling the *B-T-M Killer.* Now everything goes as planned, except there's a certain someone lying in the weeds in placid remission from his demons but has suddenly become ballistically unhappy. You guessed it, the true serial killer, a ruthless savage with an IQ light-years beyond the MENSA charts. The real B-T-M is murderously disturbed that someone has stolen his MO and returns to the game to search out who's behind the frame-up and then mete out B-T-M's patented brand of justice. Kind of a Jack the Ripper meets *All the President's Men*. My man Connor Alba trips over events and becomes a fly in the ointments of both the Washington cabal and B-T-M.

Not too shoddy, a million dollar premise if only I could get myself to roll with it. Unfortunately, for many months I'd been oddly detached, as though witnessing the coming train wreck with a third person narrative and—as my career began circling the drain, spiraling ever faster—I felt powerless to stop it. Every time I put PC to paper and began working up a head of steam, I'd realize that I'd written this very same scene a dozen times before.

"Don't worry, Sandra, I'm on top of it. Haven't you gotten my messages?"

"That's another thing, Davitt, stop phoning my office in the middle of the night. Do you think my voicemail doesn't let me know what time you called? I'm in the office till nine most nights, so when I get in at seven the next morning and see the red light blinking on my phone, it's always from the midnight man, Guy Davitt."

"I apologize for that, Sandra, but I work when the juice flows and sometimes I work all night and sleep days," I lied with forced gusto.

"Steyn wants a hard copy of ten more chapters in his greasy little fingers, so it's imperative that you send all of your *juice* to him ASAP—as in right now. You've got his address at Barnstorm, right?"

"Yeah, but a lot of the pages are stream of consciousness. Don't get me wrong, good stuff, but stream of consciousness. I won't lie, Sandra," I continued to lie, "I've had some false starts and have needed to realign the structure. Barnstorm's happy with those first three, right?"

"You mean the first three chapters we gave them when Barnstorm cut you the check months and months ago? Contractually, you've already broken the schedule."

"Rome wasn't built in a day."

"But Caesar ain't still laying the mortar, Davitt."

"Take it easy. I'll send Graham what I've got and smooth things over. I'll be the first to admit that it's been painfully slow, but it's going to be a great read, my best Connor Alba yet."

"I'm going to call Steyn in two days to verify that he's gotten the manuscript from you. And he'd better have something, Davitt. I'm not going to fuck over Barnstorm Press for you. You're not exactly Dan Brown."

"No worries, Sandra," I said before realizing she'd already hung up. The Dan Brown comment stung a bit closer to home than I cared to admit, but Kearns hadn't made much money off my last couple endeavors, and after scoring the big B-T-M advance for me from Barnstorm, I paid her back with one part writer's block and two parts laziness.

Time to buy more time. I decided to hide behind my PC. The first three chapters at the time of the advance were pretty slick and in your face, but they were generic mystery layers setting up the plot. Now I needed to get specific, name names, dream up the McGuffin, and somehow figure out how to drop erstwhile Connor Alba into the stew.

Fueled by panicky pressure, stale donuts and caffeine, I slammed out a prologue, an edgy two-pager that foreshadowed events to come. Then came my long overnighter between manic peeks out the curtains for strange cars or shadow figures indicating the potential seriousness of Scythe's threat, plus my nervous confirmations that all doors were indeed locked and bolted. Somehow I spewed out three chapters of absolute boilerplate, paint-by-numbers mush. And, feeling the pinch from Sandra Kearns's call, I then cut and pasted several more chapters from previous Connor Alba books to use as templates and stirred these together, changing names and places to fit the new book. All of this called for major editing and a clearer vision.

I didn't yet have that vision, but I had ginned up some make-do camouflage.

I absently waltzed Lady Smith around the desktop with my forefinger as I calculated my predicament. The prologue would make Graham Steyn's tail wag, make him think the book truly was progressing. The first three chapters had already made his tail wag, but that was old news and wouldn't cut me any slack, except for making the manuscript I sent him thicker. The new boilerplate chapters would, in no uncertain terms, not make Steyn's tail wag—enough said. Probably the spliced-in chapters, however disjointed, may make his tail tremble a time or two. By lunchtime I was feverishly fast-editing, hoping Steyn would not recognize my subterfuge for the crazy-quilt pastiche it was.

I printed out the 60 pages and crammed the bundle into a huge manila envelope. I balanced it in my hand and realized that it didn't weigh enough to buy me the much-needed time. I returned to my P.C. and printed off chapters 20 through 30 from *The Aristotle Analysis*—my third Connor Alba book from the mid-nineties. I hesitated, then shoved them into the envelope behind the pastiche. Hey, honest mistakes happen everyday. With a little luck, Steyn will just be so damned glad to see I've made progress that he won't even bother reading it and thus buy me another month or two to set things right.

I returned to my PC and pecked out the best fiction I'd written all year:

Dear Mr. Steyn,

I hope all goes well at Barnstorm Press and life finds itself smiling down upon you and your family.

Enclosed are the first 12 chapters of my latest Connor Alba novel (working title Return of the B-T-M Killer). My sincere apologies for any delay, but I've restructured the plotline for maximum twists and turns. I will be able to make up some lost time by redrafting earlier materials to fit accordingly in future chapters.

Please let me know if you have any questions or comments.

All My Best,

Guy Davitt

I added my home and cell phone numbers, printed it off, signed it, slid the cover letter inside the manila envelope, sealed it, and began addressing it to Graham Steyn at Barnstorm Press.

My body craved sleep, begged me to tumble straight into bed. Instead, I checked my watch…already late afternoon. Just enough time for a mad dash to the post office.

Chapter 7

"He was murdered, you know." She stood in the doorway of the pool cottage in a blue silk bathrobe, no makeup, gray-streaked hair bird-nested in no discernable style, and her huge, heavy-lidded eyes boring holes straight through me. I could smell her bourbon from across the room.

"Mrs. Thornton," I addressed her politely though startled to see her standing there. I rose from Jax's desk.

"Murdered...my baby boy murdered," she said again.

"Murdered?" my face began to flush.

"A mother would know, wouldn't she?" Tottering, Mrs. Thornton grabbed for the doorknob to steady herself, missed it, and connected on her second try. "I felt it when it happened. I did. Right here. And here." She flung her hand to her breast then to her lower belly. "Jax and I had a connection, a special umbilical. I could feel everything happening in his life. Since he was a child. Now it's...now it's cut forever. My baby boy was murdered."

"Why would you say that?"

Why?" Her eyes glazed in and out of focus, "There's always the money thing..."

"Veronica, Honey," Mr. Thornton swooped in through the open door, a nervous housekeeper following close behind him. He gripped his frail wife by the elbow, "Juanita and I've been looking all over for you."

Juanita, the Thornton's thickset housekeep, gently took hold of Mrs. Thornton's other elbow. In unison—long practice had made their choreography perfect—they began ushering her back out the door of the poolside building. Out of the late Jax's domain and back toward her crib in the big house.

Mr. Thornton paused, whispered something to Juanita, released his wife's elbow, turned and headed back toward me. "Please forgive Veronica, Guy," he stood in the space his wife had just vacated, "she keeps babbling these strange things...she's not herself. Quite frankly, Jax's death and everything that's happened...well, it's been damned rough for her."

"Completely understandable, Mr. Thornton," I mumbled to fill the awkward silence. "I should go. Come back and sort through Jax's papers at a better time."

"Better time, Guy?" Mr. Thornton chuckled falsely and held up a pair of exasperated palms. "I don't think 'a better time' will ever arrive. Not in this house. You were my son's friend, Guy, and in a certain way his mentor. So just take your time and try to make sense of all his stuff if you can. I rummaged through it a little yesterday…it's all Swahili to me."

"Thank you, Mr. Thornton. I'll try to work as quick and quiet as possible."

"Should I have Juanita fetch you some tea? Coffee?"

"No thanks, I've got some bottled water."

"Juanita and I need to take Veronica to…um…to an appointment." Thornton's shadowy and bloodshot eyes had the look of a haggard, broken man. "We'll be late getting back, so please let yourself out when you're done."

"Okay, Mr. Thornton."

Thornton Senior began to add something, changed his mind, and shuffled out, closing the door behind him.

I felt crappy about being in Jax's sanctum sanctorum. But I continued the task of sorting through his files—hard copy stuff in cabinets and electronic documents on his computer. When Thornton Senior had let me into the cottage, the place where young Jax had done his writing, the first thing I noticed was the picture above the computer. In a heavy frame of elaborately carved koawood was a shot of me with Jax at one of his book signing parties. He's all wide-eyed smiles. I, on the other hand, am a saggy-faced two sheets to the wind who appears to be toasting the camera man. I don't really remember the shot. However, I faintly recall Jax mailing me a smaller copy a couple years back. I also faintly recall folding it into a paper airplane and gliding it into the circular file across the room. Yep, being in this place made me feel pretty crappy all right—big time.

Well, the least I could do was make a thorough job of my assignment. I vowed to myself when Thornton Senior had left to take his wife to her *appointment*—what was it to be, a dry-out at the Betty Ford Clinic?—I vowed that I'd fine-tooth-comb all of Jax's materials at a later, more appropriate date, see if there were anything worthwhile Connor Alba could put to use. But for right now I had something else in mind. I wanted to see if Jax had any stray notes, records or any additional research on his *final* project. Perhaps he had something with a few more of the dots connected, perhaps something that might be of help as I groped along in the dark, bumping into the furniture.

I'd begun by reviewing all the hard copies of everything I found. No clues there. Then I went to the task of putting work papers, plot outlines, character synopsizes, and various manuscripts into a couple of those big banker's cartons I'd found in his closet. When that was done, I marked each carton's cardboard top in big red letters "Jax's Writing Projects."

Next, I'd searched Jax's computer. I had great luck. When he'd last left, instead of shutting the computer down, he'd let it go to sleep while running on low power waiting for a mouse click to reawaken the full system. Even better luck, he'd programmed the thing to automatically remember all his user names and passwords or I might've wasted time trying in vain to guess my way into his various files.

I scanned through several odds and ends, his computer desktop's random flotsam and jetsam. Came up dry. Jax had installed some screenwriting software, but it didn't look like any screenplays had been saved. Perhaps he was thinking of converting his books to film scripts with the software. I discovered the tidy little guy'd kept his working materials neatly organized, and I ultimately copied two writing folders off his C-drive onto a couple of writable CDs, labeled both, then tossed them into one of the cardboard cartons. It looked from the title of some files that he was doing research into coastal hurricanes or other tropical storms, maybe Jax's next title was The Typhooning Corpse?

The Inbox on Jax's e-mail contained a week and a half of dense clutter which had accumulated since his death. Mostly there was the usual spammed Viagra, Cialis and Levitra ads. At least ten messages from a Porsche dealership—perhaps Jax had recently entertained thoughts of upgrading the 911 Turbo-S—or more likely the dealer did. An e-mail bounce-back from Frances Whiting's Web site. Next came a couple of near-spams from some Internet writing organization and a pair of solicitations from some Web cam porn babe with the high-class name of Wendy Sukks. And then…and then a second-bounce back from Frances Whiting.

I recalled her name, she was the writer known as the high priestess of yachting mysteries, not even a remotely appealing genre for a land-lubber such as myself. I remembered seeing Ms. Whiting referenced in WatChat and on a couple of my monthly pilgrimages through Barnes & Noble. I printed off her e-mail on Jax's LaserJet and read the paper copy a couple of times. It was your basic generic bounce-back, much like the way my own Web site is set up to deal with e-mails from strangers. The automatic bounce-back that thanks the reader for writing, assures them that I'll read their message, and expresses how I'm deeply saddened that I'm unable to answer all messages personally and still fulfill my duties to publisher and public—but, hey! stay tuned, Dear Fan, for my next book's coming out in March. All of which is PR yak-kak to accompany giving the sender an instant blow-off. All successful writers need such a gatekeeper—except in my case the truth is, if I had a hankering, I could very easily answer the four or five fan e-mails that dribble in every week, but that Delete button is just too damned enticing for a lazy slug like me.

Frances Whiting's first bounce back was two nights before Jax's death. The latest bounce-back had arrived in Jax's Inbox the afternoon of his last day on Planet Earth. This second was the oldest message in his e-heap that had remained unopened. Bouncebacks are fairly quick, so Jax shoots her an e-mail, exits Outlook and scoots away to his final roundtrip, or maybe he read the bounce back in the preview panel and hadn't opened it. Either way Frances Whiting had received an e-mail from Jax mere hours before his death.

I checked the Sent Items folder to see what he might've said to her. Empty. I entered his Deleted Items folder. Nothing there either. But this wouldn't mean someone had been tampering. The server's system likely has one of those anal housecleaning programs—one that deletes such folders upon user exit, or else dumps it all every four or five days. However, I made a mental note to check with Lieutenant Neff, my resource at the Robbery Homicide Division. LAPD has techies who can sometimes go into the hard drive and pull up deletions. Perhaps an e-trail still existed that could be of help.

The only other e-folder Jax had titled was labeled Current Project. It had about seven or eight recent e-mails with his publisher regarding his upcoming *Corpse* novel, still in the gestation stage— possibly the one dealing with tropical storms. I had no idea if Jax had a second separate e-mail account, like YAHOO! or HOTMAIL, and, even if he did, I wouldn't have the foggiest notion how to hack into it. I made another mental note for Detective Neff to check with Jax's Webmaster. I knew his service was through his publisher.

Turning my attention from Jax's desktop PC, I opened the middle drawer in the desk. A messy jumble of pencils, pens, paperclips, and an electronic, palm-size thesaurus. I opened his lower left-hand drawer—the one with hanging pendeflexes—and could've wept. The thickly-padded first one was labeled "GUY'S FEEDBACK." I paged through it and realized he saved everything I'd ever given him—a postcard I'd sent from Tucson saying I'd be back in time for his Halloween party, an assortment of post-it notes he'd scribbled after our phone calls, notes from our tavern conversations jotted on soiled cocktail napkins, miscellaneous things written on the backs of our bar tabs, all of which he had, of course, paid. A paper clipped stack of newspaper snippings, reviews of all my recent books. Last of all, a few of my very infrequent, always glib e-mails to him had been tossed in here and there.

To Jax's mind, Guy was a special person—Thornton Senior had said I was the big brother Jax never had. To Guy, Jax was about as significant as the cardboard coaster under my Bloody Mary at some nameless watering hole. I choked on a thick wave of guilt.

Aw Jax, I stared at the folder, *such pitiful, silly hero-worship. A case of unrequited love, Little Buddy, pathetic and unrequited. And misplaced, considering how you were far ahead of my curve on this caper, kid. A possible real live mystery pops up and you're on it like a bloodhound, whereas I've got my head stuck up that celebrated place where the sun don't shine. I've been following in your footsteps, Little Buddy, although I did manage to score a virtual death threat from some cyberspook named Scythe. Not to worry, though Jax, I'm having a new alarm system installed and I've taken to sleeping with jars on the steps to my bedroom and Lady Smith under my pillow.*

I ran my fingers over the pages in the other hanging pendeflexes. All related to Jax's previous novels and labeled as such—a file for each corpse if you will. I pulled my folder out of the drawer, just to confirm how pompous an ass I truly am and hoping to soothe my guilt if I might trip over one or two kind words that I may have uttered to the poor dweeb. Then I spotted it.

A flash of yellow in the bottom of the file drawer caught my eye. A yellow pad was buried on the bottom, beneath the hanging folders. I shoved some files back to get a better peek. The visible part of the pad appeared to have something on it. How odd, to jam a writing pad down there. Highly inconvenient to get at every time you wanted to jot down story ideas, or anything else. Unless…unless it was something Jax didn't want lying in plain view for some reason. Maybe his treasure trove of story ideas? Or research notes? But that would be paranoid and I'd never gotten the impression that Jax was highly suspicious and secretive about his working ideas, unlike many other writers. On the contrary, he was the most open crafter of mysteries I ever met.

With difficulty I removed a thick bundle of the hanging files and set the stack on the credenza next to his computer. Then jammed the remaining files to the far back of the drawer to clear an opening. With a bit further exertion I extracted the legal size pad from the drawer bottom. I set it in on the desktop in front of me to study. The page contained letters and crisscrossing arrowed lines.

What the hell kind of laundry list have you got here, Jax?

I noted there were capitalized letters peppered about the page. Pointed lines appeared to connect several sets of the letters. In the top left was A.M. A.M.? Standing for early morning—ante meridian—was this some sort of timeline?

Below this symbol were the initials I.M.I. with an arrow upward to the A.M. a few inches above. Jax was young, but could never be confused as being the healthiest spoon in the drawer, physically or mentally. Could I.M.I. be some kind of medical acronym, like an institute? Or an MRI-like test?

Possibly I.M.I. could stand for Jax's doctor, perhaps his clinic? Had Jax set a medical appointment for some time in the morning and this was his reminder? But no exact time or date...for that matter, no doctor's name, no clinic address or phone number...was jotted near the initials. It seemed unlikely nightowl Jax would choose a morning appointment time. Plus which, Jax wouldn't bury medical appointment information beneath his hanging files...or would he? I picked up his desktop calendar and flipped through it. I found scrawled notes regarding two dental appointments and a half-dozen social obligations, mostly Jax's parties. No evidence he'd hidden a medical appointment reminder.

I turned my attention back to the legal pad. Jax's penmanship was almost as pathetic as mine—the next set of initials was either a C.S. or a C.5. or a C.8. followed by a squiggle line angling downward. Great, Jax, toss a number into the brew just to confuse things more. A few spaces lower, came T.W. with an arrow leading to an A.C. And still further down was a P.J.T. with a line to a scrawl that was either B.Q. or D.Q. P.J.T. could stand for P. Jax Thornton, Jax's own initials. What in blazes was D.Q. or B.Q. supposed to mean? Perhaps Jax intended to stop at Dairy Queen for a Bar-B-Que sandwich on the way to a morning doctor's appointment? Nonsense.

Something slowly dawned. Assuming P.J.T. represented Jax's initials, maybe all the other combinations were the same. Maybe all the scattered jottings stood for people. With that thought I stared further down the legal pad. At the very bottom of the page, this one without an arrowed line and with a big fat question mark—which had been underlined repeatedly—next to it, I saw the letters T.G.D. Those were the initials of my pen name—Timothy Guy Davitt. Why no arrow? And why the emphatic question mark?

What was intended by Jax's chart? Who were all the people represented by the random initials? I could guess at a handful, but what was the significance of the arrowed lines? Whatever this chart represented, Jax clearly had been wondering if I fit into it. I sat and pondered the hen scratchings for a long spell. Aw screw it, I finally tossed the legal pad on top of the other things I'd stacked in one of the banker's boxes.

I leaned back in the computer chair and gazed at the framed picture of Jax and myself. Not really caring if Mr. Thornton would approve, I took the photograph off the wall and placed it gently on top of the stack of Jax's materials.

The photo stared back up at me.

Chapter 8

When I got to my duplex the message light on my phone was flashing. I hit the button. It was The Judge's voice, a faint tone of urgency, "Call me as soon as you get this message. Very important. Strike that. You should drive down so we can talk face to face…yes, come just as soon as you hear this message."

That's a new one! I thought, wondering what could be so uncharacteristically urgent.

While nudging my ailing Mustang into Pacific Coast Highway's gridlocked evening traffic, I dialed him on my cell. As usual I hadn't recharged the damn thing so the battery was nearly dead, meaning I couldn't connect. It was past nine when I arrived.

"I take it something important must be up. Huh, Judge?" I asked the silver stag.

"There were traces of diazepine in his blood."

"What in hell are you talking about?"

"Look, I'm not necessarily agreeing with your wild-eyed conclusions. All your distress about the murders of mystery writers— including that Angus MacDougall chap from Canada—but after I'd thought more about it, I made some phone calls. Checked a few things for myself. Particularly the Toronto incident."

"I can't believe you did that." I was astonished at this turn of events.

"Let's just say it's the active curiosity of an aging firehorse whenever the word 'homicide' is mentioned…however implausible it might sound, and your speculations are certainly implausible…in any event, I proceeded. Well, I turned up a striking anomaly that was found inside Angus MacDougall's corpse. The cadaver's blood serum, to be precise."

"Start over and slow down for us duller-witted boys in the back row, will you Judge? Exactly what calls did you make?"

"An old Toronto acquaintance of mine. Superintendent Bolton of the RCMP."

"The Mounties?"

The silver hair nodded affirmatively," Super-intendent Bolton provided me with a copy of the Toronto coroner's report. Faxed it to my office, actually. Trace amounts of diazepine were in MacDougall's blood. It's noted in the report…here, I circled the line in red."

"What's this dizzipenis stuff, Judge?"

"Di-ahz-e-peen. Four syllables can't be too challenging even for you duller-witted ones in the rear of the class."

"Whatever. I repeat, what is the stuff?"

"Diazepine's the core ingredient in most of the benzodiazepines."

"Well *that* certainly clarifies the hell out of everything, why didn't you say so right away?"

The old man ignored me and continued in his arrogantly condescending manner, "Valium being the most notable, at least to the popular mind, benzodiazepines are the core of some of the other hypotensives as well. Also, to the popular mind, it was the base ingredient in the first generation of date rape drugs. They used to haul some real class acts before me who had plied their lady friends with Rohypnol—or Roofies I think they call it on the street..." chuckling, he added, "...y'know in my younger days a suitor courted with candy and liquor and flowers, but today's MTV generation is too impatient for courtship I suppose."

"So you are telling me the Toronto coroner found a date rape drug in MacDougall's blood."

"Is it the acoustics in this room or are you stone deaf?"

"You're kind of a Johnny One-Note with all the sarcasm."

"Just this once, my dear boy, can't you take my point and not my pianissimo? Quite frankly I'm surprised you haven't heard about Rohypnol or used it in one of your silly yarns."

"I've heard about it, just didn't know the chemistry." I vowed not to take anymore bait. At least he wasn't calling me 'Timothy' today. I added, "According to the Toronto papers, MacDougall's official cause of death was alcohol poisoning."

"Correct. I phoned Superintendent Bolton about it. He told me, quote, 'self-inflicted acute alcohol poisoning, inadvertent' is still the official verdict. Their position is eminently rational...from the RCMP's viewpoint." As always the old man's smile shaved decades from his creased face.

"You're saying what? The Toronto authorities just ignore that MacDougall's cadaver shows he'd been drugged before two quarts of single malt were funneled down his throat?"

"Not ignore, Timothy, rationalize."

"The point is why in hell would Angus MacDougall be taking dizzy dean...however you pronounce it...anyway?"

"RCMP assumed he was multi-substance abuser. Hell, Junior, almost every affluent addict in the Western World ends up doing more than one substance by the time their livers disintegrate. RCMP saw nothing remarkable to find traces of diazepine in the system of an advanced alcoholic."

"Absurd."

"The RCMP reasoned this way—the man was an alcoholic known to go on daily binges. On this occasion he probably began the binge when he was already impaired on some diazepine derivative. Thus, his internal censor system was lacking and in a brief time he quaffed down a river, thus fatally toxifying himself. Superintendent Bolton says every year upwards of two hundred of our Neighbors to the North blotto themselves right into that big vineyard in the sky by sucking in more than their metabolisms can handle in a short space of time."

"Amateurs, sure. Not experienced sixty-year-old tipplers."

"RCMP obviously assumed MacDougall didn't behave like a normal tippler his age."

"So the RCMP ignores the date rape drug in his system," I said in disgust.

"As I said, they found only trace amounts of diazepine and there's no conclusive evidence he'd been drugged immediately before the liquor, with which this poor guy pickled his medulla oblongata straight into an early grave. Just check out his BAL…I marked it in red."

"Jesus, a point six-three!" I stared at the examiner's report, MacDoogs' blood alcohol reading, which on the Richter Scale of booze would level Hong Kong. "I didn't know anyone could get that high."

"The chart also reveals a residue of unassimilated alcohol in the corpse's stomach and the coroner's throat swabs indicate traces of hooch in the esophagus."

"Meaning what?" I asked.

"This means the man's system stopped functioning before it had assimilated all he'd drunk. Naturally, this could merely indicate MacDougal over-guzzled his system's ability to assimilate the alcohol...but, and here's the rub...this residue, especially in the esophagus, could also indicate something darker. To wit, the hooch was being poured down him for a short time after his system ceased functioning. In short, after he was dead."

"With these indicators, why're they calling it an accidental overdose?"

"The forest, not the trees. Think, Timothy," The Judge tapped my temple with his forefinger, "the man was a well-known lush, he was found in the house in which he lived alone, by his day-maid. There were no signs of foul play, no hint of a struggle, nothing noticeable missing, and the booze in which he imbibed was from his private stock. Comparatively speaking, those other indicators are meaningless."

"But if the Mounties' conclusion is so bloody reasonable, if it's *de rigueur* for lushes like MacDougall to go down with trace amounts of

43

this stuff and with undigested booze in their guts, then why did you ask me to rush over here?"

"On the surface the RCMP's version is utterly reasonable. One has to give them that. But there's an equally reasonable alternative. The man may've been drugged. Meaning whoever drugged Angus MacDougall also binged him off to that far, far better place. Given the alternative premises, if I were running the RCMP I would've kept the file open awhile longer—the diazepine would've made me look into the alternative rationale—the possibility of homicide."

I looked keenly into those gray eyes. "I'll be damned…you're no longer writing me off as a victim of paranoid fantasies."

The old man sighed deeply, "Maybe I've outlived the Age of Patience, which is my method of thinking. Maybe it's not just the MTV spawn that are too damn infected with rush-rush-rush to conclusions, too damned in need of quick closure, too damn fast to leap to the climax. Maybe…just maybe…even the august RCMP has become infected with mental haste."

I studied the light of skeptical wisdom in those pale gray eyes that I both feared and appreciated. The cold skepticism that cut and hurt when focused in my insecure direction, but also a skepticism that provided warmth and a sense of steely support and safety when directed at our mutual target. Here, the mutual target was the RCMP's haste in writing off MacDougall's death as the result of self-inflicted single malt. Not pausing to account for unknown criminal forces as a possibility.

"What next?" I asked.

"Not quite sure where to go from here, Timothy. For starters, maybe you should go over with me again those other deaths you were so lathered about the other night."

Chapter 9

Lieutenant Madeleine "Maddie" Neff, fortyish with dishwater blonde hair cut short above wide green eyes and a Bob Hope nose, commanded a Robbery Homicide squad working out of the West L.A. branch of LAPD. Myself, and a double dozen other mystery writers in the L.A. area, had found Maddie a very cooperative resource. But that was for assistance in our fiction writing. My visit this morning was more serious.

"Pull up a chair, Davitt," she said while momentarily cupping her hand over the phone before returning to her call. "Bring him in as a material witness, Pickman, but don't book him yet. No, we don't want him lawyered up. Jesus, Pickman, is English your third language—you will no-bookie him yet." Maddie Neff hung up the phone, silently mouthing a string of expletives.

She brightened as she turned to me. "Do I see two el jumbo Starbucks in your mitts?"

"One for each of us, Maddie, and it sounds like you need it," I passed her the cup. "Almond cappuccino, right?"

"Daddy always warned me to beware of geeks bearing gifts," she said while popping off the lid and taking a long sip. "But in your case, Davitt, I'll make an exception."

"I was wondering, Maddie, how the heck many times have you been acknowledged?"

"Lordy, I don't know. Counting movies?"

"Sure."

"Mid thirties. Maybe forty."

"Outside of mine, any of them any good?"

"That's easy. Let's see, including yours and the made-for-TV crap—approximately none." Neff and I exchanged Mona Lisa smiles for several seconds. "Sorry to prick your hubris, Davitt."

"Very nice, Lieutenant. Very nice. Great tan, by the way. Where'd you go this time?"

Maddie Neff opened her mouth but suddenly clammed shut, wearing a self-conscious look.

"Oh no," I broke out laughing, "not another singles' cruise? Or was it a Get-Laid bus tour this time?"

"And how's your social calendar, Casanova?"

"Fair to mostly horseshit," I confessed.

"Glass houses, Davitt, glass houses."

"You ever take one of them tours to Paris—the city of love?"

"Never jumped the pond." She stared off into space as though envisioning the Eiffel Tower and Arch de Triomphe. "Perhaps someday."

"If you struck out, at least the food would still be excellent."

Lieutenant Neff leaned slightly forward in her desk chair signaling that small talk time was over, "What're you hustling me for this time?"

"Help with a murder."

"So you've written Connor Alba into another corner, you and he are both stumped, so you need my help in unstumping. It figures."

"This one has to do with a *real homicide*," I explained.

Maddie's pale green eyes glistened with suspicion. She leaned aggressively very far forward and said sharply, "If this is some story idea you're floating past me be honest about it and stow the hustle about *real homicide*."

"This time it's not a story, not about Connor Alba. God's honest truth, Maddie."

She seemed to accept that. "Who was killed?"

"P. Jax Thornton III. A minor writer. A friend."

"Don't think I knew him. Thornton, eh?...part of Jax Thornton Pools, they of the *Almighty Times* Business Section's Top California 100?"

"That's the family."

Maddie turned her chair to face the computer screen. Her fingers moved like lightening over the keyboard. "Hmm. According to our database, P. Jax Thornton died in a single car accident. Drove off West Canyon above Santa Monica. Broken neck, skull, spine, and ribs." She looked up at me, the light of suspicion again gleaming in her pale greens, "So what makes you think Thornton was a homicide?"

"Short version or long?" I asked.

"Start short, Davitt," she ordered.

"A few days before Jax's death he came to see me. He was all worked up. He thought he'd stumbled onto a string of real serial murders. All of them garbed as accidents. I didn't listen to him. Then Jax himself dies violently. Belatedly, I take him seriously and start checking things out."

"These serial killings he was so worked up about. All in Southern California?"

"Nope. One in San Francisco. One in Toronto. And I found a related pattern involving one in Connecticut."

"So your pal Thornton dies in a car crash in L.A. County, but you see this as one link in a serial pattern of homicides stretching from coast to coast?"

"Right."

"What else you got, Davitt?"

"The victims were all writers. Murder mystery writers who...."

"Dammit, Davitt, did you miss my warning? If you're in here dicking me around over some tired story idea you're cooking up I'll make sure yesterday was the last pleasant day of your life. I mean it and I can damn well do it, too."

"I'm not messing with you, Maddie. This is totally on the level. Look, Jax figured that Angus MacDougall did not die of alcohol poisoning as the RCMP in Toronto wrote it off."

"That the Angus MacDougall who writes about a mystery a month? I've read a lot of his stuff...pretty authentic as such things go. In fact, Davitt, when I was a sophomore at USC and the sages of the Music Department made it clear I didn't have the stuff to hack it as a concert cellist, I read a lot of escapism. *A lot.* And it was reading some of Angus MacDougall's police procedurals that pointed me towards law enforcement. Since then I've always had a soft spot for that Canuck's work. I hadn't heard MacDougall was dead...too bad. When?"

"Early last month."

"You say the Toronto authorities wrote MacDougall's death off to alcohol poisoning?"

"Yes."

"And why would you presume they're wrong?"

I took a copy of The Judge's fax of the Toronto autopsy report from the inside pocket of my blazer and pushed it across her desk. I quickly explained the minute traces of diazepine found in his blood. Then summarized the statistics on the absence of alcohol poisoning as a C.O.D. among affluent, long-time soaks like MacDougall.

"Hmm," was Maddie's only comment. After a moment her fingers flew back to her computer keyboard. She squinted critically at something on the screen then turned her attention back to me. "How'd you acquire a copy of the Toronto coroner's report?"

"Does it matter?"

"Not really...just curious about how sieve-like the RCMP recordkeeping is. I can't get the damn thing from the NorthAmShare Net, but Toronto may just be slow in posting stuff. So how'd *you* come by it?"

"A certain Federal Judge did me a favor."

"I see. What else you got, Davitt?"

"Well, Jax's parents asked me to sort through his office. I found a diagram in Jax's files. I clipped a photocopy beneath the coroner's report I just gave you."

Maddie Neff studied the arrows and letters for a long minute. "What in hell am I to make of this jigsaw puzzle?"

"I'm still working on that."

"You mentioned Connecticut and San Fran. What were those about?"

I quickly gave her my skimpy information on Beck Quinn's death last year and Alexandra Case's assumed asphyxiation in San Francisco last week."

"Anything more...because so far all I see is supposition. Maybe this, maybe that. Coincidences. We need something tangible, a solid motive for instance."

I was in mid-drink from my Starbucks when something flickered at the base of my brain. What was it Mrs. Thornton had said? She'd been slobbering in her drink about her emotional umbilical to young Jax and she'd said something unrelated. I put down my Starbucks and looked into Maddie's dubious gaze. "She said, 'There's always the money thing.'"

"Who said what?"

"Mrs. Thornton. Jax's mom. When I was sorting through the files in his office. She was on the sauce pretty heavy and I didn't pay much heed. She was ranting how her child had been murdered and a mother would know such things so on and so on. She mentioned money. Her exact words to me, trying to get me to take her slobbering seriously, were these: 'There's always the money thing.'"

"What money thing was she talking about, Davitt?"

"Beats hell out of me. The Thorntons are already obscenely rich."

Maddie Neff returned to her computer. Moving my coffee aside I edged forward across her desk and watched as she surfed a database or two, then brought up a Web site and worked that for a minute. "Well, seems Jax Thornton Pools, Inc. took in over $200 million, just in California and Arizona last year. And the company is global...did one-point-six billion in sales worldwide two years ago...has a Hong Kong subsidiary with very big cash flow."

"You seem less skeptical suddenly, Maddie," I commented.

"You got that right. I am a believer in Deep Throat's immortal dictum—follow the money. Especially in L.A. where even a new pair of sneakers can very well get you dead. I'd love to have a chitchat with Mother Thornton...get our crosshairs on exactly what 'money thing' she was referring to. Far as you know the Thorntons are holed up in their mountain compound above Santa Monica?"

"Yes. Well, maybe not both of them. I picked up the sense that Thornton Senior and Mrs. Thornton's nurse or watchdog or whatever the woman was…her name's Juanita…were about to haul Mother Thornton someplace. My hunch, someplace to dry out for awhile."

"I'll dig into that part, Davitt. You're totally certain she said 'There's always the money thing' in reference to her son's crash being a murder, not an accident?"

"Stack of Bibles, Maddie."

"Jot down your home and cell numbers. Once I locate Mother Thornton's whereabouts I think I wanna take you along to help me interview her…you were her deceased son's friend and she already opened the door a crack to you and so forth…okay?" I detected the momentary glint of a raw feral enthusiasm for the blood hunt in Maddie's eyes.

"Can do."

"And, Davitt, remember to keep your cell charged. And leave it on."

Chapter 10

By early afternoon I stood beside her as Lieutenant Maddie Neff flashed her LAPD Homicide badge and demanded of the Institute's assistant supervisor, "We're here to talk to a patient you've got named Mrs. Veronica M. Thornton. Of Santa Monica."

Except for what appeared to be a thin moustache of nostril hairs, the whiskerless man seemed too young for his arrogance of office as he said dismissively, "Naturally, Lieutenant, I would very much like to accommodate you but we may not even have a Mrs. Thornton here at Betty Ford, and of course, our policies won't allow me to confirm whether she is or she isn't. Also, clinic policies do not..."

"I know Veronica Thornton's here all right or wouldn't have wasted time driving down," she snapped impatiently. For the second time I witnessed the steel fist hidden inside Maddie's glove of soft velvet.

"As I was trying to say, Lieutenant, our resident patients cannot be disturbed by anyone while undergoing their rehabilitation. But if you'll leave your card, we'll get back to you if and when...."

"Look, I am here on an active homicide investigation, and you haven't any choice but to make Mrs. Thornton available. Now we'll be as sweet-tempered as clover honey but we will see her."

"I'm very sorry, Lieutenant, but our policies...."

"Call your supervisor," Maddie Neff firmly ordered.

"I don't think I care for your tone, Lieutenant."

"Call your supervisor, now, sonny!"

"Well, Mrs. Lewenthal is in the East on a trip and...well, she can't be...."

"Understand that I am telling you for the last time—make Veronica Thornton available for questioning immediately."

"And understand that I'm telling you, Lieutenant, for the last time...." began the youthful assistant supervisor.

Maddie moved in close to the sniffy young man and fast as lightning pulled a pair of cuffs from somewhere beneath her blue blazer. "Stand up please, turn around, place your hands behind you," she ordered.

"What...what is this...?" the assistant supervisor stammered.

"You are being arrested for obstructing a police investigation, sir. You have the right to remain...."

"Wait wait. There's no need. Let me just phone the clinic's lawyer and I'm sure this can all be cleared up."

"You can phone him from downtown," Lieutenant Neff barked. "You think I enjoyed making the drive all the way out here just to have

50

some snout-haired ignoramus keep me from talking to a material witness in a murder investigation?" Maddie finished cuffing him and clamped his upper arm in her experienced, vice-grip-like fingers to guide him out.

I stood back in awe, observing the petite whirlwind in action, and wondered how much of Lieutenant Neff had rubbed off on Connor Alba ever since my agent had first recommended her as one of the preeminent LAPD contacts sought by scriptwriters and novelists as a fount of police procedural information.

"You have the right to remain silent..." Maddie again started to Mirandize.

"Wait."

"You had your chance, sonny. I'll try and score you a cell with a forlorn roommate."

"Please, this is all a tragic misunderstanding," the assistant supervisor's balloon had entirely deflated, "I'm sure we can make Mrs. Thornton available to you. In one of the conference rooms."

"When?"

"As soon as you take these handcuffs off."

"Nada. Have Mrs. Thornton brought right here to your office, then the cuffs come off. You savvy, sonny?"

"Yes."

I noted how Veronica Thornton's eyes were far clearer, her face more alert and less sagging than a couple days earlier at Jax's pool house. With clean, kempt hair and absent the liquor-stained silks, and except for the slight tremble in both her hands, Mrs. Thornton looked more youthful and more robust.

"Guy Davitt? Don't tell me you've come all the way out here to introduce me to your current lady friend?" Mrs. Thornton disapprovingly eyed Maddie.

"No. Mrs. Thornton, this is Lieutenant Neff of the Los Angeles Police Department."

"Mrs. Thornton, I'm very sorry about your son. Let's all sit for a moment so we can talk," Maddie said warmly grasping Veronica Thornton's hand. She sat in the assistant supervisor's desk chair and Veronica Thornton and I sat facing her. "Guy reports you told him you believe your son was murdered."

"I said that to you?" Veronica Thornton gave me a saucer-eyed look.

"Yes, Mrs. Thornton, the other day in Jax's office. You mentioned that a mother as close to her son as you were to Jax would be able to tell if her son died in an accident or was murdered. Don't you recall saying that?"

"Oh Christ, Guy, I'm sure I did." Veronica Thornton looked around the office, from Lieutenant Neff to me, and then asked firmly, "You two are aware of where it is that you're visiting me, right now?"

"Yes," I whispered, looking down at my shoes.

"Recent days are all pretty much a blur," Veronica Thornton acknowledged. "Recent months to be truthful."

I was amazed at how much progress she seemed to have made ascending from her alcoholic sub-gutter.

Maddie took command. "Mrs. Thornton, do you know any reason anyone would have to kill your son?"

"Do people still need reasons to do horrid things? Particularly in this town?" she replied.

"Guy told me you mentioned money as a possible reason."

"I actually said that?"

"Yes," I nodded, "when I asked you why anyone would want to kill Jax you said the words 'There's always the money thing.' I wouldn't make that up, Mrs. Thornton."

"Of course you wouldn't, Guy. I know that. And if you say so," Veronica Thornton shrugged, "I must've said it."

"Mrs. Thornton," Maddie probed, "it is very important for us to know something. Very important. Please think hard. What did you mean when you said to Guy 'There's always the money thing'?"

Veronica Thornton brushed the back of her trembling hand across her eyes. "Oh…it's to do with the business and… so difficult to piece it all together. I'd like to help you but…you know it has to do with something so complicated…even when I've not been drinking I can't quite wrap my mind around it. Perhaps the lawyer could explain it."

"The lawyer?" Maddie pressed, "What lawyer is that?"

"The lawyer's name is Kuderrer. Colin Kuderrer. Of Dorsey & Kuderrer in Santa Monica. The firm has represented the family since the days of Grandfather Thornton, my husband's late father."

"And Mr. Kuderrer will tell us what the 'money thing' is?"

"Tell Colin I sent you to him. Tell him that he is to explain the trust fund, the estate…the whole sticky ball of wax. Just as he's done for me on more than one occasion. It's all an insane setup, Guy," Veronica Thornton stared at me, "absolutely insane."

52

Chapter 11

Colin Kuderrer's blond-white hair had thinned to wisps covering deeply bronzed skin that obviously saw its share of golf, tennis, and tanning salons.

"Lieutenant, if you slipped past the Praetorian Guard at the Betty Ford and talked to Veronica, you are to be congratulated. I've tried several ruses but I still can't get in, can't even reach her on the telephone."

"You've been trying to contact Mrs. Thornton?" Maddie asked.

"Have I ever. But no results. They've got her buttoned up tight…of course, I don't carry a badge…getting past her keepers I might as well be a Jew trying to get into Mecca to kiss the Kaaba."

"Why do you think she's been isolated?" Maddie pursued.

"Formally, to focus. Substance abusers are kept out of touch with the people they know, supposed to spend twenty-four hours a day focusing on grappling with their substance dependencies. That's the *formal* reason."

Maddie's interest was intense. "And *informally*?"

"Before I answer that let me ask you about lawyer jokes—you know, the kind that go 'Question: What do you call 1,000 lawyers sinking with a cruise ship in a tsunami? Answer: A good start.' That sort of thing."

"What's that got to do with anything?" I asked.

"Exactly this—I'm going to reveal some confidences. Not because I'm one of those infamous shysters you can't trust and I deserve to drown. I'm not that sort. Nor is the firm of Dorsey & Kuderrer."

"You're worried we'll criticize you for revealing some confidences?"

"The firm's good name means everything. We get done here and I don't want either of you to lump us in with the slippery sorts when you talk to others."

"I assure you we won't, Mr. Kuderrer," Maddie soothed. "Everything you say to us stays in this room."

"Good. You see, our firm has represented the Thornton family since right after World War II when the first P. Jax Thornton made his millions in construction."

"Yea, building swimming pools," I added.

"Swimming pools was only a tiny part of it and only at first, along with cabanas, golf courses, desert resorts—the whole growth of Western America following the War. My father and Old Jax were best of friends and rode the affluence express to the peak together. When Old Jax died in a boating accident down in the Keys in the late-eighties,

53

he had holdings of well over two billion. Worldwide interests in land, tankers, casinos, oil, and damn near everything else at the buffet."

"I don't get it," I said, "I'd always heard Jax Thornton I only made it in swimming pools, Jax II in pool liners."

"That's a well-cultivated urban myth."

"Myth? The late Jax III and I were friends and he never mentioned anything about the worldwide interests of the Thornton family."

"He didn't know. Jax would've been a kid when his grandpa died. When Grandpa Jax died, he left the swimming pool and cabana part directly to his only son, Veronica Thornton's husband Jax II. And to give him credit, Jax II did well, pool liners and the rest. But that was all. The rest, the bulk of the empire, was placed in what's called a generation-skipping trust for the benefit of your friend, the recently deceased Jax Thornton III."

"Mr. Kuderrer, could you put that in simple laymanese?" Maddie flipped open her notebook, pencil stub magically appearing in her right hand.

"Almost everything is in the Trust. I'm a trustee, Veronica is a trustee, and on his 35th birthday, Jax III would've been shown everything and at that time he would've become the controlling trustee and sole beneficiary."

"But what about Thornton Senior, Jax's father?" I asked.

"Thornton Senior would've kept only the pool liners and other minor pieces. Period. End of ledger."

Maddie and I exchanged looks.

Kuderrer continued, "As you might expect, Thornton Senior did not like it from the get-go. Still doesn't. Not one iota. Over the years he's questioned me a hundred times about the Trust...was there some way to break it open? What if his pool business went kaput, then what? Why did Old Granddaddy Jax name Veronica and myself as co-trustees and leave Thornton Senior out in the cold? Mostly, what ate at him though, why did his own father toss him some crumbs and put the most savory entrees into a trust for a mere kid? Candidly, I suspect Thornton Senior had more first-hand knowledge about his father's true reasons than I ever would from the outside looking in."

"Bad blood?" Maddie wondered aloud. "A family feud?"

"On the surface—tax reasons. But...let us say there was never a real bond of...in a word, love, to be blunt about it...between Grandpa Jax and Thornton Senior."

"Since Jax III will never reach his 35th birthday," I asked, "what now?"

"Legal Armageddon. Young Jax Thornton dies suddenly. Veronica Thornton, who always had a small drinking problem, suddenly right in the middle of her mourning the loss of her only child, is whisked away to Betty Ford and kept incommunicado. Meaning Veronica Thornton, co-trustee of one of America's vastest trust funds, is disabled from performing her trustee's duties. This very morning, a firm of extremely high-powered Miami attorneys—a pack of take-no-prisoners jackals—are suddenly representing Thornton Senior. These jackals served me with court papers seeking to permanently displace Veronica Thornton as co-trustee. And toss me out to boot. Also seeking to relocate the Trust to Miami, Florida. And seeking to make Thornton Senior sole trustee with sole power to exercise the Cy-Pres clause of the Trust."

"Cyprus?" I asked. "Isn't that an island in the Mediterranean?"

"Not Cyprus—Cy-Pres. Should be pronounced See-Pray. An old French term. It means there's a special clause in the Thornton Trust that says if the original intent cannot be achieved—in this case young Jax III reaching his 35th birthday and taking over the Trust—then the trustee may use the Trust assets to achieve some other goal. So long as the new goal is as close as possible to the original intent. Understand?"

"I think so."

The lawyer continued, "Under these circumstances, Cy-Pres is a nuclear device. If Thornton Senior gets into sole control of things he'll have no roadblock to handing over the keys of the kingdom to himself, since his deceased son will never reach age 35."

"What're the chances of the courts letting him pull it off?" Maddie asked.

Kuderrer pondered for a moment, then said, "I'm not a betting man, but if I were I wouldn't bet against Thornton Senior—he is one determined SOB. And he's picked a like-minded jackals for attorneys."

"Anything else we should know, Mr. Kuderrer?" Maddie asked.

"Just this. The pleadings and briefs filed by the Miami jackals are comprehensive. Detailed. Very intricate and extremely well-researched. And precisely in point with the current circumstances."

"Meaning what exactly?" I asked.

"This was not something the Miami law firm slapped together in a few days."

"You saying everything was premeditated?" Maddie zeroed in.

"I'm only saying there is no way those papers haven't been in preparation for at least six weeks. Probably closer to several months."

"You're certain?" Maddie flipped shut her notebook.

"Stake my reputation on it."

Chapter 12

Maddie bit her lips in anxious silence as she drove us away from Dorsey & Kuderrer in Santa Monica.

At length, I broke the silence. "So what do you think?"

Maddie, lost in thought, seemed not to hear me.

"A couple billion bucks is pretty tangible, eh Maddie? A lot of motive."

"You think?" Suddenly she flipped on her siren, popped on the rear window flashers, rolled down her driver's side window and stuck the blinking porta-dome atop her gray sedan. Maddie accelerated as she wheeled into a U-turn in the middle of congested LaCiennaga and roared back toward Pacific Coast Highway.

"What's up?" I asked, grabbing tight to the handle over the passenger door with white knuckles.

"Just pray we're not too late."

"Too late for what?"

"Pappa Jax is moving at mach speed on this thing. I want to preserve evidence, if it hasn't already vanished into the mist."

"What's going on in your brain, Lieutenant Neff?"

"Candles," she declared.

"Come again?"

"I learned years ago, solving a homicide is no more and no less than being a spelunker in a dark cavern. The tiniest light you can find— even the faintest glimmer of a smoldering candle—is worth the effort. Any e-mails, any documents Jax sent or received or stored may bring a little light. Now Thornton Senior gave you a standing invitation to fart around the family compound, right? Carte blanch to help yourself to the dead kid's things?"

"More or less, sure."

"Meaning you could walk in, nab his computer, his disks, his laptop, whatever?"

"Within reason, I expect so. Why?"

"Blackberries? Chip-clips? Memory sticks? Writables?"

"I had some blackberry syrup at IHOP yesterday morning...but what're all those other things?"

"If I sent someone with you, to Jax's office, to help you sort stuff? Any problem?"

"Probably not. Why?"

"Here's the thing...I'd like our techies to get a good look at the kid's stuff in the police lab."

"Why do you need me? Jax is a potential murder victim. Can't LAPD get a search warrant?"

"And you call yourself a mystery writer, Davitt?" Maddie shot.

"What?"

"'Say, your Honor, there's this schmuck who heard a dead friend's drunken mommy mumble something incoherent about her son being murdered. Can you please sign this here search warrant for the Thornton estate as, based on this mountain of probable cause, we believe Thornton Senior to be the Boston Strangler? Yea, that's the one, Your Honor, that Thornton Senior—that California Captain of Industry who dines weekly with the Governor.' Dig, Davitt?"

"I dig."

"Any judge, even one of our pro-law enforcement sweethearts would flip me the bird on this. Plus, why set off fire alarms in Thornton Senior and the entire family, them plus their army of pissed-off jackal lawyers? No, I'd prefer having you slide things out under the radar."

"I dig," I repeated.

"So, what do you think? Are you game?"

"I was born game, baby."

"Jesus, Davitt, lines like that and you wonder why you can't get a date."

"I get dates," I replied. "Sometimes."

"These brownies are really sensational, Juanita," I said while keeping the Thornton bird dog occupied. "But I really can't take a plateful with me as I'm watching my waistline. I wouldn't stop 'till they're all eaten. Thanks for the offer, though."

Maddie had hooked me up with an LAPD techie named Duante something or other. Duante had pale lime-tinted skin and looked as though the only light he ever saw came from the glare of his computer screen. Duante was a quiet fellow, introverted even, which was fine by me as we had an intricate plan for him to help me lift all the electronic data and hard drives from Jax's pool house.

Thornton Senior was in Florida for the week, which I learned from one quick phone call from Maddie's car, but Juanita remembered me well. She happily admitted me and 'my old chum Duante' into the pool cottage to finish sifting through Jax's materials. Duante had finished disemboweling Jax's desktop PC, his answering machine, and massive laser printer-cum-fax and we were getting ready to haul away the hard drives when Juanita entered with all smiles, offering us a batch of steaming chocolate-caramel brownies fresh from the oven. I quickly explained to a perplexed Juanita, as she stared over the various disconnect parts, that Duante was going to take Jax's processing unit to his computer loft in order to copy Jax's hard drive so I wouldn't have to keep pestering the Thorntons during this their period of mourning. I promised that Duante would have everything back in the morning. Then I began wolfing down what, in fact, were Juanita's Grade-A brownies.

"Jax must have loved your cooking, Juanita, these sure are excellent," I wiped brown crumbs from my lips with a napkin, "aren't they Duante?"

Duante looked at Juanita and spoke for the first time since we had arrived, "Can I take home that plateful you were going to give him?"

Chapter 13

"Yes? Hello," I answered my cell phone while returning from the Thornton mountaintop. The connection was bad and the road noise on Pacific Coast Highway deafening, so I wasn't sure anyone was on the line. "Hello!" I said again, shouting, hoping to be heard above the traffic.

"Is this Tim? Tim Davitt?"

"Yes."

"Graham Steyn here. From Barnstorm Press."

After a quick bounce off the curb, I wheeled my Mustang into a gas station-cum-convenience-mart and parked.

"Hi Mr. Steyn. Did you get the manuscript? I mailed it a few days back."

"It arrived, Mr. Davitt, but there's a problem."

His tone informed me that my idiot ruse wasn't going to buy me the time I'd hoped for. And with recent events consuming all my waking hours, I had no bone to toss the publisher. Graham Steyn was a kind enough fellow, but had always struck me as an odd duck, with his mallard-like wrinkled neck and faintly greenish tint to his complexion.

"What's the problem, Mr. Steyn?" I asked slowly.

"I was anticipating 10 new chapters, Mr. Davitt, in addition to the three I already have."

"But I sent you a dozen chapters and a prologue."

"Therein lies the problem, Mr. Davitt. I've got eight short chapters—the first three of which I've had nearly a year at this point—then several more, which, as far as I can tell, come from one of your earlier books."

"You're kidding me."

"After chapter eight, the page numbers don't even align and the header suddenly begins referencing *The Aristotle Analysis*."

"Sunnofabitch!" I made an exaggerated production of exhaling loudly before embellishing the tall tale, "Mr. Steyn, please forgive me. I picked up a new Dell last month...attempting to transfer and archive all my manuscripts on the new computer. Something got screwed up."

"Most unfortunate." Steyn's echoing silence ensued.

"Yeah." I wracked my brain. "My whiz kid nephew, Eric, is helping me set everything up. I should be back online in a couple weeks."

"I really must see those four chapters, Mr. Davitt."

"Please call me Guy."

"It's crucial that I see those four chapters as well as anything and everything else you've written, *Guy*, whether it's mid-chapters or end chapters. Everything you've written through today—I need to see."

Steyn's voice on my cell was heavy with exasperation as it bounced off the satellite and yanked me by the ear lobe.

"Tobi's had a rough month."

"And who is Tobi?"

"Tobi is Eric's mother, my sister-in-law. She's undergoing chemo."

"Sorry to hear that."

"It's been a real tough week for the family, Mr. Steyn. Heartbreaking." My flesh crawled. I despised my lying self.

"You've still got my business card, haven't you?"

"Yes."

"Please e-mail me those four chapters as well as all additional work that you've done on the project."

"Tell you what, Mr. Steyn, just give me a week..."

"I expected them months ago, *Mr. Davitt*. Three months ago to be precise."

"But Eric set up my computer system and at this point only he knows how things are arranged in the..."

"Please don't."

"What?"

"Please don't do this." Steyn's hushed voice shook as he strained to keep control—and as I strained to hear his slow, carefully measured words. "I'm in this line of work, Mr. Davitt, because I love being around original minds, being immersed in the creative process. Had I only the spark I'd be a writer myself. You have that spark, Mr. Davitt, so you have to realize and appreciate that this is an extremely difficult call for me to make...extremely difficult. Please just send me everything that you've written for *Return of the B-T-M Killer*. Everything. Nothing in this world would give me greater pleasure than to call you in two days and let you know everything is in order."

"I understand."

"Will you be able to make that occur, Mr. Davitt?"

"I'll do my best, Mr. Steyn."

I silently admitted the hard truth to myself—two days would be an impossible task even for such legendary wordsmiths as Ross Macdonald or Erle Stanley Gardner. And I wasn't even in their league's farm system.

Chapter 14

I blame Scythe. Permitless, I carry my beloved Lady Smith everywhere. Illegally. It fits neatly into the front right pocket of my sport coat, a baggy twill blazer that I've taken to wearing. Often these days, I caress Lady Smith, gently, lovingly, especially at night as I walk to and from my car. I feel like a kid in early puberty with his hand exploring things from the front pockets of his jeans. Anytime, any place, Scythe shows up, he's gonna eat the full clip—right through my favorite sport jacket. Eddie Bauer'd understand.

So imagine my surprise, just as I was sticking the key in the lock of my front door, when a figure in Levis and a jacket stepped from the shadowy hedge along the side of my duplex, a chrome-plated pistol carried at her side on the end of one thin arm.

"Are you Timothy Guy Davitt?" a female voice demanded as she positioned herself at the bottom of the 3-step landing where I stood.

Unlike my fictional alter ego, the ever-cool Connor Alba, I stood frozen to the ground, my innards atremble, dropped jaw, my eyes like deer-in-headlights, tears of fear puddling in them. Even in the cloudless moonlight I didn't immediately realize my impending murder was about to be carried out by a remarkably attractive woman, didn't note that her only detectable flaw was a yellow and blue shiner encircling her left eye. My focus was frozen on her pistol, what appeared to be a shiny automatic that hung from her hand, pointing toward the ground, invisible from the street.

"Dammit," the figure insisted, "are you Guy Davitt?"

A thousand thoughts flashed through my mind. The first thought was how much I'm going to miss baseball, my sainted Dodgers! Followed instantly was how can I make this person believe that I'm not this Guy Davitt prick even though I'm standing on his doorstep with his key in his front door?

"Scythe?" I quaveringly falsetto-ed.

"What?"

"Is it you, Scythe?"

"Who in hell is Scythe?" the figure slid what I now recognized as a Kahr's Mini .45 into her waistband.

"You're not going to kill me?" I exhaled and felt the clenched dread lift from my shoulders and evaporate into the evening air.

"Well, not today, anyhow," she smiled and walked up the steps toward me. "I kind of recognize your face from your Web site, but that picture must be very old."

"The shot's from my mother's ultrasound," I made a lame attempt at humor to cover up how embarrassingly cowardly I'd been. "I'm Guy Davitt."

"Sorry about the gun, Mr. Davitt, but I've had a hell of a week." She stuck out her hand, "My name's Frances Whiting."

What I gathered from her story, it was a pot of green tea and car keys that ultimately saved Frances Whiting's life.

She'd had a dog ass day and things just kept getting worse. She had felt a cold coming on, starting with a tickle in the back of her throat, metastasizing into a hoarseness, and finally a full blown sore throat. Next morning she faced a long-scheduled public reading of her latest book before the Borders Mystery Club at a suburban mall in Fort Lauderdale and she'd be damned if she was going to cancel. Showbiz trooper to the core, Frances said she prided herself that she had never missed a scheduled reading. And never would.

She said she had tossed and turned that night, achieving optimistically 45 fitful minutes of sleep. She chewed aspirin, wanting to stay away from antihistamines that would make her too drowsy to read, sprayed her throat with Chloraseptic, and downed plenty of liquids— orange juice, ginger ale, chicken noodle soup and a few quarts of decaffeinated green tea. Frances knew that if she could struggle through the reading, she could beeline home and sleep round the clock until her throat healed.

Originally she'd planned to deliver a lengthy forty- minute read from her most recent Sally Kerentine mystery, but she downsized that on the way over in favor of a page from her best chapter, then quickly open the floor for Q&A. Her voice was all but gone, but the bookstore provided a microphone and a table for her thermos of tea beside the podium. Apologizing profusely to an audience she'd likely made uncomfortable by forcing them to witness her awkward struggle, Frances soldiered on and got the job done. Then—like a zombie from a C-grade horror movie—Frances had hung for an hour to sign autographs, Borders actually sold quite a few books that day and her eventual cut would about pay for her lozenges and gasoline.

The ride back to her shipboard home at Snail Bay Marina had been miserable, traffic was bad, her hacking continuous, but the worst thing—the very worst thing about the ride—was that Frances really needed to use the bathroom. She'd gone to the restroom right before leaving Borders, but the manager had caught her arm on the way out and spent ten minutes saying the flattery that writers want to—no, make that *need* to—hear. By the time she'd sprung from her parking slot in Snail

Bay's lot, checked her mail in the community room, and double-stepped down the dock, her back teeth were floating. The final 20 yards she'd broken into a sprint. She needed immediately to get to the restroom on her 45-foot yacht, a Carver Mariner II, where she lived.

Frances described how she'd hurdled across the foredeck, dropped her mail on the bar table as she lunged frantically toward the master head. She nudged open the door with her shoulder, began undoing her skirt when she noticed the toilet seat was up. Frances explained as how she lived alone, had no cleaning service, never shared her keys with any previous boyfriends or repairmen, and is more anal about toilet seats than Felix Unger. There was no possible way the seat should be up. And—by the way—what's that faint odor? My god, is that coming from the propane tanks?

Her first thought was burglary, some teenagers had been caught last spring kicking into Hyman Lasky's Voyager over on the next slip, stealing booze and punching out windows to celebrate their testosterone. Frances, fearful that her yacht'd been vandalized, really worried about the Dell computer which contained a not-recently-backed-up copy of her latest Sally Kerentine draft, spun around in the bathroom doorway to see if it was still sitting on the desk across the room. She spun just in time to see the huge man in the Marlins baseball cap and red hornrims rushing toward her.

Reflexes kicked in and Frances, a second degree black belt, threw a hasty throat strike that bounced off his chest just as he sent a roundhouse into her temple that smashed her back into the bathroom. She hit the back of her head on the sink and sank to the floor. And then he was on her, his hands in surgical gloves, his iron-like arms squeezing about the small of her spine, picking her up like a rag doll, dragging her out of the head. He was crushing her in some wrestling hold, she couldn't breathe and stared at his nostrils, his shoe-polish black moustache, his clownish red framed glasses. And as if things weren't bad enough already, she felt her bladder release, warm wetness soaking her thighs and skirt and against her assailant.

About the time of the great bladder release, Frances realized she still had her keys in her left hand and began pressing the Car Find button on her key fob, frantically, furiously pressing the button, praying her Lexus LS wasn't out of range. As the crow flies, it couldn't have been more than thirty yards away. Miraculously, the Lexus' siren, a piercing honking began. Marlin Cap twisted, his head turned towards the sound. A slight pause in his death grip gave her the chance she needed. Frances jammed the car key for all she was worth into the soft throat tissue underneath Marlin Cap's chin. There was a bloodcurdling shriek, Frances dropped as Marlin Cap grabbed his hemorrhaging throat.

Freed, Frances sprinted off the starting blocks, raced back up to the foredeck, but he was like a panther, bounding right behind her. Frances leapt left, darted toward the railing, and dove overboard. Let Marlin Cap try and catch this Florida 200 meter Freestyle State High School Runner up of 1990. He stared at her departing form for a moment, and then rushed back inside.

Frances said she swam to the dock across the way, pulled herself up, and screamed for help until the Ridleys, as usual cocktailed to the gills by noon, came rushing over to see what was wrong.

At this point in her narrative I said with gusto, "My favorite part is where you peed on him."

"Hmm," Frances studied me with a cool detachment that fast mutated into condescension, "and of course it would be, Mr. Davitt."

"Guy. Please. So what did the police say?"

"That it was an attempted rape. We all went back aboard my Mariner. No one was there. Propane gas smell was strong so we opened all the windows. Blood puddles on the floor and deck."

"What did the police do?"

"They found a loosened connection on my propane tank. They wrote a report. Took samples of the blood, and tried some random fingerprinting, but, as I told them, the perp had worn surgical gloves. A sketch artist drew a picture of a guy in a Marlins cap with a black moustache, looking for all the world, you know, like every other guy of thirty-something in Florida."

"What about the red glasses?"

"Pure theatre. As my guts were being squished out, I remember how the glasses didn't appear to have lenses. The moustache wasn't real either. I wouldn't even be surprised if the guy had orange peels inside his cheeks."

"You didn't stay on your yacht, did you?" I asked.

"I put my laptop and a few things into the Lexus's trunk and departed when the police did. Haven't been back since. After seeing an E.R. doctor about my eye and some bruised ribs, I checked into a hotel, showered, ate three room service orders of tomato bisque soup, then slept for two days. Did wonders for my cold."

"Then what?"

"Went online from the hotel, logged into my site, and checked my e-mail. Hadn't done that in a week or two. I try to respond to my fans...of course, I ignore the vulgar ones."

"Funny, I only respond to the vulgar ones."

"Of course you would. Anyway, I found an e-mail from a Jax Thornton, whom I've never heard of, asking me to call him immediately—saying it's very urgent, so, of course, I delete it and go on to the next hundred messages. But I eventually find another one from Thornton with the subject line *Mystery Writers Are Being Murdered.* Which hit me sharply. I read his message. He attached names of authors who had died recently from *alleged* accidents. I'm about ready to hit Delete when he states that Angus MacDougall was just murdered and it was made to look like alcohol poisoning. He thought the murderer's M.O. might be a riff on *Lady Mesmer's List* and that's why Jax sought me out."

"Lady who's lisp?"

Frances gave me a disapproving stare, "You've never read any of my books, have you?"

I blushed, "Boating's not really my thing."

"That particular book was quite popular about four years ago. The villain in *Lady Mesmer's List* used alcohol poisoning to murder a well-known lush."

"Jesus! I think I may've short changed the yachting mystery genre."

"In the interest of full disclosure, I've not read any of your Connor Alba novels."

"Sacrilege. Connor should be taught in every school."

"Pre-school, perhaps," she retorted.

"Sure, any school that pays hardcover retail."

She continued, "Anyway, Jax Thornton ended his last e-mail by saying that I needed to contact either him or you as soon as possible. He left phone numbers and addresses."

"He wanted you to contact me?" That part was puzzling. "Did he make it sound like he and I were investigating this thing together?"

"He used your name, which I did recognize, but he may've thrown in everything and the kitchen sink to try and grab my attention."

"Jax was dogged about this…" I studied Frances' black eye as I murmured remorsefully, "…and I blew him off."

"Imagine my surprise when I did a search of his name, and discovered that Jax Thornton III had just died in a car accident, mere hours after he sent me his last e-mail."

"It was no accident."

"You are preaching to the choir, Guy. Something tells me that if I hadn't gotten away, I'd be another notch in a serial killer's totem."

"I can just see the WatChat buzz, 'Poor Frances Whiting, she had everything going for her—why'd she have to light a cigarette when the furnace in her boat had a horrendous propane leak?'"

"That's exactly why I jumped in the Lexus and cross-country'ed it out here."

"Not to pry or anything, but why'd you hide in the bushes with that gun."

"A simple matter of priority, Guy." Frances scratched at the yellow bruising below her eye, "I had to make sure *you* weren't wearing a Marlins cap."

Chapter 15

I had a vodka and ice, Frances a diet Pepsi. We sat on my patio looking at the huge Century plant, my landlord's pride and glory, now in hibernation.

"Y'know, the killer could be a deranged fan," she speculated aloud. "Think Hinckley. Think Mark David Chapman."

"Chapman…I'm still pissed at that moron. To get so close, yet completely miss Yoko and hit John."

"You're very sick, Guy."

"Only kidding, I own all her music."

"Who amongst us doesn't?" Frances took a sip of her drink, "Didn't George Harrison and his wife, some years back, have a hellish struggle when some fanatic broke into their mansion in the middle of the night?"

"Yea, George was damn near stabbed to death."

"Gruesome," Frances said. "How about sociopaths like Andrew Cunanan who went on a kill spree and capped it off by murdering Versace?"

"But Cunanan, Hinckley, and those other boys were all mental." I rose to pace the patio, staring at my feet, something I often find myself doing when plotting a story sequence. "Our killer has methodically stalked a variety of mystery writers in a variety of locations and has made all their deaths appear accidental. And at least in MacDougall's case seems to have used a murder M.O. from your story. That calls for considerably more brain matter than the unhinged shooters you mentioned."

"Not really true, Guy. Did you know Hinkley's raw IQ was at MENSA levels? Plenty of sociopaths operate on a very high order of logic. Their starting premises are wacko, naturally."

"Hmm. Fitting," I muttered aloud.

"What are you thinking?"

"It occurs to me, Frances," I resumed pacing, "our killer has to be very bright. I mean, this scheme is ingenious, actually, a Rubik's Cube of homicide. And he could be somebody in the writing community…I'm thinking of my e-penpal Scythe."

"You called me that when I showed up on your steps. Exactly who is Scythe?"

"I got a virtual death threat from some e-jerk named Scythe in WatChat—you know, the mystery writer's chat room?"

"I went there once. WatChat, a chatroom populated by undersexed geeks, losers one and all."

I shot her a sharp glance of disapproval.

"What?" she snapped.

"Nothing. Fact is, I don't go there much either...only went to WatChat this time to bounce some of the names off the group and see if anyone knew anything. While I was online, someone named Scythe sent me a chiller of a message."

"Is that all? One of the WatChat dinks was messing with you, Guy."

"No...not likely. Scythe named a novel, *Dead Man Typing*, by someone named Justin Way."

"Don't think I've heard of that book. But the writer sounds fam..." Frances gave me an eye-widening pause, "...you live on Justin Way."

"Yup."

Swallowing hard, she said, "Oh oh."

"Odds are Scythe's the key, Frances. Scythe builds a detailed dossier on a mystery writer—sadly me. My guess, Scythe also did one on old Angus and on Jax and Beck Quinn and Alexandra Case. Quite frankly, Frances, I think you met Scythe wearing red hornrims without lenses."

Frances rose and stared through the patio door into my living room as though taking everything in for the first time. At length, "Go with that for a moment...I'm still at a loss for motive. And apart from his dossier he'd need means and opportunity, this would entail coast-to-coast homicides. Think of the logistics it'd take. Think of the traveling money he'd burn."

"Oh shit! It just occurred to me," I exclaimed.

"What did?"

"What if there's more than one?"

"But how would that work, Guy—serials almost always work alone—too paranoid to trust a partner. Of course, there was that mother-son team out of rural Nebraska in the mid-eighties."

"Yeah, but incestuous freaks like those two Nebraskans are a whole different breed of animal. I don't think sex freaks fit our pattern. You agree?"

"Agreed."

"Frances, I'm wracking my brain, and everywhere I turn I keep hanging on motive." I picked up the pace, "Let's go the opposite way. Forget sex. Forget envy and reject all the other Freudian voodoo. What's wrong with the good old standby—in short, why couldn't dollars be the motive?"

"*Cui bono*—to whose benefit?"

I paused, undecided whether to bring her into the Thornton Family snarl. I decided, and gave her a fast thumbnail sketch of the

Thornton Trust can of worms. Frances seemed unimpressed, didn't see how that predicament—that family feud—could possibly connect the dots to her. I then pursued another line of thought, something I'd been vaguely tinkering with since Jax's funeral.

"Go with me on another money angle for a second. What if there's more to it than some *I'm rabidly insane and must kill every mystery writer in North America* sort of nutjob. Couldn't some publisher stand to make millions once the news of this hits the press?"

"I don't know how."

"Think of this…there are vast fortunes to be made, such a thing could hype the living hell out of the market. Once word seeps to the media that such a serial killer is at large, there's going to be O.J. Simpson-level coverage of this on cable. It's Geraldo Rivera's wet dream."

"Sounds like an Oliver Stone conspiracy theory. Maybe Kennedy was murdered by some oil patch communist mafia king politician."

"Stay with me on this, Frances. Think about the tabloids running wild. And normal newspapers, and magazines. It'd be topic number one at every dinner table in America. Every office coffee room or water cooler, every bedroom. A free trillion dollars of publicity for your product. Your company's mystery publishing flies into orbit…I mean, suddenly all of the backlogged books are jumping off the shelves, the presses can't keep up on reprint orders. All of Middle America wants to wallow in the clue hunt."

"But I don't think that MacDougall, Beck Quinn, Alexandra Case, or Jax Thornton had the same publisher."

"Well…maybe a cabal of multiple publishers?" I suggested.

"Reel it back in, Guy, scores of people would be involved. Remember Ross Macdonald's old dicta—the chances of getting caught increase exponentially with the number who are in on the caper? No one with business motives would take that risk, so we can dismiss your cabal of publishers' notion."

"Your theory?" I asked.

"Haven't got one. For all we actually know it's a tier one writer who's fallen off their keyboard. Grown tired of merely writing about killing and has decided to take things to an entirely new level."

"Oh great, one night my bedroom door'll blow open and the last thing I see is John Sandford rushing at me with a pick ax."

"Remember, Guy, it was you who said Scythe had to be someone in the writing community," she added with more than a trace of triumph. "Well, the first tiers would certainly have money and plenty of free time—no nine to five jobs to hobble them—both means and opportunity. Plus," Frances added, "the unsuspecting victims, they'd all welcome a first tier to their bosom with open arms."

"True. Mary Higgins Clark shows up at my door, I'm gonna grill her a steak. I'd be marinating the zucchini and Mary Higgins could sneak up from behind and stick the ice pick in my neck."

"I was being facetious," Frances replied.

"So was I," I said. "We need to think smaller. I couldn't afford to be-bop around North America, popping writers, and making their deaths look like accidents. Third tiers like us wouldn't be able to..."

"What's this 'third tiers like us,' Kemo Sabe? I'm firmly second tier."

"Trust me, I know this and now is not the time to be vain."

"I made high six figures in royalties last year."

"You did? High six?" my head spun.

"I've a loyal fan base and an excellent publicist."

"Maybe I should start writing yachting mysteries."

"Do you know how to sail?"

"I wouldn't know the starboard jib from my ass, but my dear friend Google does."

"Second tier or third tier, I could easily afford to have done the traveling needed to knock off those writers."

"I'm pea green with envy but, Frances, what if there is some failed writer out there, some wannabee with rejection letters up to his eyeballs, living with his rich mother while his manuscripts are drowning in the slush piles of a dozen publishers? He's forever brooding, fermenting in his own bile. And one day he snaps and figures that, by God, I'm going to make them successful bastards pay."

"So now we're back to the deranged fan." Frances glanced at my side entryway. "Guy, why are all those empty bottles sitting there?"

"I set those in front of the doors at night so when John Sandford and his ax come for me, I'll be able to wake up, grab Lady Smith, and plug him."

"Jesus, and I came to *you* for help." Frances put her head in her hands and groaned, "I'd be safer sleeping under a bridge."

"Don't worry, Frances." I tried to make this as socially unawkward as possible. "You can stay in my guest room until this thing gets sorted out."

"Here? With Scythe stalking you? Sorry, toe tag, but when they're hauling bodybags out of the house on Justin Way, I don't intend to be in one." Frances looked up, "Let Scythe, or whoever, try to find me at an Embassy Suites."

"Well, now that you've scared the absolute hell out of me, do you think the Embassy'll have something near the ice machine for me?"

70

Chapter 16

Fortunately my credit card didn't bounce and I was able to secure a room at an Embassy Suites. Both starved, we went out for a bite. Frances and I had just ordered when my cell jangled. It was Maddie Neff, very excited.

"Where are you right this moment, Guy?"

"Maggios."

"The seafood spot on Harbor?"

"Yep, we're at the very dive."

"We...? Who's with you?"

"Frances Whiting. The writer."

"Oh sure, I read one of her books on one of those singles cruises you always give me shit about. Sadly, reading's about all I did that trip. Tell her Maddie Neff says 'Hi' and bring her along."

"Along? Where? We just ordered dinner."

"Cancel it. I'll have a squad car there to pick you up in four minutes."

"Frances," I flipped the cell back into my pocket, "You're about to meet Lieutenant Madeleine Neff."

"Who's that?"

"The L.A. homicide cop they send writers to," I said. "Think Ed McBain in lipstick and a bra."

When we got to Maddie Neff's office, she wasn't alone. Detective Pittman and his bulging paunch was cramped into one chair at the round conference table in the corner. Next to him sat an emaciated, longhair blonde kid in wire rim glasses and a green T-shirt, who wore an LAPD photo ID tag on a lanyard dangling above his concave chest. During Maddie's fast introductions, I learned the blonde guy was named Einerssen and was LAPD's newest computer whiz kid.

"Our young e-guru here crawled all through the two hard drives. Both yours, Davitt, and P. Jax Thornton III's. We may have hit pay dirt. Explain what you found, Einerssen."

The blonde kid nodded, and spoke in an almost pre-pubescent soprano. "Some of the nano-byte technology I used is pretty advanced...classified...we got it on a license from the Pentagon and they made me sign something sez if I ever discuss it with anyone I'll lose my reproductive organs among other things. But generally, here's the deal. I went into your hard drive, Mr. Davitt, and found some quite interesting stuff."

"Such as?" I asked.

"In the past month have you yourself removed that hard drive, Mr. Davitt?"

"No," I chuckled, "I'd as well know how to give myself a tonsillectomy. Plus, it's a fairly new computer."

Einerssen pushed me on the subject. "Ever loan your desktop to anyone? Leave it at a shop for repairs? Give someone access to where you keep it?"

"No to the first. No to the second. As to the last, only my landlord. The owner of the duplex has a key, he's an eighty year-old retired stevedore with gout. Why do you want to know?"

"Davitt," Maddie interrupted, "I took the liberty of having one of our CSI teams check out your place this afternoon."

"Thanks for asking first," I shot back.

"I tried to ask but I couldn't get you on your home phone or your cell. I didn't figure you'd object and we needed to be sure if you were okay. Don't worry, Davitt, we left the *Playboys*."

"Is this leading someplace?" I began to blush. I could kick myself for leaving my cell phone in the car for most of the day.

Maddie scowled, nodding vigorously, "You bet your ass. Our people found evidence someone has been picking your lock."

I stared at Maddie then Frances. "When?"

"CSI can't tell when exactly, but under the microscope the chambers in the tumblers on your front door deadbolt showed definite scratch marks. The sort a springneedle would make. That's a professional lock pick made of titanium. Fairly recent scratch marks."

"Great," I whispered.

"Brace yourself, Davitt," Maddie continued, "our CSI people are convinced from the number and depth of the scratch marks on the lock tumblers, whoever picked the deadbolt and entered your place did so on repeated occasions."

I felt the hairs on my scalp prickle. "This just gets better and better. There's a killer roaming around who threatens me on the Internet and breezes in and out of my place without my knowledge whenever he fancies." Frances reached across from her chair and squeezed my arm in a consoling, albeit an *I-told-you-your-house-was-unsafe*, manner.

"There's more," said Einerssen.

I looked at Frances. "What'd I say? Better and better."

"When I was exploring your hard drive I found clear evidence it'd been wiped," Einerssen explained.

"Huh? You mean a virus or something? It was working OK yesterday," I protested.

"Not a virus. Someone tried to erase all of your deleted e-mails and all of your net tracks."

"Oh, is that it," I breathed with relief. "Every ten days my Internet provider automatically deletes all the stuff I haven't saved. They call it courtesy housecleaning. Nothing sinister in it."

"Nope, that's not what I'm talking about. Even with your provider's timed scrubber program nothing is completely deleted, all standard deletion programs always leave traces behind, enough to reconstruct big parts of most deletes. When I was inside your hard drive I found footprints of something far more sophisticated. Someone used a very advanced cleansing program."

"Meaning my hard drive is cleared of all old e-mails and Internet activities? Totally?" I asked Einerssen.

"Meaning somebody tried very very hard to do exactly that."

"*Tried?*" Frances asked with a surprised look.

"Yes, tried. Tried as hard as any ordinary mortal can."

Frances smiled with a trace of condescension as she said, "But being from Planet Krypton, Mr. Einerssen, you accomplished the impossible?"

"Sure did. By using that technology I was telling you about I found most of it anyway," Einerssen announced proudly.

"More to the point," inserted Maddie, "is the Scythe question, Einerssen, so zip up your fly and explain that part."

"Sure thing. Lieutenant Neff had asked me to sort through trace records and see if I could locate an exchange from a particular chat room on the Mystery Writers Association's Web site. Involving you, Mr. Davitt—or I suppose I should use your WatChat name, CAlba—and another person using WatChat by the name Scythe. I eventually filtered through fragments of the exchange, which was tough going. But I located it. Then came the trickiest part. Tracing the source terminal used by Scythe."

"You do that?" asked Frances.

Einerssen gave Lieutenant Neff a questioning gaze.

"Speaking from…ah you know…simply hypothetical standpoint," Neff picked up the conversation, "I imagine a person with the correct tools and know-how could theoretically jump a firewall and run a program to find the desired data record. Then it becomes, I assume, a simple matter of tracing back Internet providers, kind of how the Secret Service tracks down the loonies who send virtual e-threats to the President. Of course," Neff continued, "this is all academic as in California law enforcement would need either a search warrant, or full cooperation from the affected Web site to accomplish such a task."

I looked back at Einerssen, "And you found…?"

"Scythe was using a terminal in the Human Resources department of Pentathlon Productions," Einerssen announced with a crooked grin.

I exchanged glances with Maddie Neff.

Frances blurted, "I sold Pentathlon the film rights to three of my novels."

"I sold them one…and it was one too many," I replied.

Maddie flagged me to be silent as she spoke up forcefully. "Thanks very much for the report, Einerssen. I'll take things from here."

Einerssen departed, leaving myself, Maddie Neff, Detective Pittman, and Frances alone in the office.

Chapter 17

"**Pentathlon brokered a TV script** they'd ginned up after buying the rights to my first Connor Alba novel," I explained, "and sold it to one of the networks. Result—the network's made-for-TV flick butchered my piece worse than they did that novel by Robert Savage," I said bitterly, adding, "'the Made-for-TV-ghetto'...wasn't that what Savage quipped after they ruined his...if there was any honesty in network hype they wouldn't call it Made-for-TV. They'd call it Made-for-Pigfeed. Actually, the real culprit that let it happen was a Pentathlon Vice Prez named Oliver Robbins."

"Small world," said Frances. "I dealt with Robbins when I sold Pentathlon the film-TV rights for my *Compass to Deathward* trilogy...but after hearing what happened to Savage I didn't even watch the resulting Pigfeed."

"Hold on. Back up a minute," ordered Maddie Neff. "I think we just tripped over an intersection."

I noted the thick ridge of glower on the lieutenant's forehead. Detective Pittman leaned forward in his chair.

Maddie snapped up a yellow pad and pen, then very businesslike, "Tell me all about your experiences with Pentathlon Productions. And this Robbins guy you mentioned. Ladies first, Frances."

"Well, about three years back my literary agent connected me with Oliver Robbins..."

"Is that R-O-B-B-I-N-S?" Maddie interrupted.

"Right. Anyway, Robbins wanted to buy a seven-year option for the film and TV rights on *Compass To Deathward*. My agent had a couple companies interested and tried to start a bidding war, but Robbins cut through all of that, offered a take-it-or-leave-it high six figures and I said okay and took it. That was that. Later on I heard they'd done three Made-for-TV scripts and sold it as a trilogy to a network...meantime everybody in the trade was talking how abused Bob Savage felt about the Pigfeed the same network had made of one of his and how he'd vowed never to sell them another one. So when Oliver Robbins sent me an invite to a pre-screening party at Pentathlon for the first of the three, the one titled *Death Overboard*, I declined. To this day I haven't seen it. And they never filmed the other two, so what does that tell you about the quality?"

"Davitt, was this same Oliver Robbins the key man in your instance?" Maddie asked, while scribbling furiously.

"Same guy, same story. Except I made the mistake of watching the result. I clipped out the worse of the telecast's reviews and sent them to Robbins stapled to my business card so the bastard would know that I knew what monkey vomit he'd made of things." As I explained this to Maddie Neff I realized just how hot I still felt over the five-year-old incident, which I had assumed I'd long since buried.

"So Robbins produces shit films, huh?" asked Detective Pittman.

"Much worse than that." I collected my thoughts and looked at Pittman, "Shit films are campy…they make the midnight matinee…frat boys skip class and drink to shit films. The critics write hilarious essays about them. Shit films are memorable. Robbins makes Gerber's—bland tempo, bland acting, bland dialog. His films are unadulterated mush, instantly forgotten on the drive home from the theater or the walk upstairs to bed. For my money, give me a shit film any day of the week."

"And you sent a letter telling off this Oliver Robbins at Pentathlon?" Maddie Neff paused in her scribbling and looked at me inquiringly.

"Not a letter exactly…just clippings of reviews, which universally nominated the show as the year's worst. And enclosed my card. Robbins couldn't mistake the meaning—I'd never deal with him or Pentathlon Productions again."

Maddie looked at Frances then at me. "Let me ask you this. Is there some place, on the Internet or otherwise, where I could find out about other mystery writers who've dealt with this Robbins fellow? Or with Pentathlon Productions?"

"When exactly? I mean, what time period were you thinking of?" Frances asked.

"Ever."

"That's a tall order. Any way to narrow it down?" I asked.

Maddie replied, "Timewise? No, I don't think so. But how about narrowing it down by author. I'm mostly interested in knowing if any of certain recently-deceased writers also had dealings with this Robbins—ever? I am, of course, referring to Angus MacDougall, Beck Quinn, and Alexandra Case."

"Let's not forget Jax III?" I saw exactly Homicide Lieutenant Maddie Neff's thinking. Someone, using the Internet moniker "Scythe," had hacked into WatChat, and using WatChat had sent his threat to Guy. From a computer located in the very same office suite where Oliver Robbins operated from. In addition, both Guy and Frances had had unpleasant dealings with Robbins and Pentathlon Productions. Robbins, or someone else at Pentathlon, whoever Scythe really was, is deeply implicated. Scythe had also gotten access to Guy's home desktop, seemingly had repeatedly picked the lock on Guy's duplex door. It

76

didn't take a nuclear physicist to see who was likely next on the killer's list to meet with an untimely accident.

Now Maddie was trawling to find other connections—apart from Scythe's Internet threat to Guy, was there any linkage between Oliver Robbins and the late Angus MacDougall? And/or Beck Quinn? Alexandra Case? P. Jax Thornton III?

"How about this, Guy?" Frances suggested, "You could ask your friends at WatChat, ask if any of them ever heard of the deceased authors dealings with Pentathlon Productions?"

"Scythe may be prowling WatChat, Frances."

"Oops, I stand corrected," Frances responded. "Okay, how about this? Why not contact the dead authors' respective literary agents—for example I'm pretty sure Alexandra Case was represented by MACA as am I. Any literary agent using oxygen would surely know if their client had dealt with Oliver Robbins at Pentathlon."

"You're at MACA? Make that at least three of us," I added.

Frances brightened. "I think MACA can be one-stop shopping. My personal contact at MACA is old Bertie Ellis. Bertie's been around since Lindbergh flew the Atlantic, knows everyone and everything about the business. He's a living encyclopedia and best of all, Bertie loves me and loves to gossip with me. I'll bet I can find out most of what we want from Bertie. Want I should give it a shot, Maddie?"

"Yeah, I like that," said Maddie. "But with this stipulation—you must not, under any circumstances, breathe one syllable about what we're really looking for and why—the last thing I want is tipping off...."

"Hey, consider the dots connected, Maddie," I interrupted. "It's become abundantly clear that Frances and I are high on Scythe's list."

Maddie turned to Frances, "You've met Robbins in person, so he's not the guy on the boat?"

"Actually, I never met Oliver Robbins face to face. My agent set up a handful of conference calls between Pentathlon and Florida, a dozen e-mails, a FedEx, and a fax or three." Frances looked at me excitedly, "How tall is he, Guy?"

"Taller than me. A bit on the plump side, though."

"But that was what—a few years back? This is California, Guy, home of eight million distinct diet regimens and a fitness center on every block. What color is his hair?"

"Darkish brown."

"Damn," Maddie Neff began playing with her computer once Frances confirmed that she'd never met Robbins in person, "a lot of text hits on Robbins, but no pictures. Wait, here's one from Pentathlon's Web site, but it's a small face shot, kind of like a high school year book, maybe taken some years back."

The four of us crowded around Maddie's computer. Frances' face was a blank, "I don't know. My attacker wore a hat and fake glasses, but I could tell he had dark hair."

Maddie back paged to the Internet search engine and went through a dozen more hits on Oliver Robbins before landing on a crowd shot at the Academy Awards from ten years back. "There he is in the back row on the left. You see him, standing next to Warren Beatty?"

"The picture's too far away to be clear, but he's definitely tall enough to be the attacker."

Maddie surfed another dozen hits that proved to be text references only, "The guy sure is camera shy for a major Hollywood producer."

"Especially with his Hindenburg-size ego," Frances and I walked back around Maddie's desk. I sat in a chair and yawned.

"One more thing, gang," Maddie threw in the towel on the picture search, "We're gonna move both of you to the Star Motel in West Hollywood. We use it as a safehouse for informants and various types of undercovers...not exactly flashing red alert security...more bright orange. But there's always some police presence hovering about. And don't give me any pushback, you hear me Davitt? Because I plan on keeping you two numbskulls under my wing."

Chapter 18

The midnight banging at my Star Motel room turned out to be Lieutenant Neff.

"Need to talk. The three of us. Frances Whiting and you and me."

"Frigger-snickler," I mumbled, or syllables to that effect. I'd been dead asleep, exhausted from a long day spent retrieving gear from my tainted duplex, showing Frances a few sites in the City of Angels, and enduring a particularly frustrating phone conversation with The Judge. I tried to keep my eyes open as I beckoned Maddie in before realizing I was wearing only my boxers. "What's up?"

"Your question invites a double entendre, Davitt, but I'm in no mood to be funny. It's those asshole bureaucrats in the Prosecutors' office. Where's Frances' room, we'll talk there."

I looked down and realized I wasn't presentable. "She's in 222. I'll put on some shoes and a lampshade and join you in five minutes."

"Those pencil-dick lawyers. I took them all the data from the computers, said I wanted to get blanket warrants to search the offices of Pentathlon Productions. Seize all their computers. Bring in Oliver Robbins for grilling."

"How'd you finesse the warrant-less trace to Pentathlon?" I asked.

"Whatever are you talking about, Davitt?" Lieutenant Neff gave me a quizzical look. "Our *conjecture* from last night led me to instigate a dialog with the Mystery Writers Association first thing this morning. They became astoundingly obliging after I impressed upon them how their chat room has been used to issue death threats. And Einerssen's been working with their most cooperative Webmaster since lunch and, voila, damned if it doesn't turn out that our *assumptions* were 100% accurate."

"It's as though we were clairvoyant," I noted.

Eyes boring into Maddie Neff, Frances asked, "What were the results of your meeting with the brass?"

"Ought to be able to shoot the gutless political shysters on sight," Maddie grumbled, "every one of them, the metrosexual pussies."

"Translated, means no-freaking-help, I surmise. Right?" I asked.

Maddie nodded. "They ordered me to steer clear of Robbins and everyone else tied to Pentathlon. I demanded to know why. After wetting his Pampers, the Deputy Chief Prosecutor was very explicit; he said we'd need far more hard evidence than quote 'some half-assed, thinly-veiled threat' traced back to Pentathlon's IPN."

"To which you said...?" I asked.

"I told gutless that in other cases Homicide'd interviewed material witnesses, suspects, and the rest without anything near a threatening message."

"To which Pampers said...?" I pursued.

"A ton of double-speak about new higher court standards...which I asserted was 200-proof mule piss...eventually we shouted our way to the truth. He screamed at me about how we cannot jackboot into a West L.A. media-connected business, loaded with politically wired-in people like Robbins, as if he were nothing more than another East L.A. gang-banger. Gutless said if we did we could all kiss goodbye to our careers in running L.A. County and start washing cars in the private sector."

"Jesus," I whispered softly.

"Mother Mary and the Step-Dad, too!" Maddie, her face now purple with anger, spit out the words.

"Do I have this straight, Lieutenant?" Frances asked. "The criminal justice system of L.A., from the top down, considers certain suspects off limits?"

"Damn straight," shot Maddie, then sang, "Hooray for Hollywooood."

"Silly me," Frances shrugged, "I thought Stalinism was dead."

Maddie grunted her agreement then, cooling down, she slumped into a chair and added, "But we're only in check, not mate. More evidence, come up with something closer to a smoking gun, that'd unleash the honest cops. Problem is, Oliver Robbins is so damned connected with the politicians who run this town—hell, they all go to each others' parties and play polo together and golf with each other and join each others' causes and all give money to the same causes—the whole damn system is inbred. Only difference between this place and a backwater county in Arkansas, in West L.A. incest is money and power, not sex. Some days I think the sex sorts do less damage. Fuck it, I oughtta take early retirement and tickle my cello for the next 20 years."

"So we're screwed," Frances said quietly.

"Maddie," I had an impulsive idea, "let's get creative and think outside the box."

"Don't use that yuppie-puke jargon, Davitt. What are you driving at?"

"Well...you've spent what 10-12 years in Homicide...isn't there any other way you can think of for a concerned citizen, meaning me, to get more evidence so that you *can* act?"

"Davitt, you know any evidence obtained by a civilian agent of the police force would be tossed out in a blink."

"Firstmost, if I turn up something, maybe it could lead to other information that would not be tossed. Maybe."

"That part's true. Very true," Maddie nodded. Then a smirk began to split her freckled Nordic face, "But it's your secondmost I really wanna hear."

"I'm merely an interested citizen. I was a longtime friend of Jax Thornton III. And another close colleague of Jax, Frances Whiting, has also told me things that corroborated Jax's suspicions. So...what I did was not for LAPD...but solely as one very threatened, very concerned private citizen."

Frances replied, "Guy Davitt was not playing LAPD's Oliver Twist slipping through the rear transom to unlock the door, but simply Guy Davitt, self-help Sherlock Holmes, ably assisted by Frances Whiting, because we were both pretty damned disgusted with LAPD's inertia."

Maddie and I both stared at Frances, who coolly returned our gaze.

"Precisely so, my dear Watson," I said finally.

"Then you'll go along?" Frances asked me.

"Dealing yourself in, Doctor Watson, could prove dangerous to your health."

"No shit Sherlock," Frances returned my smile, "but dangerous as compared to what? The way I see it, not nailing Scythe or whoever the killer is would be conclusively lethal to my health."

"So you two amateurs want to grab some costumes and put on a show in the old barn?" Maddie's surgeon-like eyes examined us both. "Just for the record, I have absolutely no idea what either of you are chattering about. But if you want to play trick-or-treat out of season, it's a free country and not my style to dissuade you. However, if in a few days you come to me with some new information, useful information, seeking LAPD's assistance, well that's an entirely different matter. First and foremost, can we agree that those are the ground rules of the game?"

"In a heartbeat," Frances said.

I nodded my accord and asked, "Secondmost is the part I really want to hear, Lieutenant Neff."

"Secondmost, concerned citizens, I'm jotting down the phone number of a trusted old friend, a retired detective who once was my mentor. Ben Zemke. Ben can be of help."

Chapter 19

Past 70, fully gray and with a widening paunch, Retired Detective Ben Zemke resembled a sledgehammer, only lacking the quiet grace. His craggy face was pockmarked enough to interest me in rock climbing. His paws were the size and texture of baseball mitts and, feeling his vice-grip when we shook hands, I realized that getting punched by Zemke would be a life-altering experience.

We stood in his garage, a cluttered gunshop-cum-police-warehouse-cum-workshop. "Which of you is going to wear the wire?" Zemke's voice had a dried tobacco leaf rasp.

It was something Frances and I hadn't discussed. I gallantly asserted, "I should go in alone, Frances. If Robbins is the man who attacked you, if he's Scythe, you can't take the risk."

She shook her head, then said firmly, "Risk? In broad daylight? With you along, Guy? In Robbins' business office? Besides, dammit, I need to look over Robbins for myself. If he's covering his throat with an ascot or something, BINGO, because my key drew so much blood the wound will be a lot more than a touch of makeup could hide."

"No, Frances, because…"

"Not negotiable, Guy. I'm the one who made the appointment, the person he's expecting to see."

"The thing of it is…"

"Plus, Robbins is anxious to deal for rights on a couple more of my yachting mysteries for Movies-of-the-Week—without me you might not even get past his door. Ergo, I'm wearing the wire. End of discussion. Case dismissed."

"Okay, Frances, but if Robbins is the man from the boat, give me some kind of signal."

"A codeword to clue you in so we can make a skillful retreat?"

"Codeword, huh? How does 'Jesus! It's fucking Scythe!' sound? And at that signal I'll kick him in the avocados and we'll both run like hell."

"Works for me. We'll phone Lieutenant Neff's cavalry from the lobby," Francis said with a victorious grin. She looked very pleased at having stamped her will on the situation.

"Is the Vaudeville over?" Zemke looked hungry, but I imagined he always did.

"Yes, sir." I immediately came to order.

Zemke belched in response. I could smell the pastrami.

"Okay, lady. Take off your blouse and we'll start from there."

"Umm. Slight problem. All my trip laundry's dirty, so, ahem…no bra today."

I said, "Looks like I'll be wearing the wire after all."

"Not so fast, toe tag," Frances responded and began unbuttoning her blouse.

"That's my cue I suppose, I'll go in the house until you're through."

"No need, Guy, just grab a stool and face the wall while *Doctor* Zemke here performs his surgery."

Zemke commented as he worked, "I need to use plenty of tape, to keep the wire, mike, and recorder in place. I remember once when Maddie Neff was a rookie Narc and was wearing a wire. She'd went undercover in this Colombian drug case—and the recorder wasn't properly taped down 'cause she'd put skin lotion on after her shower that morning—the damn thing come loose under her slacks. Looked like she had a tumor the size of your fist on her thigh. Course in those days we used those big ass tape recorders weighed over a pound—those old clunkers're only good for retro parties and museums—not itsy bitsy micro chips like now."

"What happened?" Frances asked. I pictured her making a mental note of the image for future use in a novel.

"The Colombians wouldda killed Maddie soon as they spotted the damn thing but that woman moves quicker'n a cat on uppers. Whipped out a gun she had taped to her ankle and drilled 'em both right in the teeth."

"No kidding?" I said to the wall while caressing Lady Smith in the pocket of my sport coat. "Maybe I had better wear the...."

"Forget it, Guy," Frances shot back.

"You got body lotion on, Lady? Your skin looks kinda shiny."

"Unfortunately, yes."

"Okay. I'll haffta use this solvent here. Smell goes away pretty quick. Gotta wipe down certain places. Between your...umm...excuse me, Lady...aw shit, you do it. Here's the rag. Along there, good, now way down the small of your back. That's right." Ben Zemke's rasping voice was softer, grandfatherly and entirely professional but try as I might to restrain my thoughts, unbusinesslike images of what was happening kept bubbling up from my hormones. Deep into my thirties and here I am starring in some bad sequel to *Porky's*.

"Okay, Lady. Now towel off with this rag—no no, dab your skin don't wipe—okay, that should do. Now I'll tape in the mike, the wire, and the chip pack at the rear. Now listen up—while you're recording the mark, and this is important—keep facing the target."

"Why?"

"The mike is multi-directional, but that really don't help much. Buried between your, uhh, your bosoms like this, only the sound from the front will get picked up. Got that?"

"Sure," Frances laughed, "you going to tape a pistol to my ankle so I can blow him away if he gets wise?"

"Naw, nothin' like that. Next thing, this wafer battery is the kind they run hearing aids on, and the chip's got enough storage for the World Almanac. So they'll run almost until next election year. What I'm saying is, don't rush things. Keep relaxed, there's no need to get jittery about running low on tape or power like in the old days. Just take your time, be natural—don't feel you gotta force things outta him— that's a dead give away, with the emphasis on *dead*."

"Will you be parked in a nearby van also picking it up?" Frances asked.

"You seen too many TV shows, Lady. The amount of microwave interference we get nowadays would give us noises like a grizzly digestin' an Airedale. So all you'll have is this recorder taped in the small just above your...ah...rear end. So? Feel about right?"

"Fine."

"Don't forget, you haffta be able to sit back in a chair all natural-like. How's that?"

"Fine, Doctor Ben. You're really good."

"Thirty years since my wife said that," came Ben Zemke's laughing rasp. "Okay, let's test. 'You pickin' me up you little flea?'"

Zemke must've flicked the replay switch, an almost perfect sound of his voice, but very low in volume, said, "You pickin' me up you little flea?"

"Now, Lady, reach back here—feel this slider switch with your pointer finger?"

After a moment Frances said, "The grooved thing? Is that it?"

"You got it. Up is on, down is off. Now here's the best routine...before going in to record you go to a rest room and make damn sure she's slid to up. Then let the equipment do its job, don't fuss with nothin'. You copy that?"

"Copy."

"Okay, Cowgirl, suit back up now."

Later, as we sat around Ben's kitchen table drinking lemonades out of cans he ran through the do's and don'ts several more times.

At length he pronounced in his Lucky Strikes rasp, "I think you two have it all. What time's your meeting with the target?"

"Three this afternoon," Frances replied.

"Where?"

"An office complex in Universal City," I said.

84

"You better get rollin'. Good luck."

"One other thing, Ben," I added, "I'd like to write you a check."

"No charge. I'm doing this out of friendship for Maddie Neff."

"That's exactly my point. Your work with us has nothing to do with helping an old LAPD pal—Lieutenant Neff never entered into it—you are doing this solely for the money. Frances and I happened to find you on the Internet list of retired LAPD officers with experience in undercover. We paid you the going rate for this."

"What the hell are you talking about?" Ben Zemke coughed loud, personal umbrage in his tone.

"See, if we go in there with any connections to LAPD, Ben, then anything we get will be excluded in court. Maddie made that part crystal clear…Frances Whiting and Guy Davitt are totally freelance citizens going in."

"So how in hell can anything you get be useful to the police?" Zemke asked quite reasonably.

"It's like this, if Nick and Nora Charles—that is to say a couple of regular citizens—come to the police only after the fact, with taped evidence, then it's usable in court. See?" Frances explained.

"Crissakes! Ain't that dumb as hell? Glad I retired from the force before all this PC bullshit took over police work. Crime rates keep risin' but the courts keep loading down the good guys with more procedural formulas than Mah Jongg played by Hong Kong rules."

Chapter 20

We took Frances' Lexus to Universal City; I drove because she needed to crouch forward at the hips to keep some slack in the tightly taped wire she wore.

"I wish I'd found this problem when Ben was taping me up. What's worse, I'm starting to feel prickly heat on my skin—everywhere I rubbed off my body lotion with that solvent—I'll bet it's giving me a rash. I'd give anything for a hot shower and a bottle of Calamine lotion."

"Rash? Sounds awful, Frances, but too late now," my inner angel sympathized earnestly with her plight, but Devil Davitt secretly felt Frances' discomfort was ironic justice for her elbowing me out of the way so she could enjoy the prestige of wearing the wire.

During the drive we rehearsed the scenario we'd invented hoping to draw out Oliver Robbins, get him to misspeak, give us something. Anything. I could see that, doubled over like she was, Frances was only half concentrating as she kept squirming this way and that, seeking the least irritating position for her body.

At length she burst out, "Good God, Guy, this is absolute murder!" Her voice was garbled and she choked back tears.

I swung off La Palma half a mile from the offices of Pentathlon Productions and eased the Lexus into the parking lot of a Tony Roma's rib joint. I turned off the motor. Looking at her doubled over, tears now streaming openly I said, "Get out your cell phone. Call Robbins' office and reschedule. You can't go in there like this."

"No way! It's now or never, Guy."

"Look in the damn mirror…you're a masque of agony…there's a bright pink rash crawling up the front of your neck, your eyeliner's running, and you can't sit up straight more than five seconds. Robbins'll wonder when you got Parkinson's."

She flipped open the mirror in the Lexus' sun visor. "God help me I have to get this itch weed off, dive-bomb into a shower, and rub on some lotion."

"So call and cancel," I repeated.

She dialed Robbins office but clicked off. "Better idea. You go on in alone. I'll check into a room at the Universal City Hyatt and take care of this nightmare. Then elevator up and join you."

"I can't go in alone."

"Why not…chicken?"

"Chicken?! What is this, third grade recess?" I shot her a look. "I am not chicken."

"Thou doth protest too much."

"Look, I'm not wired. If I get anything at all, we need it on the wire. Evidence's gotta be more than he-said, he-said."

"You're right." Frances grabbed my raincoat from the back seat to cover herself as she began a feverish struggle to remove the equipment. "Get me to the Hyatt while I squirm out of this. You go in with the wire—find some way to hook it up. Your inside breast pocket might work. Pedal-to-metal, Guy. Stat!"

Twenty minutes later I was in the elevator heading to Pentathlon Productions and Oliver Robbins' suite on the 22nd floor. Twenty minutes after that a leggy blonde in a leather miniskirt was ushering me into Oliver Robbins' office, which looked half the size of Jamaica. The deep-pile carpet and elegant koawood furnishings were incredibly astounding…which was, of course, their intended effect.

"Hey, if it's not Big Guy. Good to see you again, been way too long. Frances just phoned, said she'd be a little delayed and catch up with us as soon as she could. Something about a fender-bender on the highway." Evidently, the man hadn't sampled one of California's eight million distinct diet regimens as the 300-pound, big bear that was Oliver Robbins rose behind his desk. His power gaze seemed to penetrate my every cell.

"Good to see you again, Oliver," I instantly saw beneath the man's open collar Tommy Bahama golf shirt that his throat was not bandaged. We shook hands while my brain scrambled to improvise. "I suppose Frances already told you what we had in mind?"

"No. Actually she talked to my assistant, not me. Hey, let me offer you a Cubano El Majesto." He proffered a cherry-wood humidor where a couple dozen stogies of Churchillian proportions were carefully stacked. "Fresh from Cuba. Fidel's nephew sees that I keep a big supply…his Uncle's my close personal friend, of course…met the great man twice while down there. Hey, wasn't one of your detective yarns set in Havana?"

"A piece called *Deus Ex Gringo*. The book wasn't overly kind to El Fidel, perhaps that's why it didn't sell its own word count." I said it with a pleasant nod as I removed a Cubano and took a long sniff of the stogie. Then, studiedly casual, I used the gold combo snip and lighter Robbins offered. As I leaned back to inhale the illegal smoke my mind raced. Eventually exhaling I smiled, "Ahhh. Like Groucho Marx said, 'A woman is only a woman…'"

"'…But a good cigar is a smoke.' George Burns, actually. So what are you and Frances up to that you wanted this meet?"

As I opened my mouth to answer I was saved by the buzzer. "It's Ms. Streisand on two, Mr. Robbins, returning your call."

The big bear grabbed the phone and spun his desk chair to face the windows that stared onto palm-tree lined La Cienaga. "Well, Hello Dolly! How's everything in Saville this month?"

As Robbins scored social points on the phone with the famous singer, my mind raced to come up with a new stratagem. Go with the truth…part of it…garb it as the pitch for a story idea.

Eventually Robbins hung up with, "*Hasta luego*, Baby." He spun clockwise back to face me, "Sorry about that, Big Guy, but Babs and I've been telephone-tagging since she flew to Europe last week, about her appearing at my big Rally for Humankind in August. Now then, what were you and Frances…hey, Big Guy, tell me if I'm being too personal but are you and Frances…?" he made a pumping gesture with his clenched fist, "Are you two a number?"

I wasn't sure where to go with that one so I shot a boyish grin and shrugged.

"I caught her photo spread in *PEOPLE* magazine last year. Frances reminds me of a young Kathleen Turner, you know, before Turner went Willy Wonka. So, are you and Frances a number?"

"In a sense, but so far only a business number." Frances scored a photo spread in *PEOPLE* magazine, I thought to myself, I really need to work on my marketing. Or get a publicist. Or something.

"Keep workin' the problem, Big Guy. Skirt's never been born can't be unzipped… that's my experience."

"I'll keep it in mind, Oliver."

"So what's the deal?"

"You see, Frances and I've come up with a story concept. Kind of a co-author partnership, you know what I mean. She suggested we should see you about a doing a two layer deal…line up the film rights first and then write the novel. Then aim for a timed joint release of both, sort of. Wish Frances was here, she has a better handle on details than I do, but basically, that's the concept."

"Why are you pitching me?" Robbins leaned back and placed his cigar in the ashtray on his desk. "I remember receiving a suppository gift pack of reviews from you regarding how crappy we handled your Connor Anal book."

"Alba."

"Huh?"

"His name is Connor Alba."

Robbins smiled, his reptile's tongue darting out like a python, "Whatever. Seems you were pretty anal about our treatment, so I'm having great difficulty understanding why you're camped out on my doorstep."

"The way it was filmed there was no pacing, Oliver, no pulse whatsoever. Say, I haven't seen that director's name on anything lately, has he returned to industrial safety films?" I guess I'd been blocking that debacle a bit more than I'd let myself believe and suddenly the dam had burst. "That actor you defibrillated to play Connor—if you can call his rigor-mortis acting—must've phoned it in between breaks at De-Tox."

"It served its purpose."

"What was *its* purpose?" I cocked my head to check the skin under his chin, praying to God I'd glimpse a stitch or two.

"Purpose? Put butts on the couch for the car ads."

"What about the art?" I prayed he wouldn't notice how much he was getting under my skin.

"Art? Art who?" Under the haughty smile, the reptilian tongue darted out and back in again.

We stared at each other for an eternity, trying to see who'd blink first, when I realized I'd led the meeting entirely off-message.

"Art who…cute one," I blinked.

"So when am I going to hear the pitch?" Robbins leaned back in his chair, stuck the cigar back in his mouth, and clasped his hands triumphantly behind his head.

I wanted to kill the bastard with his own gold letter opener, but what's that old saying? Never wrestle with a pig, you'll both get dirty, and only the pig will enjoy it. I forced myself to get back on track, "Right. Actually, this came to Frances and me out of real events. You see, Oliver, there was this mystery writer, a minor leaguer, died in a car crash recently. But the same week he died, he contacted both Frances and myself, about something, which led us to the story idea."

"Who was the minor leaguer? I might've known him."

"P. Jax Thornton III."

"Jax Thornton. The swimming pool magnate?"

"Same family, but young Jax wasn't in the family business. He wrote murder mysteries."

"Get on with the pitch." Oliver Robbins glanced at his gold Rolex. I detected unease in the man's confident exterior.

"Okay. Jax Thornton figured that there was a serial murderer offing certain mystery writers." I studied the nervous flush that invaded Robbins fat jowls. "After Jax's death, Frances and I did a little checking. Depending on whether you count Jax himself, it does seem three or four mystery writers have died in recent *accidents*."

Again I paused to watch Robbins. The power-gazing eyes were now avoiding contact with mine, seemed intensely distracted. I shoved harder, "So Frances and I decided it made a good spine for a story. Someone's murdering a series of mystery writers. What do you think so far, Oliver?"

"You'll have to excuse me for a second, Big Guy, I forgot to send something and I need to be sure my assistant gets it into the late FedEx pickup. Enjoy the cigar and I'll be back faster'n a bounced check." Robbins hurried out.

I was disappointed. I'd sensed the narrative had Robbins right to the edge of...of what?...of hitting the panic button? Of revealing some weakness for the tape mechanism in my breast pocket? Something? Now the man was out of the line of fire, collecting himself, getting his bullshit in order. Not good, but the best I could manage on the spur of the moment. I patted my breast inside pocket, the small recording device was there and the mike still firmly pinned to my coat lining. I hoped the sound pickup was working, but so far Robbins had offered nothing remarkable.

Truth be known I was angry, still pissed off from the way our conversation had played out. In my mind's eye I strangled Robbins, unfortunately it brought no closure. I continued to inhale the rich Cubano and scanned the office, gazed over his glass desktop, desperately trying to locate a treasured heirloom, or perhaps a beloved trinket from his fascist chum in Cuba that Robbins had on display, something I could *accidentally* snap in half or, better yet, steal. I then heard a commotion in the outer room. It sounded like Frances had arrived. I cocked my head and listened.

"...to finally get a chance meet you in person and put a face to a voice."

"The pleasure's all mine, Frances," Robbins boomed from beyond the door, "all mine."

Robbins re-entered, escorting Frances Whiting and her wide smile above some heavy liquid makeup on her throat. "So very sorry I'm late, gentlemen. Chain reaction accident on the freeway. Ambulances, fire engines, the works."

"Welcome to California," shrugged Robbins.

"Guy, how far did you get in the concept?" Frances gave me an almost imperceptible shake of her head, signifying that it definitely hadn't been Robbins on her boat. Damn, the pleasure at that point of punting Robbins in his seeds would most definitely have been mine. All mine.

"I was just describing to Oliver our story idea based on the things we'd heard from Jax, about a possible serial killing of mystery

90

writers. And your notion that we do a film deal first, before we actually co-write the novel."

Frances nimbly grasped the situation. As she slid, a little gingerly, into an overstuffed chair she said, "I think it's a dynamite concept, Oliver...and I was so pleased with that movie of the week you produced of my yachting yarn *Death Overboard*...so I insisted to Guy we bring this to you first."

"Interesting idea. Query, you two, who would be the killer? What kind of motive?"

"One of the lines we're working on," I replied, "would be the psychotic spin. A complex nutcase is thinning the herd, so to speak."

"Another homicidal psychopath? Beaten to death already," Robbins pronounced dismissively.

Frances cut in, "I told Guy the very same thing. Even though the twisted sociopaths always have traction in the marketplace but it'd be hard to compete with Thomas Harris or John Connolly in the deranged killer genre. My preferred path at the moment would be serial killer with a money motive, Oliver."

"*Money motive* for serial killings?" Robbins head popped up, he stared at Frances and then quickly spun his chair around to gaze out the window, "How in shitdom would something like that work?"

"I can't supply final details for certain, Oliver, but here's the gist..." Frances was inventing things as she went along and sounding smoothly persuasive, "...a ruthless businessman who sees people as digits in his market curve. Same mentality as those Detroit bastards who put out the exploding Pinto. Popping writers somehow helps the tycoon corner the market."

"I like that—a typical Wall Street fascist! That's solid," Robbins spun back to face us. "But exactly what sort of business is the guy in? And don't tell me another arms dealer or pharmacy company. Those've been kicked to death as well."

I could've kissed Frances for hitting Robbins' hot buttons. Her inspired improv continued, "Publishing. A big publishing mogul. Some global capitalist kingpin with an empire of books, magazines, and newspapers—think Rupert Murdoch. The murders of the various authors are simply part of his business plan."

"Wouldn't that put ten million butts on the couch, Oliver!" I exclaimed, much to Frances' confusion.

Again, Robbins' eyes started to dart away and again he became preoccupied, lost somewhere in private thought. "Y'know I just remembered I have a meeting I'm late for over at Dreamworks. Sorry, guys. But I think your idea has merit, especially the part about the Wall Street fascist with the soul of stone. Hey, how's that for a title—*Soul of*

Stone—think I'll get one of our staff people cranking out a script to use with it. Get Chris Walken...have him do his ruthless bigshot shtick...hell, maybe even go A-list and get Sean Penn or Tony Hopkins."

The big bear rose from behind his desk signaling that our meeting was over. He came around, shook my hand and gave Frances an overly attentive hug, then escorted us out. "Let's leave it this way, Frances. Big Guy. I am very interested in whatever you two can come up with. Very very interested. Why don't you two sort through things, put something down on paper for me, an outline—two or three pages, tops—then we'll talk more."

Later, sitting in Frances' Lexus in the Universal City parking ramp I said, "Couple times I felt he was right on the verge of spouting something—then he'd break things off and regroup his pitter-patter." I looked at Frances. "For whatever it's worth, that's my radar's impression—both that and God Almighty how I hate that arrogant fat ass."

"My radar told me a tad bit more than yours, Guy. The man was secretly sweating bullets when we started into the details. Especially when I said the murderer was a ruthless businessman. Remember how he immediately tried to bend that thrust towards some stone-souled Wall Streeter, pushing the focus 3,000 miles from Hollywood."

"Radar or not, what he said for the tape won't do shit to help Neff force the L.A. Prosecutor's hand," I said.

"Nonetheless, Robbins' body language and non-verbals screamed that he's hiding something, Guy."

"Oh he's hiding something alright, Frances, but Hollywood's a town full of skeletons. Hell, a snake like Robbins probably built his empire on them."

Chapter 21

"It's him!" Frances barged into my bathroom at the Star Motel.

"Maybe you noticed I'm showering, Frances." Because of the transparent plastic curtain I held the hotel washcloth over my genealogy.

"I know who attacked me."

"How'd you get in here?" Even though we both had keys to the adjacent door between our rooms I knew I'd locked the bathroom door.

"Easy, I introduced Ms. Lock to Mr. Paperclip, Guy. Now shut up and listen. The bad boy who attacked me is named Charlie Pizzaro. An old mug shot of him is in the morning newspaper."

"The *LA Times*?"

"Right."

"Why's he in the paper?"

"Charlie Pizzaro's dead, Guy. The man's been murdered."

Minutes later, Frances handed me the *Los Angeles Times* and a cup of coffee when I came out of the bathroom, robed but still damp.

**AQUEDUCT BODY IDENTIFIED
BY POLICE**
Remains of Minor Crime Figure found
Nude & Disfigured in DWP Piping
by Mike Needly, LOS ANGELES TIMES
Staff Writer

Police today identified the body of a man found shot to death as known Los Angeles felon, Charles Vincent "Upchucks" Pizzaro. Pizzaro had an extensive juvenile record and had also served time for warehouse burglary, car theft, drug dealing, and had a trial pending on aggravated assault charges.

A police spokesman told reporters that Pizzaro had been considered "a career criminal." Pizzaro was rumored to have once been a lesser associate of the Manfusco crime family.

Pizzaro's mutilated body was discovered yesterday morning by four workmen for the Los Angeles Department of Water and Power according to Wilma Coffy, spokesperson for DWP. She said that the workers were on a routine repair assignment of several flume pipes at Big Tujunga Reservoir northwest of Burbank. They called DWP officials and reported finding a man's nude body wedged into one of the flumes. DWP immediately contacted authorities.

According to the coroner's office, medical technicians from LAPD's West Hollywood branch spent most of the afternoon recovering the disfigured remains. Absent clothing or other means of identification, fingerprints were used and the corpse was established as that of Charles Vincent Pizzaro, age 36.

Morton Bingerson of the Coroner's Office said Pizzaro's face was entirely disfigured due to the severity of several gunshot wounds to the face and head. According to the coroner's report, Pizzaro had been dead about three days and placed the time of his death around dusk Tuesday. When asked whether the death looked like a gangland style murder, Bingerson declined to comment.

A reliable source, now retired from LAPD Homicide who asked not to be identified, said the shooting appeared to be the work of paid professional killers. The source went on to say that it was likely drug related.

Pizzaro's only known family, an unmarried sister, was thought to live in New Jersey but had not been reached at press time.

Although no arrests have been made, police are following up on several leads. Anyone with information regarding the shooting is asked to contact the Los Angeles Police Department.

Maddie was waiting for us at the station. She was the one with the incredulous look on her face. The guy sitting next to her had a dark complexion and one of those excessively bad combovers that seemed like he must have brushed hair up from his armpits to grace his dome.

"Guy Davitt, Frances Whiting," Maddie stood and pointed to the two open chairs across her desk, "this is Detective Masloski. He's working the Pizzaro shooting."

We mumbled fast greetings.

"Lieutenant Neff mentioned that you believe Charlie Pizzaro attacked you in Florida a week or so back, Ms. Whiting."

Frances nodded, "When I saw his picture in the paper I felt like I'd been slapped in the face."

"Pizzaro wasn't known to work Florida. He'd been strictly a creature of L.A. in the past. Lucky us." Detective Masloski took two pictures out of a folder, evidently snapshots of Pizzaro from better days, and placed them in front of Frances.

"Yes," Frances again nodded her head, "that's him. Even though he had a bogus moustache and glasses, I was this close to him," she held her hands a foot apart.

"You're certain, then?" Masloski queried.

"Absolutely."

"Seems like whenever we turn over a rock, there's always some worm like Pizzaro staring up at you," Maddie Neff added sarcastically. "This guy was a work of art."

"Yea, the lug was a real winner," Masloski agreed. "Charlie Pizzaro. AKA Charlie Upchucks. Arrest record as long as my thigh. Robbery. Dealing. Assault. Extortion. A little B&E tossed in for shits and grins. Word on the street was even S&M hookers wouldn't get in the sack with him. A double-striker with a lit fuse."

"Guess Pizzaro won't have to sweat that third strike," I said. "What in hell happened?"

"Someone had him exterminated. Quite professionally done," Masloski replied continuing, "one helluva mess—what was left of Charlie Upchucks looked like his nickname. The hitter blew off most of his head and his genitals. Stuffed the rest in the old aqueduct south of MacArthur Park, the middle of nowhere. A couple of workers spotted his arm hanging out of an old bypass pipe yesterday morning."

"How twisted," Frances commented.

"Not twisted—a business signal most probably—the Russians and Colombians like to do grisly crap like that as a warning to others. In this case six rounds point blank in the head from a .357 so we had to use his prints for ID—didn't hack off his paws 'cause they wanted him known."

"Where'd he get the nickname?" I asked. "'Upchucks' sounds like some local wiseguy O.D.'d on Tony Soprano?"

"Not that elevated—Pizzaro got around but he wasn't made. He was, shall we say, limited. Mob wouldn't touch this dumbass for anything serious with a ten-foot pole. Let's see," Masloski flipped through his notebook, "the nickname came from his first stint in prison…seems he ate soap to get out of a laundry detail."

"His mug shots do have that generic shithead look," Maddie piped in.

"Any leads?" Frances asked.

"Not unless you're here to confess," Masloski grinned. "Between you, me, and the walls—this one'll never get solved. We got no witnesses. No shell casings. No one's talking about it. Sure, we'll push the rock uphill for a bit, but the explanation's plain on its face."

"Namely…?"

"Charlie Upchucks dicked with someone he shouldn't have," Masloski responded. "Our working hunch is that Pizzaro was just another hump in the ongoing turf wars. He pissed off the Colombians or the Russians—definitely the wrong people to anger—and they used him to make a statement, said statement being, 'Don't fuck with us.'"

Detective Masloski paused as if to collect his thoughts, "Look, Ms. Whiting, I'm not saying it's impossible that Pizzaro was in Florida last week, it's just seems so very highly unlikely."

"How tall was he?" Frances asked.

"Until two nights ago he was about six foot two. Now he's maybe five six and it ain't from the South Beach diet."

"Six two would be about right for my attacker."

"We searched his apartment, which, by the way, was an armpit of empty beer cans, taco wrappers, dirty dishes with half-eaten enchiladas heaped neck high in the kitchen—a maggot mariachi group was rehearsing in his sink." Detective Masloski didn't attempt to hide his disgust. "Anyway, we found a sock full of credit cards in his underwear drawer. Some of them even had his own name on 'em, but none showed any Florida activity. After Maddie called me, I checked air flights. Couldn't get any hits on him going back a full year."

"He could have used a false ID. Or driven," Frances said.

"No charges from his cards indicate any road trips. Could've paid cash, I suppose, but, like I said, L.A. was pretty much his playground. Fortunately for us, recess is permanently over for Upchucks Pizzaro."

"I'm certain Pizzaro was the man aboard my yacht," Frances insisted.

Maddie began gingerly, "Pizzaro had broad features. The right size, too. But, Frances, I read his file and quite frankly, this guy killing writers? I'm not sure if the beefslab could even read."

"Maddie, if he was into credit card fraud, he could read," I noted.

"You know what I mean, Davitt," Lieutenant Neff shot me an irritated look. "If Pizzaro had a literate bone in his body, I'll eat your next book. He might've read the racing form to set up his bets, but even that's a stretch."

"I find it odd that he was killed in such a manner that the identifying mark I left on him would be obliterated," observed Frances.

"These gang bangers are complete psychos, likely hopped on Mexican crack—that is, methamphetamine," said Masloski.

"Crystal Meth is a god-awful problem," explained Maddie, "jails spilling over with addicted prisoners, it's pouring in from homelabs and Mexico."

"And you're sure Pizzaro dealt methamphetamines?" Frances asked.

"I'd need a scorecard to keep straight with what Upchucks had his fingers into," Maddie replied. "No way he's bright enough to cook it—his meth lab'd gone boom-boom long ago."

"Five years ago Pizzaro got snared farming—selling pharmaceuticals—mostly pain killers, narcotics like OxyContin. Would've done more time, but he dimed his supplier—some plastic surgeon from Burbank. And who knows," Detective Masloski volunteered, "he could've been moving Ecstasy, pushing the nightclub scene. Heroin and crack cocaine are making a comeback, dealers killing over that pipeline never went out of vogue. Blasting off a face and a hunk of the skull is about par for the course these days."

"Don't forget the .357 circumcisions," Maddie said.

"Is the physician Pizzaro sold for still in jail?" Frances asked. "This could have been a grudge killing."

"The surgeon has an airtight alibi—on account've his being dead for half a decade," Masloski answered. "He hung himself in the waning days of his trial."

"I guess things weren't going his way," I shrugged.

"His wife had left him, he lost his license, and he was about to lose his freedom. I think the good doctor may have had some performance anxiety about his upcoming stint in prison." The homicide detective tried not to laugh at his own joke. "All things considered, Ms. Whiting, chances are Upchucks Pizzaro was a lower drawer goods jobber. He knew people that could connect with other people."

"Maybe the competition decided to cut out the middleman." Maddie raised another scenario. "Or, hell, Upchucks mighta been outsourced by his own people."

The balding homicide detective turned from Frances to face me, "Did you hear about that shootout in a Chinatown warehouse last week? Four dead, a couple more on life support."

I nodded, vaguely remembering some sound bite from the nightly news.

"That was over 10 kilos of marijuana." Masloski shook his head. "Now ask yourself this, who goes O.K. Corral over marijuana these days? Well, it turns out the dope was laced with embalming fluid."

"Good lord, what genius dreamt that up?" I asked in amazement.

"Lacing it with formaldehyde creates a powerful hallucinogenic," the detective clarified, "probably a first-rate rush—once you get past the brain damage and vomiting. It didn't help in this case that the shooters were sampling the goods."

"The beat goes on," Maddie added dryly. "Day in, day out."

Masloski absentmindedly pushed some more side hairs up toward the top, "As long as no kids get caught up in the crosshairs, these turf wars actually provide a much needed public service. Small loss—none of these nutsacks were developing the cure for cancer anyway—if you know what I mean."

"Can you do anything with Frances' assertion that this is the man who attacked her?" I asked Masloski.

"Look Ms. Whiting, I can talk to Florida and have them send a blood sample from your boat to our lab. Quicker that way, but it'll take a good week. Also, I can't promise you anything, but I'll poke around and ask some questions. In fact, I'm meeting with Pizzaro's parole officer in about an hour." Detective Masloski shot Frances a cockeyed grin, "But let's say for the purpose of discussion, Ms. Whiting, that Upchucks, for whatever reason, jumped in a car, caught I-10, zipped cross country to Florida, hid on your boat, and then tried to kill you." He paused to smooth another loose hair up the side of his head, "You can take heart in the fact that he won't be performing an encore."

"How'd the trick-or-treating with Oliver Robbins go?" Lieutenant Neff asked us after Masloski had left.

"Nada. Nothing. Zero." I added more descriptive words, "Zilch. Bupkiss. Squat. I could go on."

"Nothing solid to give you, Lieutenant." Frances was much more formal. "But Robbins certainly acted fishy. He seemed distracted at times, spun his chair around so he wouldn't have to face us, and even cut our meeting short."

"I hate to take more air out of your tires, Frances," Maddie said, referring to her notes, "but I did a little checking on Oliver Robbins after our last meeting and found out that he was in Cannes, you know—making preliminary arrangements for the French film festival—when your friend Jax died in the car crash and you were attacked. I'm starting to think maybe Scythe is just some asshole having fun at your expense, Davitt."

"But you traced it back to a computer at Pentathlon," I said.

"And you did business with Pentathlon once. I'm sure some tasteless twit could find your address laying around there somewhere or other."   Maddie crossed something off in her notebook, "Frances, did you get a chance to talk to your agent friend over at MACA?"

"I spoke on the phone with Bertie Ellis for an hour yesterday."

"Did you find out if Case or MacDougall or that Quinn writer ever had any business relationships with Pentathlon?"

Frances looked defeated, "Nada. Nothing. Zero."

Chapter 22

"I absolutely know it was Pizzaro. For damn sure."

Frances and I were catching sandwiches and coffee at Chasens. "Look, Frances, I've got two older brothers that look a lot alike. If one attacked you, you could easily pick the other one out of the line up."

"Don't *Gaslight* me, Guy. It was him. I was a foot away from his ugly face when he tried to take my life."

"I understand, and I know your gut-check is screaming 'Pizzaro,' but we need to consider that it's a second generation ID, you know, from the picture in the paper and the pictures Masloski showed you."

Frances irately bit her lip and stared away from me.

I decided to broach the subject that had been clanking about in the back of my mind. "Consider this—it's absurd the amount of Thornton Trust money that's involved. So what if Jax's murder turns out to be inapposite?"

"Inapposite?" Frances said, her angry stare yielding to her curiosity. "Go on."

"Let's just say there's something out of sight at work on Jax. An undercurrent. Okay? Jax comes to me with a story about mystery writers getting bumped off. Two days later he dies in a car accident. But suppose that Scythe never meant to add Jax to his list. Hell, Jax is such small fry he's not even on Scythe's radar. Suppose instead Jax got taken down by an entirely unrelated undercurrent. Do you see what I mean?"

"You're saying there's Scythe and the rest of us, but that Jax was murdered separately over his trust fund? And the timing is wholly fortuitous?"

"Something to think about is all I'm saying."

"But wouldn't Thornton Senior have it done for him? That is, he'd hire a thug—a Pizzaro-type—to do it for him. Right?" Frances asked.

"I imagine Thornton Senior would get someone, sure. Point is I owe it to Jax to pursue this line of thought. And the key may very well lie in Florida."

"In Florida?"

"Frances, you're from Snail Bay—that's near Fort Lauderdale?"

"Mmhmm, Snail's just north of Pompano Beach."

"Do you happen to know of a Miami law firm named Carlos Tapia & Associates?"

"The scorched earth boys. Who hasn't heard of that crowd? Around Dade County they're called the Sons of Attila…and that's the sanitized version."

"They play rough, eh?"

"Very. I actually used Carlos Tapia once."

I worried about the implications of her statement. Would Frances have divided loyalties about the situation involving Thornton Senior trying to snarf up the entire family trust? I decided to slowly feel out the ground. "I understand this Miami firm is involved somewhat in a matter, a legal tussle, which might cast suspicion on Jax's father."

Frances put down her guacamole BLT on toasted sourdough, Chasen's Wednesday specialty, and stared evenly at me. "Tell me more."

"Well…it probably doesn't mean a damned thing…" I soft-pedaled, "…but like I mentioned before, with Jax dead there's a court fight shaping up for control of the family fortune. I heard that Jax's dad hired Carlos Tapia. I wondered if you had any read on the lawyer?"

"Rabid, frothing at the mouth junkyard dogs fear Carlos Tapia…the guy performs living autopsies on anybody he gets under oath and relishes every drop of blood he sheds…that's how he got the nickname 'Attila.' That's why my agent had me retain Carlos in a business matter a few years ago."

"Really? Did you have extensive dealings with him?"

"Oh yes. I watched Carlos in action. Firsthand. Even took notes for a character…wait, make that *caricature*…seeing as how raw he can be. When Carlos takes a case he goes for blood all the way, and after the enemy's fallen, he plows the soil with salt so nothing grows for six generations."

"What sort of case did you use him in?"

"I found out my former publisher—the mega house of Avis & Crowle—had hired some hack to do knockoffs of my yachting stuff and crank them out using the house's subsidiary printer in the Philippines. Similar enough covers and story titles to confuse buyers…for their hack's *nom de plume* they invented 'Fran Whiten.' We learned during pre-trial discovery it was actually part of Avis & Crowle's nefarious business plan to cannibalize several of us who had developed lucrative niches for our writing."

"And Carlos Tapia was your hired gun to stop 'em," I added.

"And did he ever! Of course Carlos took his 50% off the top of the settlement, he's a very greedy gator but he got enough to make all our tails wag. We got treble the knockoff profits Avis & Crowle made, which was only a couple hundred thousand. But Carlos also got me punies—full refund of their net profits on all six of my previous novels they'd published, plus interest, with all future rights returned to me. Plus my release from all future contractual obligations I had with the Avis & Crowle vultures. And an agreement setting out a lifetime prohibition against them."

"That's out of this world, Frances. You recovered champagne and Beluga caviar."

"There's even more. A certain scum puppy who was Avis & Crowle's general manager at the time had a near-fatal heart attack. You see, during depositions Carlos frightened him into signing our settlement or facing his formal criminal fraud complaints to the prosecuting attorneys of every state they did business in. In other words, Carlos threatened their management with fifty state prosecutions. I later learned making such threats to force a settlement is flat out unethical for a lawyer, but Carlos Tapia is not the sort to lose sleep over trivialities."

"Sounds like you've got major reasons to trust Carlos Tapia."

"*Trust Carlos*? Sooner trust a water moccasin. Yes, he gets results, and he's smarter than any two other lawyers in the room, but he lies, cheats, double-crosses, concocts evidence, coaches his witnesses like a Broadway director—his life motto is 'Anything to win, Baby.' Don't get me wrong, Guy, I'm exceedingly happy with his results, I truly dread to think what might've happened if Carlos had been sitting on the other side of the table. But trust Carlos Tapia?" She suppressed a laugh as she answered her own rhetorical question, "Never."

"Let me share a few details with you...." Earlier I'd given Frances a much-abridged version, but once that scaly son of a bitch Robbins danced onto the radar, my unconditional hatred of the man gave me tunnel vision. For the next ten minutes I told Frances everything I knew about the saga of the Thornton Trust, Jax's father's connivances immediately following young Jax's death, the family haggling, and the legal battle that was shaping up. Finally I said with emphasis, "I've been assured by the Thornton family attorney that the court papers which were just filed would've taken a long time to prepare—long before Jax's death—and a basic legal premise of the whole thing is Jax never living to reach age 35. Hmmm?" I raised my brows at her and added, "What's at stake is several billion worldwide."

Frances hung keenly on every word. When I finished she asked, "I gather the Thornton Company isn't merely those swimming pools and liners being hawked on late night infomercials?"

"Not by a long shot. The empire's an iceberg of money and the pool stuff's only the tip—pools are Thornton Senior's endeavor—but when you hear Thornton Trust, think Onassis."

Frances grinned, "Carlos Tapia would be on it like sharks on a chummed corpse. To Carlos, 50% would be a ton of Viagra."

"So Carlos measures his manhood by the bucks he can stuff in his bank account, and not the ripcord between his thighs?"

"That would not be incorrect," Frances nodded.

"I think Jax's murder could be traceable to the Thornton Trust battle," I said, not quite perceiving all the implications. Frances was two steps ahead of me.

"Hold it right there, Guy. Let's consider this—Thornton and his lawyers—Florida. Pizzaro's attack on me—Florida. Jax killed in L.A.—Pizzaro an L.A. homeboy. Therefore…?"

"Therefore linkage."

"Guy, where this leads is there's a strong possibility that Thornton Senior killed his only son over the Thornton Empire. But also there's a secondary possibility that this entire murder MacGuffin, this making mystery writers an endangered species…"

Could be part of Thornton Senior's…"

"Scheme," she concluded the thought, "something to throw the police off the trail in case they didn't buy the car accident scenario. I picture Thornton Senior killing off a string of mystery writers just to fake a pattern in order to knock his son off for the trust money."

"In which case both undercurrents eventually converge into one, like tributaries feeding into a lake—only Jax's death is primary and the rest of us are simply decoys to throw off the authorities." I leaned back and tried to unboggle my mind, "Anyway, I'd love to get a peek inside."

"Inside what?" she asked.

"The lawyer's files, the Carlos Tapia-Thornton Senior gameplan."

"Hmm…worth shining a flashlight into that black hole, isn't it?"

"More like a 30,000-watt klieg light," I agreed. "If I can just figure out a way."

Frances took a long sip of Chasens' green iced tea and then leaned toward me, "Guy, I have an idea that might help."

Chapter 23

Before ordering air tickets to Miami, I decided to float Frances' cunningly elaborate con past Lieutenant Maddie Neff. Maddie had no reservations.

"Strikes me that Frances Whiting could keep our Fraud Unit hopping if she hadn't chosen to be a writer."

"It's certainly ingenious."

"Davitt, I have this contact who's a senior detective at Pompano Beach P.D. I'll call him and tell him you and Frances are flying down and ask him to cover your ass-side and help out if needed. His name's Philbrick, Sgt. Herbie Philbrick. But remember, I have absolutely no idea what you two are up to. Anything you may have mentioned I took as just another one of your lame-ass jokes, naturally."

"Naturally. This tape self-destructs in five seconds. But I need one other favor, Maddie. A pretty big one."

"What now, Davitt?"

"It has to do with Frances' attack."

"Yup, I've gone over the report from the Pompano police. Frances still think it's that Pizzaro asshole?"

"Yes. Thing is..."

"You want me to have Sgt. Philbrick check on things—see if there's been any progress."

"Now that you mention it, that'd be excellent, thanks. But I actually had something else in mind."

"Spit it out fast, Davitt," Maddie made a production of glancing at her wristwatch.

"It'd be a great comfort to Frances, and me...you know, just in case...to have a gun for protection while we're in Florida."

"You're asking me to arrange a gun for you to use in Florida?"

"It'd probably be a bit of a hassle to cargo our guns on the plane but maybe you..."

Maddie cut me off. "If the killer exists and is tracking your movements—a mighty big *If*—and if he clairvoyantly finds out which hotel you'll be staying at in Florida, he might be prompted to try again. Right?"

"Well, I just thought that maybe you'd..."

"Davitt, I find myself more and more frequently contemplating what flavor village idiot you are. A neo-idiot? A pseudo idiot? Or a post modern one?"

"I take that as a no."

"And when you blow away the pizza boy who mistakenly knocks on your hotel room door, they'll place you in a concrete room with no air-conditioning and feces smeared on the walls and they'll grill Guy Davitt over and over again like a broken record to say where he got the gun. Now I know you have this steely core of moral stamina, so you'd hold out about eight seconds before they'd know I'm your accomplice in the great pizza boy hit."

"I won't shoot any pizza boys, Maddie. Pinky promise."

"I like the concept of being employed, Davitt. I get free coffee here. Thoughts of a pension dance in my head. Plus which, they won't let me bleach my roots in prison and I don't do gray."

"I didn't know you dyed your hair," I replied.

Maddie sat back and impatiently checked her watch again.

I broke the silence. "I've got a great idea, Lieutenant, what do you say we both go through life and mutually pretend I never brought this gun thing up to begin with?"

"As you leave, Davitt," Maddie squinted at me, "wipe that shit-eatin' grin off your face before I do it for you."

I wiped the shit-eatin' grin off my face before she had to do it for me.

Sgt. Herbie Philbrick was waiting for us at the gate when Frances and I de-planed at Miami International. Philbrick was shaved bald and bone thin. If not for the glare off his dome, when he turned sideways I wouldn't notice he existed at all, being thin as a shadow must come in handy on stakeouts. During a quick round of introductions Philbrick hustled us out via a security corridor that led to the rear of the terminal. We climbed into his gray unmarked Ford, Frances nabbing the passenger seat.

"I'll run you up to Pompano where I made your hotel reservation."

"We appreciate this very much, Sergeant," said Frances.

"Hey what the hell, I sail every weekend and naturally I've read all your books, Ms. Whiting." Philbrick smiled a perfect row of snow-white crowns.

"Please call me Frances," she turned on the charm as she asked, "You ever read any Connor Alba books?"

"Connor who?"

"Detective mysteries by Mr. Davitt here," Frances cocked her head at me, "run of the mill stuff, actually."

"I have a couple items for you—a supercharged white Pontiac from our impound lot—I got it waiting for you at the station. Also, a couple vials of pepper spray that Maddie Neff wanted you to have are in the glove compartment." He looked back at me, "Maddie said to go easy on the pizza delivery boy, whatever in hell that means."

"We're most grateful for both items, Sergeant," I said.

Philbrick didn't acknowledge I was in the rear seat. "Ms. Whiting...Frances...I looked into that attack on you aboard your boat up at Snail Bay. No real progress so far. Couple of male E.R. visitors who matched the size you reported showed up shortly after with throat and face wounds but they both had alibis that checked out. Forensics came up with zero for stray prints but they found some blood puddles...Type A-Negative...it's my understanding they sent a sample to L.A. That's about it."

"Thanks so much," Frances said.

"Best thing if you don't go back to the boat unescorted by police. Particularly after dark...or otherwise for that matter...obvious reasons," cautioned Philbrick.

Frances replied, "Haven't any plans to go there. Could you spell out your personal take on the attack, Sergeant?"

"After Lieutenant Neff phoned, I drove down to Snail Bay, went through your boat, checked out the Marina area generally. And talked to the Marina security stump, no fear of that fence-post-in-a-uniform ever setting the world afire by the way. Openly picks his nose while he talks to you. I had to turn away in case it was his first course. Anyway, the stump says he was making his regular rounds when the perp slipped through. No word of other attacks. Or of other boats being burgled. The police report says the attacker surprised you, big lug you thought, maybe 220-230 pounds. You said nothing appeared stolen, no drawers rummaged. To me that means you were personally targeted by the assailant and he didn't even bother to make it look like a burglary. Scary stuff, Frances. The timing—and his slipping in that way and escaping without being seen—the bastard did his homework, knew exactly what he was doing. Adds up to a professional with one object. You. As I see it, you're flat out lucky you survived."

"I see things the same, Sergeant," Frances shrugged. "Did Lieutenant Neff tell you about Charlie Pizzaro in L.A.?"

"I really don't know what to make of Pizzaro. Maddie sent me a couple scanned jpegs that I showed to your neighbors, but no one could place him. Sorry."

"I'm dead certain the attacker was him."

"The blood test will be conclusive one way or the other." Philbrick looked at Frances, "You don't think he stole anything, but I'll bet you a nickel you're short at least one beach towel. A jogger running with a towel wrapped around his neck would be much less noticeable around here than some beach bum oozing blood."

"You're probably correct, Sergeant. But if it's ever recovered, I don't want it back."

"Listen you two," Philbrick said, finally acknowledging my presence as he handed me his card, "while you're in the area do me a favor. Check in with me a few times a day. Cell and office are on the front and my home number's written on the back."

"Can do, Sergeant. We're both very grateful," I said, noticing Frances's mind was now preoccupied. I assumed her thoughts were lost in intimations of her own mortality.

Chapter 24

Carlos Tapia was a well-groomed simian of a man, swarthy, gym-bought muscles fitted in tailored silk dress shirts. Something told me if I opened enough of the doors that composed his firm, I'd find a private weight room and a personal trainer reading a power lifting magazine, instantly ready at Carlos' beck and call. Tapia had card dealer eyes; the kind of man a Vegas pit boss sends in to end some rounder's string of luck. He seemed delighted that Frances had made an appointment for us to see him and was obviously fond of her. His wide grin flashed the signal that one of his front teeth was exquisitely framed in gold.

After introductions, his receptionist brought us tall frosted tumblers of ice tea with crushed mint, we settled at a round conference table in one corner of Tapia's massive office.

Tapia's voice was warm and humorous, "Frances Whiting...my favorite victimized author. Another row with your publishing company? Say, did I ever tell you I celebrated our happy outcome with Avis & Crowle by buying a pair of matching Rollses, baby blue for myself and pretty pink for my lady friend?"

"A pink Rolls to celebrate the win! Carlos, I certainly hope she appreciated the gift," Frances said, then added with suggestive charm, "and the giver."

"Only momentarily, like everything else in life," he chuckled. Tapia clearly relished repartee with Frances. "Actually, that particular self-centered wench is my former lady friend. Fear not, Frances, she didn't get keepsies on the Rolls. Right now I'm with a redheaded jockey lady and I'm buying a stable full of thoroughbreds."

"To answer your question, Carlos, I'm not in a fight with my new publisher. In fact, Guy and I are here for advice about an extremely touchy business matter."

"Touch away, Frances," Carlos winked at her. "I wish all my clients were as smart—ask for the legal advice prior to getting their short and curlies caught in the door crack—so tell me exactly what is the problem?"

"Guy here was *best* friends with Jax Thornton III, the young writer who was killed in a recent car crash."

Tapia immediately began to size me up and I took that as my cue. "Both of us being writers, Jax and I used to exchange ideas, trade gossip, go to each other's launching parties...that kind of thing...you know?"

"Mmhmm," Tapia said with a tone of suspended suspicion. As Frances and I'd planned I kept a rube-from-bumpkin creek look of doe-eyed innocence painted on my face.

"Anyway, after the funeral, Jax's father invited me up to the estate. The family's big California place in Santa Monica Canyon. Mr. and Mrs. Thornton were really broken up—as you can well imagine—what with losing their only offspring and in the prime of his youth and all. You know?"

"Mmhmm."

"Well, Mr. Thornton asked me to sort through Jax's files—young as he was, the kid had amassed a ton of notes and story ideas and all the rest. He had a real mountain of stuff. You know?"

Tapia, picking up on my non-threatening naiveté, began to loosen with me and nodded, "I can imagine."

"Jax's dad, Mr. Thornton II, told me to take whatever seemed useful or else it would go to waste. Of course I didn't want to at first, Mr. Tapia, it seemed so ghoulish. A dead friend's work product. You know?"

"Understandable. Please call me Carlos. Tell me, did Mr. Thornton mean for you to have it all as a gift? Stuff you found useful?"

"Carlos, you have an unerring talent for cutting right to the heart of things," Frances responded. "Guy, tell Carlos what you found," she prompted, playing the perfect foil to help set up the scenario we'd mapped out in considerable detail on the long flight from L.A.

"Sure. When I started digging through Jax's files, I figured there'd be pretty standard stuff, story lines jotted down or proposals typed up. Miscellaneous rag-tags of research, magazine clippings, so forth. Frankly, at first I expected to find nothing of much use."

Tapia's interest was obviously getting piqued. "You said *at first*. But later?"

"Right. At first nothing exceptional, nothing hugely useful. But then I began to find more and more of…well, when I explained the situation to Frances and showed her some of Jax's rough files…"

Frances inserted, "I named Jax Thornton's idea pile 'The Mother Lode' and as you know, Carlos, I never hand out undeserved praise."

Tapia leaned forward across the table intensely interested, "Define 'Mother Lode' for me, Frances."

I leapt in, "I saw that many of Jax's concepts showed real inventiveness. Real imagination and—well, at least from my perspective—real diamond-in-the-rough genius."

Frances interrupted, "The damn shame of it, that Jax was cut off so early before he could…well…anyway, the more we dug the more I started to doubt my own eyes. Not only was the vein rich, it was huge. It looked like I could spend the rest of my own writing career realizing Jax's concepts into books and still have plenty left over."

"Mother-friggin'-Lode, huh?" Carlos muttered, still struggling to get his arms around what we were telling him.

Frances gave his thinking a boost, "For most of us, Carlos, us journeymen writers, we might spend six months or a year sweating bullets to come up with one halfway writable idea. Then add on the hard work of research and the actual writing. But Jax was an idea fountain like nobody since Erle Stanley Gardner. There's got to be three dozen top-drawer ideas—I can see seven-digit potential for each. Books, TV, films, sequels. A firehose pouring out liquid gold."

"Give me an example from Jax Thornton's files." Carlos directed his inquiry at me. I hadn't expected the question. But Frances, bless her inventive little heart, came to the rescue.

"Take for example, Carlos, and just one of many that grabbed my own brain, was a few pages, not even titled, where young Jax had jotted out a murder plot. Based on a very dysfunctional family."

"Dysfunctional family." An enthused Carlos nodded, "I had a drink or two with that Mike what's-his-name, the big shot from Broadway, at a party one night and Mike said at its core every good story's really about a dysfunctional family."

"Exactly!" I enthused.

Frances continued, getting absorbed in her inspired lie, "The husband seems cold, remote, too busy with his career, keeps a secret girlfriend on the side. The wife—an Earth Mother Theresa type—rearing the kids, always brimming with love and good humor but then one Christmas season the husband begins to plot her murder, cunning and methodical. As the story bounces back and forth between the holiday preparations, etc., and the husband's scheming the reader begins to pick up on another side of the dysfunctional marriage—the seemingly longsuffering wife isn't really Mother Theresa at all—more a Lady Macbeth-type shrew trying to give a saintly image to the world. As a writer you need to do something very rare, you shift sympathies so the reader starts rooting for the killer to succeed—oh, the twists and turns the hubby encounters are breathtaking—and then the story breaks the reader's heart when the hubby is led away by the homicide cops. Jax's working title was *At Home for the Holidays*."

"I know that bitch well!" Carlos laughed, "my third wife! I'd buy the book on the spot and rent the movie."

"To cut to the chase on why we're here, Carlos," I picked up the cover story, "I was doubting my own judgment...could Jax's stuff be as good as it seemed?...I knew Jax and I had a mutual acquaintance in

110

Frances, so I got in touch with her. Asked her to go through Jax's files, give me a second opinion on the stuff."

Tapia stared at Frances, and grinned. "Mother-friggin'-Lode, eh? You recall my fee structure for all business transacted—fifty percent of net. Off the top."

"I recall," Frances nodded pleasantly.

I shot Frances a quick look as if to ask, is this guy for real? But then I remembered F. Lee Bailey from the O.J. trial and gave it no further thought.

"Mother lode," Carlos repeated.

"Sixteen carat," Frances said absentmindedly, then rapidly added, "so Guy and I started to brainstorm aloud about some of Jax's ideas. We came up with the notion of being partners, putting the ideas into books. So I had a chat with my agent about it and she gives me this big legal concern...didn't young Jax's estate still have some rights to those files? Even though Thornton Senior told Guy to use anything he could?"

I quickly added, "I recalled one of them, Mrs. Thornton I think it was, had mentioned in passing something about a Thornton Family Trust. I asked her about it and she gave me the name of some musty old money Santa Monica law firm. So we drove over there to talk about it. But the stiff we saw—some tightlipped Swede named Colin Kuderrer—was completely unaccommodating. Brushed us off totally."

"But Kuderrer mentioned your name, Carlos," Frances supplied, "not sure of the context, but since I knew you pretty well I told Guy we ought to fly out here and have you look into things for us."

Carlos Tapia drained the last of his ice tea, then said finally, "What you're really asking me to find out is what sortta deal you should make with Jax Thornton's estate—or maybe with the Thornton Trust—right?"

"Precisely," Frances nodded.

"That's easy, or will be by this time next month. Look, I've got to run to a Board of Directors meeting, there's a certain about-to-be-former CEO of a Fortune Five Hundred Corp who doesn't know it yet, but he'll be on a suicide watch by tonight..." Tapia gave a carnivorous grin, "and I do so relish delivering the coup de grace firsthand." He then flipped open his day planner. "How about we all meet back here later for drinks, say eight-thirty tonight, and we'll go over the problem. And a little fashion advice, Guy, you're in South Florida now, so in the evening lose the friggin' tie-and-coat."

Chapter 25

While bouncing rubbery pasta around my plate with a fork I said to Frances, "Most lawyers I know would've tossed us out. Pretty blatant conflict-of-interest for Carlos Tapia to represent Thornton Senior in capturing the family trust and entertaining you and me waltzing in with the request for him to help us cut a deal for all of Jax's soon-to-be-bestselling story ideas."

Frances laughed, "Say exactly that to Carlos and I guarantee he'll dance a soft shoe all the way to the bank, fobbing off as how it's perfectly okay and.... Hold on, I have an idea."

"What?"

"The thing we really want to accomplish is to pump Carlos about Thornton Senior's planning."

"Particularly how long ago did Senior decide to sic Carlos Tapia on the Thornton Trust?" I added.

"But also what result Thornton Senior's looking for? What he might've told Carlos about his son's demise? Soak up any possible juice about the father's involvement with young Jax's death?"

"Tell me what I don't know, Frances."

"How's this for a gambit? I know the office layout of Carlos's HQ pretty well from before."

"So...?"

"So when we're with him tonight, you ask Carlos your question about conflict of interest. I'll excuse myself to go powder my nose— always hated that euphemism—and scout the file room for anything we can use. Luckily the firm's a smallish boutique and everything's clustered together on one level."

"You're kidding me, right?" I asked skeptically. "You think my question will buy you enough time to snoop?"

"I expect it to take Carlos 20 minutes or more to give you an elaborate answer—which will be no more than a royal run-around the mulberry bush but phrased eloquently. And, Guy, while you're at it, keep on stirring the pot, even argue with him to buy me extra time."

"Yeah right, Frances, no one's going to notice you lurking about and then you'll show up 90 minutes later—70 minutes after Tapia's gone looking for you—with a wad of files jammed into your pantyhose." I suppressed a giggle. "Have you got anything better up your sleeve?"

Frances began shoveling the shrimp scampi into her mouth, "Better hurry, Guy, if we want to make our eight o'clock appointment."

"The meeting's at eight thirty."

Smiling, Frances shook her head, "I clearly recall Carlos said eight. And we want to be early so as not to keep the man waiting."

En route to Carlos's office, Frances insisted I pull the Pontiac from the Pompano P.D.'s impound lot into a Best Buy and double park by the entrance.

"Back in a flash," she said, clambering out of the passenger door.

"Where are you going?" I glanced nervously at my watch. "You wanted to get there early, remember?"

"Gotta grab something, Guy. Two minutes. Tops!"

"At Best Buy? Grab what, an HDTV?"

"No, a Mata Hari Kit."

"Mata Hari? What in hell are you talking about?"

"Guy, if you were even semi-literate you'd have read my stuff and then you wouldn't have to ask such dim-bulb questions," Frances called over her shoulder from the store entrance. "Sit tight and stop fretting."

"Mata Hari got shot by a firing squad," I called after her. With no apparent effect.

That time of night we had to sign in at the Security desk in the lobby, then a beefy guard accompanied us up to the Carlos Tapia & Associates suite. A barefoot young female in Levi cutoffs and a tanktop unlocked the twin glass doors to let Frances and me in and then ushered us to a large conference room. She introduced herself only as "Sofia"—like we should know the rest—and mentioned how we were early and how Carlos had just called to mention he was running behind. "Sofia" explained that she was in the office working late, finishing an urgent brief on her computer. Her office was down the end of the hall on the left if we needed anything or had any questions.

"There's plenty of coffee, tea, cold drinks in the sweets alcove. Just turn right and you can't miss it. Restrooms are that way, too. Make yourselves at home and holler if you need me," Sofia called while quickly retreating down the hallway.

"It's a fortress mentality really," Frances explained in a quiet voice, "designed at keeping moles out. They've got video cameras at all entry points, even by the fire exits. Anything disappears, they can review the tapes. Security cards allow only employees to walk in and after six at night the elevators shut down and the employees must use their cards to make them work and to enter the office. Nifty, 'cause a computer tracks your movement."

"How about once you're inside the castle?" I asked.

113

"Far more lax. After all, these are hotshot attorneys with massive egos. They wouldn't want to feel like they're auditioning for an episode of *Miami Vice* every time they walk down a hall or use the toilet." Frances went to the door. "If anyone shows up, say I went to find the sweets alcove—say it loud and do that goofy yammering thing you always do."

"Uh-uh," I yammered in a hush, "I'm on this safari, too—which way to Carlos' office?"

"We won't find too much there...Carlos's filing is kept by two secretaries in the big file room directly across the hall from his office." Frances paused, "This'll actually work...if someone spots us, we're early so I'll say I'm just giving you the nickel tour of their impressive layout."

"Lead on," I said softly.

"Don't whisper," she whispered, "it makes us sound guilty to anyone who stumbles in."

We found the file room unlocked and slipped inside. The walls were lined with lateral files of gray steel, reaching nearly to the ceiling. There was also a gray steel portable stepladder on rollers that was fixed in an overhead track that circumnavigated the room. The ladder had steel side rails for balance, very much like those I'd used for reaching the tallest stacks in the bowels of the Library of Congress and some of the other research repositories I hung around in the days P.G.—Pre-Google.

"Archivist's heaven!" I said in awe.

"I know," Frances said. "We better get cracking. You take the top half, I'll take the lower."

"Any idea how the place is organized?" I grabbed the rolling ladder.

"I know the file on my lawsuit against Avis & Crowle was indexed by my last name."

"Where do the A's start? These damn laterals are unlabeled."

Frances stopped in her tracks and began to look about her. "Recalling how it goes could present a problem—I think the filing is based on some of these being criminal cases and some being civil suits—I think civil and criminal are separated. And then alphabetical...no, wait, I think broken down by the State, or maybe the County of the lawsuit...but then maybe alphabetized by client's name. Or maybe...."

"Life is a Cabaret, Old Chum," I said, and stopped listening.

Climbing to the topmost shelf nearest the door I flipped up the hinged lid of a lateral file which, luckily, wasn't locked. I pulled out the first massive red file and found the title: *State of Arkansas vs. Baroni*

Industries. I peered at the title—quickly deciphering the system. Obviously this was a criminal case, located in Arkansas, a state starting with an "A." Carlos Tapia & Associates were a private sector firm so sure as a Miranda Warning the State of Arkansas wasn't his client. Meaning Baroni Industries was paying the freight. So this row of files must be criminal cases, alphabetized by state of prosecution, and sub-alphabetized by client name.

I slid Baroni Industries back into the lateral, flipped the lid down. Riding at the top of the rolling ladder, without dismounting, I pushed along from lateral to lateral by using my hands to shove against the top edge of each unit. Until I reached the far corner. I flipped up the top lid—again not locked—and pulled out the end file.

"Guy, you find the rhyme or reason yet?"

"Patience, Young Jedi."

"Okay, Obi-Wan—but exactly what are you up to?"

"Hush, Frances." Holding the heavy red file I studied the title. *[DADE COUNTY] Barker v. Barker.* Okay, the filing system had switched. Once we'd moved out of the criminal case section and into civil lawsuits, the files showed the county—oops, not quite right—Dade County was Florida. I checked the next file, then the next. That was it! The schizoid archivist who'd organized this maze had grouped all the *Florida* civil cases alphabetized by county, then by client name, situated immediately following all the criminal case files.

I tried to penetrate the logic behind such a jumbled mishmash. Something glimmered. Files of non-Florida civil cases, such as a Federal Court sitting in California's L.A. County, our schizoid genius would have put them in….

"Talk to me Guy!" interrupted Frances driving out my thought. "Clock's a ticking."

"Frances, does your Sally Kerentine babble incessantly in times of crisis?" I felt her eyes burning into my spine and knew I'd pay dearly for that remark. I held up my left hand and closed my eyes and tried to resurrect the glimmer. It was lost. But another, much simpler hunch came sneaking in.

Again, perched atop the rolling ladder and pushing myself along by hand, I circled the room, repeatedly testing the top row of lateral drawers. Finally, in the middle of the third wall and about fourth row from the top, I found what I thought a candidate. The drawer was locked. "Damn."

"Guy," Frances whispered, suddenly on tiptoe at the bottom of the ladder. She was holding up what appeared to be some kind of dental pick. I leaned down and grabbed the tool from her. The metal end looked like a flattened needle with a slight swerve. I stared at her.

115

"What?!" she asked.

"You never cease to amaze me." I turned my attention back to the lock.

"It's not as if these file locks are Fort Knox. Jiggle the pick in softly, then apply a little pressure and twist right."

I spent about 20 seconds jiggling and twisting every which way. In the end the lock popped open. I lifted the lid. The row was empty except for four thick files. I pulled out the first and read the title: *[FED. CT. CALIFORNIA, L.A.] Thornton Family Trust.* "Eureka, Frances." I handed the first heavy file down to her.

"How did you figure the system, Guy?" she asked in a subdued tone.

"If you were even semi-literate and read *my* stuff, etc. etc." I quoted sarcastically.

I pulled out the second file, sat on the ladder, and began to sort through it. The file was jammed with drafts of pleadings and a fat legal brief. Nothing in here that Colin Kuderrer of Dorsey & Kuderrer couldn't supply. I slipped it back in place and tried the equally meaningless third. Then the last.

"Good stuff this—the true Mother Lode," Frances said, avidly sorting through the file I'd handed down to her. "Guy, I'm going to need time to take shots of this. Could you be an angel and check on Carlos, try to waylay him in the conference room while I snap some digital pix of these?"

"Okay. Remember, when you put that file back up there, top row, far left. And push down the lid and slide the handle to re-lock it. And roll the ladder to the opposite wall but leave the lights on, like when we came in."

"Yeah yeah yeah don't worry."

I marched down the hallway, checking my watch. Half past eight exactly. The conference room was still empty. As was Carlos's office. I marched down to the far end of the corridor. Sofia was at her computer, typing feverishly. I stuck my head in and smiled. "Decided to get myself a cold drink while we're waiting. You want anything from that sweets alcove, Sofia? Coffee or anything?"

"No thanks. Sorry he's late," she said not looking up from her keyboard.

"No problem, Sofia," I said with studied casualness. "Frances and I are plotting out story ideas in that conference room you put us in. It's good fun."

"Whatever," Sofia muttered abruptly, still not looking up from her computer. Under normal circumstances, I'd have been insulted.

After a few minutes I checked Carlos's office—found Frances in front of his computer screen.

"Are you nuts?" I looked again at my watch.

"I'm looking to see if his password is on a post-it note or somewhere on his desk."

"You're pushing our luck, Frances."

"I entered two of his ex-wives' first names, but they bombed out. I fear another strikeout will lock his PC and he'll need desktop security to unlock it. Then he'll know someone was here."

"Fuck that," I glanced down the hall, "let's go."

"One second more. Where else, where else?" she murmured.

I walked over and lifted up the keyboard. Nothing there. I turned it over, found nothing underneath, and then set it back down in the exact position. I did the same with his phone and calendar while Frances was frantically scanning his side desk and the backs of pictures.

She finally patted me on the arm, mouthed *Let's Go*, and headed toward the hallway with me on her heels. Right before the open doorway Frances spun around, pressed me against the wall, leaned in and kissed me full on the mouth. Her lips were soft, full, her hips tightly flush to mine. I melted. Reflexively my hand went to the small of her back as I pulled her tighter yet. The scent of her perfume and smell of her hair was enticing, seductive. I began to react more than mouthwise. She stepped back.

"Frances," I whispered and leaned forward for a second kiss when I spotted Carlos Tapia, arms crossed and glaring at us from his doorway.

"Carlos!" I felt as though my skeleton had jumped out from my skin.

Frances jerked and spun, "Oh my God, Carlos. I was...I was...giving Guy a tour of your firm, and we just...um, it's...I'm so embarrassed..." she stammered and looked down at the floor as she hurried past Tapia in the doorway, "...please excuse me."

"Not to worry, Frances," Carlos called after her. "But if I'd been two minutes later, *that* would've been embarrassing."

Carlos turned back to me. I stood frozen to the ground, likely a pale white. Carlos had a stern look on his face. I braced for the worse, but slowly his face relaxed into a sparkling grin that showcased his glistening gold-framed incisor, "You rascal—I am so jealous—how long have you two been a pair?"

I breathed a heavy sigh of relief, "Quite recently."

"Ahh, the hungry stage," Tapia nodded, "I love the hungry stage."

"Let me apologize for all of this, Carlos. It was entirely my fault." I looked at him conspiratorially, "I just can't keep my hands off that woman."

"No explanation needed among gentlemen," he lightly batted the side of my arm with a loose fist. "You've got some lipstick on your face."

"I need to go after her, Carlos," I rubbed my sleeve across my lips. "She probably got Sofia to work the elevator and is waiting for me in the car, blushing."

"Tell her that Uncle Carlos says to think nothing of it, nothing to be ashamed of. Hell, Guy," Carlos and I walked toward the front of his firm, "the stories I could tell you about some truly embarrassing scenes in my office would curl your hair."

"I bet. But you know how publicly prim and proper Frances is," I said. "Expect a 50-page letter of apology from her first thing in the morning, my friend. Single spaced."

"Miami is for lovers...at least that's what I always tell the new ones."

"By the way," I turned toward him, "was there anything important you had for us?"

"Actually," Carlos said, "I will need to check into a few issues before we can plan a strategy. Did Jax III leave a will or die intestate? Any contracts for future books? And is there anything in the Thornton Trust bearing on this?"

"Ahh...about Jax's father, your client on the Trust matter," I interjected, thinking about the conflict of interest pawn I hadn't yet used, then thought better of it and closed my mouth.

"What about his father?" Carlos asked.

"Ah...well, Carlos...you probably want to give him a call," I feebly improvised, "you know...check with Thornton Senior...make sure he asked me to take Jax's files and use what I could...you know, be certain I'm being straight with you, Carlos."

"Oh hell, why bother. I know you're not lying. But I do need a little more time to look into the Trust document. Where you two staying?"

"The Hyatt Marina," I said.

"Okay, I'll phone you there in a day or two when I've got something." Carlos walked me to the elevator. "Take good care of her, Guy," he swiped his magnetic card in front of a black rectangle, "Frances is a woman to be placed on a pedestal."

"I'll try, Carlos, I'll certainly try."

"You know, Frances, since I've met you I've had a gun drawn on me, I'm near to filing Chapter 11 over hotel charges, my precious literary creation has been dragged through eighteen different hues of mud, and now I've just burgled an important Florida law firm that likely has ties to mobsters."

"Great first date, huh?"

"You femme fatales are all alike."

"We do aim to please."

"Why do I get the impression that a second date would somehow involve my being drawn and quartered? Although, that groping part makes me look forward to getting caught again."

"I heard footsteps and saw Carlos' shadow approaching," Frances explained needlessly, "so I kissed you on the improv."

"Rather Tapia busts us as adulterers than for corporate espionage."

"Adultery's his native tongue. I had a character do something similar in a book once. Contrived, but effective." Frances looked over at me, "I just don't want you to get the wrong idea, Guy."

"Wrong ideas are the story of my life, Frances."

Chapter 26

It's impossible to get lost on Key West, a skinny tail of land with the aquamarine waters of the Gulf on three sides and a causeway to the other Keys and eventually to the mainland on the Northeast. We quickly found the impressive Thornton compound, three pink tile villas surrounded by a high fence. I told the gatekeeper, a smiling old man with limited English, I was a family friend and I was bringing a lady acquaintance along to introduce to the family. He waived us through.

I parked our Pontiac at the head of the circle drive in front of the largest villa. The tall windows and massive front door were wide open, probably to catch the cool sea breezes that swept the neck of the Key from south to north. A chattering housekeeper, whose Spanish was three times faster than my ear and brain could assimilate, led us through to the rear pool and *cabaña* area.

"Senorita Bella," she addressed the bronzed Hispanic Amazon in the white thong-bikini who was sunning herself on the diving board and gestured toward Frances and myself, then rapid fired another paragraph or two in her native tongue.

"Okay, Rosa, I'll take it from here. Bring us some cold drinks." The leggy Amazon, loudly cracked a wad of Doublemint, rose languidly and moved to us, pulling down her sunglasses to get a better look. "You two seem familiar…we met before?"

"I'm Guy Davitt, a friend of the Thorntons. This is Ms. Whiting, a friend of Jax. The late, younger Jax."

"Hi ya," said the Amazon who looked to be in her mid-twenties, and appeared to have leapt off the screen from the kind of movies commonly viewed at Bachelor parties across the nation. "Let's set our asses in the shade under one of the umbrellas…damn sun's started to microwave my skin 'n I don't wanna look like some shishkabobbed spic. It's not even two and I've already used a quart of SPF-45 today."

"And you are…?" Frances asked.

"Me? Oh, about five-ten and a half barefoot. Why you wanna know?" Again the Doublemint resounded.

"No, I meant your name."

"Oh. I'm Mirabella."

"Mirabella? Same as the big hurricane in '04?" I asked.

"Big Jaxie always says stuff like that, too…," she laughed, "at bedtime he calls me his Little Tropical Storm. But you can just call me Belle, like Big Jaxie's pals all do."

"Mr. Thornton's pals?" I asked, glimpsing Frances's look of surprise.

"Yeah, his big poker gang on Fridays. Big Jaxie'll be flying in tomorrow. Which reminds me, I better have Rosa check the stock of booze and start bar-b-cuein' 40 pounds of ribs in the morning."

"So Mr. Thornton's still in California?" Frances asked. "Guy, I think we might've gotten our dates wrong."

"You guys were meeting him here today?"

"Well...not formally. Just wanted to stop by since we were in the Keys and see how he's been doing since the funeral."

"Ohh...wasn't that so sad? Little Jaxie checkin' out like that in a car wreck? I'm really gonna miss the little fella. I wanted to fly to L.A. for the funeral but Big Jaxie said it wouldn't look right...I mean his divorce not bein' final and all. Did you go to it?"

I nodded. "Yes. Very sad."

Rosa bustled in with a tray full of icy lemonade.

"Big Jaxie didn't say too much about it. I could tell he took it pretty hard. Little Jaxie was a writer you know. Little Jaxie wrote three or four mysteries."

"Yes, we know that," said Frances.

"Mainly I read Harlequins, a few mysteries of course. Hey, now I got you figured!" she stared at Frances, "I seen your picture on the back cover of a paperback I bought in an airport. *The Tropic of Homicide.* It was really good, especially the way she got her loverboy to chum up her husband's body for sharkbait, but naturally before I could finish one of the Friday night gropers snatched it and the cheap shit never gave it back to me."

"I'll send you another copy. Autographed."

"Wow, great." Smack went the Doublemint.

"Belle," I asked casually, "did young Jax keep any of his things here?"

"In the old days Little Jaxie had one of the houses and kept an office there...but that was before Big Jaxie and Junior had this doozie of a fight. Little Jaxie moved out lock, stock, and typewriter."

"Do you know what their argument was about?" I probed.

"Me, I guess," she pouted as though she'd misplaced her navel ring. "Big Jaxie thought...you know how possessive men can get sometimes?" Mirabella looked at Frances for confirmation, "You know?"

"Thornton Senior was jealous of his son?" Frances asked.

Mirabella nodded her faux blonde head. "Funny thing, too. Big Jaxie never blinks an eye when I mess around with some of the Friday night poker guys, but just let me flirt the tiniest bit with Little Jaxie!"

"So, Mr. Thornton went ballistic?" I inquired of the Florida bimbo.

"Balls-to-the-walls ballistic!" snapped the gum. "You'd of thought Little Jaxie had robbed an armored car or kilt the President...and all cause he'd follow me around like some lost puppy and ask me silly questions."

"Silly questions?" Frances probed.

"Little Jaxie always wanted to know about my life and my past. But there really isn't that much to tell. What you see is what you get." She arched her back and a mischievous look crept across her face. "Sometimes I'd lean forward and give Little Jaxie a peek."

"And all of this angered Mr. Thornton?" Frances followed up.

"What is it about fathers and sons anyway, when I was still in high school my Old Man nearly kilt my half brother for copping a quick feel in my jeans—the Old Man chased poor Rudy with a butcher knife for a mile beyond our trailer—I didn't see poor Rudy again for four years until he got outta the Navy."

I rose and asked, "Mind if I use the lavatory? Long drive back to the mainland and the lemonade...."

Once out of sight of the poolside patio I explored the villa. I found Thornton Senior's office—massive desk, large fax unit, and several tall file cabinets. All locked tight. The desktop PC was locked down and off. I knew my technical skills weren't proficient enough to try and rev her up, break the password, and take a quick look. Nothing pertinent in any of the unlocked desk drawers or closets.

When I returned, Frances and La Airhead were laughing loudly over something. I made our excuses, asked Mirabella to give my card to Thornton Senior and tell him we'd dropped by.

As our Pontiac crawled down the circle drive toward the gatehouse, Frances said, "Belle is the most honest call girl I've ever talked to, told me the whole arrangement without even blinking an eye. Turns out Thornton Senior pays her two grand a week plus room and board to manage the place and—quote, 'haul his ashes when Mamma Thornton ain't around,' unquote—which is most of the time, Mamma prefers an apartment they own in Savannah—and Belle gets a cash bonus every Christmas of five thousand Andrew Jacksons."

"Hmm."

"You sound distracted, Guy."

"Just thinking about how Jax never talked about his family."

"Does family ever come up when two guys talk?"

"Not much, but the fact is he never told me a thing. He introduced me to them on a couple occasions, sure, but that was the extent of it. Blank slates. I've talked to them more since his death than ever before."

"Can you blame him?"

122

I glanced at Frances, "I do know that name, though...Mirabella."

"From where?"

"I'm sure I saw it in Jax's files someplace."

"Interesting."

On the causeway I punched Lieutenant Neff's office number into my cell phone and got through to her on the second ring.

"We're still in Florida. Key West to be exact," I explained.

"Key West? You two gone Marlin fishing?" crackled Maddie's voice over a poor satellite feed.

"Need a quick favor, Maddie. Can you hear me okay? I'm getting an echo and a lot of static."

"Fine on my end...what favor?"

"Those disks from Jax's office...his writing stuff? You know, the shoebox full of rewritable CDs and memory sticks Duante and I glommed from his office for you?"

"I'm looking at them right now, Davitt. They're stacked on my table. I started cataloging them last night. Why you ask?"

"One of the disks is marked 'Mirabella Force Five'...something like that...you got it?"

"Just hold on and I'll..."

With a screeching protest that sounded for all the world like the feedback from my high school's defective microphone at a pep rally, my cell went dead. "Oh, shit." I tried redial but the damn electronic marvel was D.O.A.

"I'll try to get her back on mine," Frances offered.

Traffic was light but reception was balky until we reached the Key Largo leg of the causeway.

"Me again, Maddie. Sorry about that."

She sounded out of sorts. "I've got that hurricane disk you asked about. 'Mirabella.' Now what?"

"Could you e-mail it down here ASAP?"

"Right away, Sir," from Maddie's tone I knew the sailing would be anything but smooth, "oh, wait a minute, I almost forgot, I ain't your secretary and it ain't my lot in life to help you play grab-ass with story ideas."

"I think the disk may be relevant."

"Such as...?"

"Until just an hour ago I figured 'Mirabella' was only Jax's research into tropical storms. It's far more."

"Huh?"

123

"Mirabella's not merely the name of that monster hurricane a few years back."

"Oh?" finally there was a definite spark of interest in her tone.

"Let me clarify—we ran into Mirabella at the Thornton's Key West compound—this Mirabella runs about 38 by 23 by 38 by nearly five-eleven by twenty-something—and by the look of her tan swims au naturelle."

"The playthings money can buy, huh, Davitt? Hold on a minute...I'm popping the disk in my desktop and...okay, here it comes. *Mirabella And The Force Five*,' it says. What in hell? This looks like a book manuscript. Listen to this. 'Chapter One. Welcome to the eye of the tempest. Welcome to the P. Jax Thornton tribe. If family dysfunction was ranked by the science of meteorologists, instead of the carnage toted up by the high priests of psychiatry...' Look, Davitt, I have to fly outta here to make the first meeting of ILMAC, so what did you want me to do with this drivel?"

"Ill Mack?" I asked wondering if I'd misheard her. "Who's ill and who's Mack?"

"Get this one, I'm LAPD's new deputy liaison for the committee *du jour*, ILMAC—Intercounty Liaison on Major Crimes—get it? I just wish we were half as effective in fighting the bad guys as inventing acronyms which make for nothing but sexy press releases—'Mayors of six cities laud ILMAC Taskforce.' Your taxpayer money at work."

"Sounds dreamy, but before you leave can you attach Jax's Mirabella file to an e-mail and send it to me?"

"Gimme an address," Maddie replied.

"Send it to..." My eyes searched the causeway, fruitlessly, trying to find a Kinko's at curbside rather than the Gulf of Cuba.

"Screw it, Davitt, the thing's four meg, runs nearly 200,000 words. Let me encrypt this to Herbie—you know, Sergeant Philbrick."

"Great idea, Maddie," I agreed.

"In my cover message to Philbrick I'll ask him to print out a copy and have it waiting for your arrival. Gotta run, Davitt."

Chapter 27

Ten minutes into reviewing the printout I thought, Jax, you poor, blind, dumb bastard, poor, poor Jax. You opted for the wrong genre. *Mirabella and the Force Five* was not a crime book, but a gripping personal account—autobiographical—of the horrors of growing up Thornton. An hour into it I knew that his intense page-turner throbbed with raw sexual tensions whirling though Jax's family cast…a brutally lascivious father and Svengali grandfather, pill-popping whore-mom, the father's series of trailer-trash bimbettes, and the bittersweet flavor of curdled childhood innocence. A further smorgasbord revealed questionable offshore business ventures, union payoffs, Thornton-owned politicians, child neglect, mom's revolving rehabs, abortion, and family suicide. Jax's brew would've turned Jacqueline Suzanne and Jackie Collins neon green with envy. Poor, blind Jax, the quintessential mystery wannabe whose personal tales exploded off the page like *Peyton Place* on angel dust.

As I passed another page to Frances I shrugged, "Jax old kid, your mysteries violated the Writer's First Commandment…write what you know! You poor dumb bastard."

"Amen," Frances affirmed. "A piece this raunchy, Guy—this would be every reader's guilty pleasure, it'd double Amazon's stock quotes overnight."

It was almost dawn when we'd finished our review, each taking separate chunks of the manuscript and speed-reading like crazy. We sat limp on the motel bed gaping at each other.

Frances spoke first. "What do you think, Guy?"

"I believe every single word of it, right down to the apostrophes and semi-colons." I decided to share, "I recall first meeting Mrs. Thornton at one of Jax's parties—just think the *Gatsby* crowd, only more booze—anyway, she shook my hand, told me how nice it was to finally meet me, and continued holding my hand, said how much she enjoyed my books, and continued holding my hand, said how she dearly hoped we'd meet again very soon. I was way past three sheets to the wind, but I still felt her heat. I was thankful when Jax tore me away and steered me toward some colleagues."

"I never even knew Jax and I'm ready to weep," Frances said. "No wonder the poor guy read mysteries, it took him away from all…all this human desolation…if even 10% of this is true, our suspect Thornton Senior possesses all the compassion of a starving barracuda. There's even a hint Thornton Senior may've arranged the demise of his own beloved father during the late eighties. And staged it to look accidental…sounds familiar, doesn't it."

I shrugged with exhaustion. "Maybe, Frances, but I figure it was snuff or be snuffed between those two jungle panthers. Poor Jax, it wasn't enough he had to cope with being a near-dwarf, but growing up with carnivores like Grandpa Thornton and Daddy Jax as his male role models."

"Mamma Thornton did more than her share, Guy, a sexual passive-aggressive alcoholic, a pill-addled schizoid who twisted her kid's psyche into a pretzel," Frances commented.

"Toting things up, this manuscript and Carlos' files could prove that Thornton Senior's scheme to takeover the Thornton Trust pre-dates Jax's death."

"As a journal of Family-from-Hell, this manuscript's motive enough its ownself to implicate either or both of his parents," she added.

"Plus a string of expensive Mirabellas stretching back for decades."

"Plus Jax's suspicions about the departure of his aged grandpa," Frances added.

As to Grandpa Thornton, according to Jax's manuscript the old man had gone sailing every morning at 5:00 A.M. sharp. One day Grandpa Thornton simply didn't return. By lunch they went looking for the old man and all they found was his empty and overturned catamaran.

"A great premise for one of my yachting series, maybe someday I'll..." Frances said, "then again, maybe not."

On that dark note I decided it was time to turn in and rest my weary eyes and brain.

I spent a sleepless night as scenes from Jax's manuscript haunted me, repeatedly forcing themselves into my mind. Moral qualms are not my natural condition, so I wondered with real surprise about having some. Why was I suddenly squeamish about using what I'd learned from Jax's manuscript? Why did I feel haunted about the dark foibles...in a more judgmental era we'd have called them "depravities"...of the Thornton family? Squeamish or not, I knew I must do all I could to solve young Jax's death. Which meant getting to the bottom of Thornton Senior's possible involvement. Which meant using the moral rot in the manuscript to pry out the truth.

"I need to do this alone, Frances," I told her over our El Grandes from Starbucks I'd fetched around ten, after confirming Thornton Senior would be at the Key West compound that afternoon.

"You're making no sense, Guy."

"I could try to explain it a dozen times and you'd still think that."

126

"Confront Thornton Senior alone? From what we learned last night the man is ruthless. If Senior killed his only son and set up a series of other murders to throw off the scent, what's to keep him from making a creampuff like yourself, who wanders into his spider web, simply disappear?"

"I've got that pepper spray."

Frances started laughing, "It'll be a fair fight then as long as the bad guys stay within one yard of you."

"It's what comes after this meeting that I'm worried about."

"Okay, Guy. But you promise to call me from Key West every hour on the hour."

I agreed.

"If you miss a call, Guy, I'll immediately phone Philbrick and the Coast Guard so they can snare the bastard as he dumps your body in the ocean."

"I think I'd much prefer a shallow grave."

"That ain't how it's done here on the Gulf, M'dear creampuff."

Chapter 28

Thornton Senior looked far better than the strife-worn shell I'd seen in the days following the funeral.

"Guy, I told the chef to fix us a late dinner. Lobster bisque and fresh fruit salad. I assume the drive over the causeway worked up your appetite. Always does mine."

"Did Mirabella tell you we'd stopped by on Wednesday?"

"As soon as I arrived. Belle said a Miss Whiting was with you—Belle was very happy that she'd promised to send her an autographed book. Were you two visiting Miami?"

"Yes. That's one of the matters I needed to discuss with you."

"We can chat over dinner...I see Rosa has everything set...cold bisque is not something you'd want to try."

Once we were settled and Rosa had finished serving the steaming meal, I looked at Thornton evenly and asked with faux candor, "Did Carlos Tapia call you?"

"How do you know Tapia?"

No need to invent a new lie when the old one is still perfectly serviceable. I told Thornton how Frances and I hoped to expand young Jax's papers into a series of books and since Tapia had been Frances' lawyer on other matters, we consulted him. Then added my ennobling touch, "Although Tapia and Frances were satisfied with the deal I wanted to touch base with you personally. After all, Mr. Thornton, it was your idea I sort through his files in the first place."

"Thought I made it clear, Guy, you have my permission to use whatever you can of my son's work. In any case, that's what I want." His bored eyes, the lack of interest in his voice, loudly proclaimed indifference...if loud indifference isn't an oxymoron.

"How about Frances Whiting being my partner in the project...?"

"I see that as your business, not mine."

"And the profits that might come?"

"If you want me to have a share, give the money to charity...in fact, I'm starting a fund for driver safety in memory of my son...plunk something in there if you want."

"You're very generous."

"No—just too goddamn busy running the Thornton businesses to give a rat's ass about chasing pocket change from some publishing magilla you and Ms. Whiting may gin up. Have some merlot, great with Rosa's bisque sauce. Say, you play poker, Guy? Ballsy Stud, of course, not that candy-ass Texas Hold 'Em crap you see on TV, which is strictly for tourists, the Vegas masses, and other amateurs."

128

"A little. Two-dollar limit…I'm not in your league."

Thornton brightened suddenly, "Here's an idea, you stay over 'till tomorrow and by noon my poker crowd'll start drifting in. I run three tables, everyone buys a hundred thousand in chips, then we play 'till the last man's standing."

"A hundred thou? Too many royalty checks for me, Mr. Thornton."

"I'll back you. You win, we split 50-50. You lose, my bath not yours. What do you say?"

"It's very tempting. But there's another item of business— unpleasant—and you may not want me around after we talk about it."

For the first time Thornton's eyes showed genuine interest in what I had to say. "Another item?"

"Yes. In Jax's files, I found something we should discuss."

"I'm all ears."

"Jax had a big, completed manuscript."

"Another *Corpse* mystery?"

"No. Autobiographical, of sorts."

"No kidding?"

"Yes. It was the tale of three generations of Thorntons. Very steamy, very sensationalistic stuff. Told from Jax's viewpoint, as a kid growing up, treading stormy waters actually, in a sea of dysfunction."

"About me?"

"Oh yes."

"His mother?"

"Oh yes. And his legendary grandfather, Jax the First."

"Define dysfunction as used in his book."

"The full Jackie Collins litany. Every kind of promiscuous sex. Drugs and booze, wealth and power. Brutality. Child abuse."

Thornton violently threw his napkin onto his plate. "You weasely son of a bitch, you're tryin' to shake me down!"

"No, sir, I'm not."

"Bullshit, Davitt!"

"If you think I'm here to blackmail you with the manuscript, sell it to you for seven figures so it'll never go public, well, think again."

"Seven figures my ass. I know the goddamn marketplace, for six figures I could have you killed, everyone you've talked to about this, and all your cousins in Kansas!"

"The number was a figure of speech, Mr. Thornton, not the start of an auction. I'm not here for blackmail, hadn't even thought of it until you brought it up."

"But now that you think of it, if I agree to wire two million in U.S. to an offshore account you set up in your sole name in return for the manuscript…?"

"You could wire two *billion*…I don't want your fuckin' money."

After a tense moment of eyeball-to-eyeball, Thornton relaxed and laughed. "Goddamn, but I believe you. Now you must join my poker club, Guy, if you're not one ballsy liar you're a sheer lunatic. Tell me more about this manuscript my son is alleged to have written, okay?"

"What do you want to know?"

"Was it any good? And be honest now, because you know my thoughts about his other scribblings."

"Very good, Mr. Thornton. Of its type, first drawer. It would sell like hot buttered popcorn."

Putting down his wine glass, Thornton leaned back and locked his hands behind his tilted head. A serene smile settled on his face as he blinked at the ceiling. After a long minute's pause he said, "I know some of the board members at Random…Christ yes! Let's do it, Davitt."

I couldn't believe what I'd just heard. Thornton read my thoughts.

"Don't look like you've been abducted by Martians, Davitt, I'm serious. In fact, publishing the goddamn thing would mean a great deal to me…my kid finally made it. Tell you what, you do whatever clean-up work is needed on the thing and…"

"Not much needed."

"You take a secondary byline—by P. Jax Thornton III and Guy Davitt.

"No sir. This opus is pure Jax."

"Has the thing got a title?"

"*Mirabella and the Force Five.*"

"Ahh, Belle—he *was* awfully fond of her—but what's *Force Five*? Sounds like a third-rate war movie. What's it mean?"

"It's comparing the pathology of the Thornton family to the meteorology of tropical storms."

"I'll be goddamned. That's really apropos. Damn!"

"Mr. Thornton, you can have it published or not. You don't need me. I had a different purpose in raising the subject, but your enthusiasm got me completely off my track."

"Which was?"

I returned to my original scenario. "Jax's manuscript is already in the hands of the police. They snarfed up all the files I had because of another case, and it was in there."

130

"What case?"

"Jax may have been murdered, not an accident."

Thornton leaned forward and his eyes flashed with feral anger, "You're saying some son of a bitch killed my boy?"

"I think so."

"Jesus! The kid never hurt anybody in his entire life, all he wanted was to be loved. You know that, Davitt."

"Some will think the motive's in the manuscript, Mr. Thornton."

He stared at me blankly. Slowly a thought pattern began to form behind his eyes, then moisture. "Sick as she is, she'd never do that. Never hurt the boy. Never."

"Your wife?"

He nodded. "If she found out what my son and I were planning to do…she's a bipolar alcoholic, Guy, with a stubborn tendency to tumble off her meds…the Swiss doctors told us anything's possible with her. For a long long time, before she fell off the edge of the world, his mother loved that kid. As much as I did. Despite the booze, which had her by the throat since before he was born. Ever wonder why Jax was barely five feet but every male in his mother's family and mine are over six-one?"

"I figure he lost the gene lottery."

"Oh no—the mommie lottery. While she was pregnant she put away more brandy, gin, schnapps and—if the cupboard was bare—more mouthwash, than the British Navy. And afterwards, when he was finally out of the incubator and she wanted to nurse the little guy."

"I don't quite…"

"Baby's neural tissue's susceptible—pituitary and some other glands—fetal alcohol syndrome. Time we found out what her booze was doing to him it was too late.…" His gaze was far away, a mix of torment and cold hatred.

I tried to say something but my mouth couldn't form the words. The older man looked at me, "For godsake, Guy, I'm talking about dysfunctional mommies in Southern California. Don't look like you've never seen fire before."

I collected my thoughts and asked softly, "You mentioned you and your son were going to do something about her?"

"Let me give you a little Thornton family history. My father, Jax I—the late great empire-builder—was an unrepentant brute. A sadistic despot. Damn near killed my mother on two separate occasions. I sat by her side in the hospital room for days after her *falling* episodes. Try this on for a first memory, Guy." Thornton had a distant look in his eyes and spoke more to the past than to me, "This may surprise you, but as a very little boy I was late to toilet train. Can't imagine why, what

131

with growing up in that blast furnace—but to my father it was a sign of weakness. So one day he walks by, yanks off my pull-up and dabs it in my face. *'There, you pissant little shit, now how do you like it?'* he screams at me. Quite frankly, Guy, I didn't like it and I remember to this very day staring cross-eyed at the brown glob on the tip of my nose, and wondering what on God's green earth I'd done to wake the monster that particular day?"

"Jesus," I mumbled.

"Dear old dad, the demigod, ruled with fire and brimstone. The Word to which he bestowed all devotion was *control*—his absolutist control—and if you didn't wear his yolk, he'd fester, burn, twist and boil, and when he'd finally explode, all hell rained his clenched fists and nobody was safe. The goddamned tyrant beat the living shit out of me—right up until mom's death. He'd use a belt, his fists, a telephone, anything close at hand, actually. Check out my nose, Guy, doesn't seem terribly straight, does it?"

Thornton Senior looked lost, done in, but he continued anyway. "When I was seventeen I came home from school one day and found her—upstairs, lying on the bed—their bed. Cold. The blood had already begun to settle, ghastly sight, but I sat by my mother's side one last time, worshiping her, before calling for help. My saintly mother—the only woman I've ever truly loved—had taken enough sleeping pills to put down Whirlaway—meantime, her husband was off screwing his Vegas call girl flavor of the month."

"I can't begin to imagine how hard..." I began, but Thornton Senior waved me off.

"The son of a bitch not only drove her to it, but walked her down the pathway and did everything but open the casket lid. After the funeral I asked to speak with him, privately, in the back parlor. I broke his jaw, and then his nose just to see how he liked it, a rib or two, even ruptured one of his testicles. I started to kick out his eyes when the chauffer and funeral director burst in and yanked me off him. But I'll never forgive myself for not doing it sooner...for not taking a stand..." Thornton Senior's voice wavered, "...for not saving my mother."

Awkward seconds ticked past as he composed himself. He rose and stood looking down at me.

"Naturally, the bastard hated my guts forever after ending his reign of terror, so he pretty much cut me out of the empire. Last thing the fucker did was make my son and rum-soaked wife co-trustees of the Thornton Trust...the seventh largest dynastic trust in the universe in *her* hands? After the Switzerland institution, I talked Jax into helping me get her off the trigger and several months ago my boy and I quietly got the lawyers cranking. Figured worst-case scenario she'd go down fighting like a banshee to stop us. But when Jax died suddenly I had them switch our tactics to name me alone as trustee."

I thought in silence for a long time as I fit the pieces in place. Carlos Tapia had a running start on the court case not because Thornton Senior had planned to murder his son to preempt control of the Thornton Trust, but because father-and-son had collaborated to preempt Jax's mentally disturbed, chemically-dependent mother. Swiss clinics, Tapia's law firm, the facts Thornton had poured out so voluntarily could be easily checked against the pilfered law files. Not that I needed confirmation. He wasn't lying. No one, not Crowe not Brando not Depp could've pulled off an acting job to match the pain and panic, love and loss, I'd just seen in Thornton Senior.

I asked slowly, already sure of the answer, "Is it remotely possible, in her condition, she got wind of the Trust fight and hired the murder of her own son?"

"Absolutely not, Guy. Never in a million years. Jax's death has destroyed her, and she was a busted sparrow to begin with. Assuming she was rational enough to find out about the Trust matter, and think things through, she'd have had me killed, not the boy."

"Or the both of you, maybe?" I added.

"Naa. Half her brain's burnt out, she just doesn't have the candle power to have planned any of it. Now it's your turn, Guy. I demand to know why you think my boy was murdered."

Now trusting Thornton Senior completely, I poured it all out. How his son may've been just one in a series of killings targeted against mystery authors. Of the little we knew so far I told him all.

"The police wrote Jax's death off as an accident. They've mentioned none of this to me."

"There nothing's solid at this point, Mr. Thornton. And…well…" I hesitated to finish the thought.

"And I'm suspect numero uno. I see. That's fine, let them do their job." Thornton Senior sat again, played with his fork, and made a mental note aloud. "Poker's off. I'm flying back to L.A. tonight. I've got a team of special *security* people on the payroll and if it turns out my boy was murdered, and if my people find the person or persons responsible," Thornton looked at me dry-eyed and with bitter determination in his voice said, "you sure as hell won't be hearing about it on the eleven o'clock news." Thornton rose once more, walked to the window, and stood staring into the dark waters of the Gulf.

I stared toward the window that looked out on the moonlit waves and pondered the overturned catamaran of the Thornton patriarch. "It's a deep ocean," I murmured.

"Yes, Guy. Deep and unforgiving." His voice told me Thornton Senior knew everything about the uses of the deep.

He slumped down into his dining chair. Suddenly Mr. Thornton looked weary. We sat in silence awhile before he sighed. "My poor boy wasn't really a mystery writer—from what you said his true forte was high profile scandals, like us carnivores of the Thornton clan. Dysfunctional families, isn't that what you said?"

"Mr. Thornton, by my lights, one way or another all families are dysfunctional."

"You're a goddamn tactful liar." Thornton Senior shot me a grin. "Now, Guy, I really must insist on your joining my poker club someday."

Frances was waiting for me in the Hyatt Marian lobby.

I cut directly to the chase. "Thornton Senior didn't kill his son."

"How do you know?" she asked.

"Long story, and I'll tell you every detail on the plane, but," I shrugged my shoulders, "I've managed to place us into a bizarre episode of *Beat the Clock*."

"What do you mean?"

"If Thornton Senior finds the killer first, no one will ever know but the sharks."

"That works for me," Frances replied.

"Don't get me wrong, I'm not *necessarily* against vigilante justice. But neither of us wants to spend our lives looking over our shoulders long after Scythe has been fed to the fishies."

After tapping the necessary numbers into my cell phone to check my home voicemail, I visibly cringed as I heard Sandra Kearns rasping out her curt message. Barnstorm Press was pulling the plug on Connor Alba and expected the advance returned as soon as possible lest their attorneys be fed. Kearns also informed me that as of immediately she would no longer be representing me.

I took a long drink from my bottled Evian and thought about my financial future. In a month or two I'll have to get the Mustang tuned up in order to sell it. And I'd likely need to hit up The Judge for a small loan—boy, won't that make for an enjoyable conversation. Then I can decipher the LA transit system in order to figure out which bus to take to whatever community college will allow me to teach creative writing in its adult ed classes. Or, alter-natively, to scrub their lavatories.

Chapter 29

Right after arriving back in West LA, more emotionally exhausted than physically, Frances and I sat across from Lieutenant Neff and filled her in on our findings, papering over any felonies we may have committed in the law offices of Carlos Tapia. Maddie listened intently, made some scratches on her notepad at various points in our narrative. My report on Thornton Senior riled her.

"That's great, Davitt," Maddie snapped at the conclusion. "Just what LAPD needs, mercs roaming the streets."

"Mercs?" Frances asked.

"Mercenaries. Hired guns." Maddie frantically scratched some more in her book. "I'd better talk some sense to Mr. Thornton, nip this silliness in the bud."

"I doubt he's going to listen," I said.

"This town's volatile enough as is, we certainly don't need him dumping kerosene on the fire." Maddie bounced a couple fingers off her desk, "Hey, before I forget, your great friend Oliver Robbins is back in play."

"But wasn't he out of the country at the time of Jax's death?"

"That's what the flight itinerary at Delta indicated, but it turns out Robbins never showed up for his return flight…Pickman did some digging…turns out a studio jet flew a planeload of Tinseltown glitterati back five days early, of which your pal Robbins was onboard."

"So what's it mean, Lieutenant?" Maddie now had Frances' undivided attention.

"It means he was back in town two full days before Jax's car crash."

"Greetings!" A two thousand dollar Armani sporting shoulder-length silver hair met us in Robbins' outer office. "I'm C. Tackford Howell, Pentathlon's general counsel, but please blow off the 'C' and call me Tacky. Everybody does."

"Hello Tacky, I'm Frances Whiting."

"Oh, don't I know it!" Tacky Howell enthusiastically pumped Frances' hand and patted it for emphasis. "My wife reads all your books. I keep meaning to pick one up, but Oliver has me jumping so fast day and night I've completely forgotten what free time looks like." Tacky Howell turned to me, "And you must be Tim Davitt?"

"Call me Guy, Tacky."

"Guy and Tacky—your nicknames sound like a pair of Mickey Mouse Club alumni," Frances chirped, much to Tacky Howell's head-bobbing guffaws.

"Would either of you like coffee, we've Starbucks? Or perhaps a fresh squeezed juice or an Evian?"

Frances chose the coffee. I requested water while wondering why Pentathlon's lawyer was meeting with us. Frances had contacted Robbins' secretary to set our follow-up meeting. We'd bagged using the recorder after last time's debacle, figuring LAPD would just have to believe two upstanding citizens in case Robbins got a wild hair and decided, on the spur of the moment, to confess to murder.

"Grace," Tacky Howell said to one of Robbins' secretaries, "can you get Ms. Whiting a coffee and a couple of Evians for Guy and myself? And if you'll put a lime twist in mine, I'll appreciate it boundlessly at Christmas bonus time." We followed Tacky into Robbins' inner sanctum.

Faintly resembling Jaba-the-Hut, Robbins sat behind his glasstop desk, a Pentathlon coffee mug in front of him and what looked like a script sitting on his desktop. On the side couch sat a scrawny young fellow in a green *Wallflowers* t-shirt, intently studying his Adidas.

"Welcome Frances," Robbins beamed, came around his desk and gave her an extended hug. "Big Guy," he nodded my way before retreating back behind the desk and looking toward Tacky Howell.

At that point Grace glided in with a tray containing our drinks and mounds of blueberry scones. Frances and I took residence at a coffee table adjacent to Robbins' desk. Tacky Howell stood and sipped from his drink. The room was silent.

"We've completed the outline you requested," I volunteered.

Robbins pointed toward the young man on the leather sofa, "First, let me introduce you to Yogi Mosset. Yogi here is one of our in-house writers. Does brilliant work, a true up-and-comer."

"This is an absolute honor for me." Yogi Mosset popped to his Adidas, walked over and limp-shook our hands, turned to go, but then turned back. "Mr. Davitt, when the drug runners had Connor hooked up to the truck battery in *The Night Imposter*, I had no clue how you'd get him out of it. I stayed up all night finishing the...."

"No time for shop talk this morning, Yogi," Robbins leaned forward in his chair and looked at his general counsel. "Folks, Tacky's going to lead this meeting. I'm afraid I stepped in it the other day, and I don't want to bollix things up any further."

A red flag as well as the hairs on the back of my neck went up.

I glanced over at Frances. Her eyes were blue consternation. Both Frances and I redirected our gazes toward Tacky Howell.

136

"Here's the problem." Tacky Howell sat on the opposite side of the couch from Yogi Mosset, placed his drink on a coaster, and began, "As you know, Pentathlon is a huge and complex operation. We have production departments specializing in film, television, cable, video, video games, some industry magazines—that's a secret goldmine, by the way—and radio production, although radio may not necessarily be long for Pentathlon."

"Radio production's got a high PIA factor," Robbins cut in, "pain in the ass—with goddamn little return to show—and if I get my way, this time next year Pentathlon'll be out from under that albatross completely."

"Pentathlon's foreign market is even bigger than the domestic—Britain, Italy, Japan, French TV—it's mind boggling all of the different markets we've been able to tap into."

"This all sounds like great news for the shareholders' meeting," Frances replied, "but what does it have to do with us, Tacky?"

"I just wanted to give you a little background on how hectic things can be. Concepts, story ideas, plot lines buzz about here like a thousand bees on honey." Tacky Howell paused for emphasis before resuming, "You know, amazing how we're able to juggle so many balls in the air at one time. And the credit for that goes largely to Oliver. And," Tacky Howell chuckled, "at the risk of having this come back and bite me, I'm going to state that Oliver is the most anal-retentive micromanager I've ever met. Wouldn't you say that's a true statement, Oliver?"

Robbins raised one hand, "Guilty as hell."

"I head legal and Oliver somehow finds ways to micromanage my department. I can just imagine how you creative types deal with him, Yogi."

Yogi Mosset smiled sheepishly.

"Just as I'd assumed." Tacky Howell's corporate ass-kissing chuckle was beginning to grate. "Anyway, after you two met with Oliver last week, where he liked your story idea, he got to thinking that it sounded somewhat familiar, that he'd bumped across it before."

"What's he talking about?" I asked Robbins directly.

"Quite frankly, Guy," Tacky Howell forced the spotlight back to himself, "serial killers are so 90s—every other movie, novel, or made-for-TV had a dogged detective hunting down a psychopath—wouldn't you both agree?"

"Yes," Frances responded.

"So there exist the derivatives of derivatives of derivatives of derivatives all across the industry." As he spoke Tacky Howell actually ticked off derivatives on each of his well-manicured fingers. "That's a

137

given. The challenge for you artists is to discover that unique angle, that new approach with which to breathe new life into a worn-out genre. Now the concept of a serial killer stalking mystery writers is so rich in irony—it was the mystery writers who first turned serial killers into an art form—sheer brilliance. You must be congratulated. However..."

"Here it comes," I said.

"Please hear me out, Mr. Davitt. The reason it sounded so familiar to Oliver is that in a brainstorming meeting some time back, Yogi here tossed something similar out as a premise for a film."

I looked at Yogi Mosset, who was nervously analyzing his Adidas.

"Cock-and-bullshit," I blurted.

Tacky Howell turned to Yogi for corroboration. "That's correct isn't it, Yogi?"

"Well...I ahh..."

"I repeat, cock-and-bullshit. Robbins recognized a great concept and immediately started thinking about how he could screw us over."

"Watch what you say, Mr. Davitt," Tacky Howell shifted in his seat, "that's prima facie slander."

I focused on Mosset. "Hand on the bible, kid, is any of this true?" The guy had probably worked in the basement mailroom until yesterday and this was his ticket upstairs. "Is it true, kid?"

Mosset glanced from his feet to Robbins, and then settled on me, "Well, yes. Sure, sir."

"Hey kid." I ignored both Robbins and Mr. Smooth in the suit, "Did you get market value?"

"Well, I'm a staff writer so I'm salaried and..."

"No, Mosset, not for your work. For your soul." I pointed at Robbins with an accusing index finger, "Did this heap of lard pay you market value for your soul?"

"Ms. Whiting, I strongly suggest you talk some sense to your partner," Tacky Howell said. "There's no need for recriminations, we are all civilized people here."

"I'm going to fuck you for this in open court." I glared at Robbins.

"I'll quote you on that, Mr. Davitt, should this ever go to a jury." Tacky Howell stated calmly.

"Feel free, pal. I plan on suing son of flubber here into a size 30. Everyone knows you're a dung beetle, Robbins, but I'm gonna tattoo it on your forehead."

"A lawsuit is certainly your prerogative," Tacky Howell's nervous laugh had vanished and his eyes narrowed as his voice became

138

thick with intimidation and I began to see exactly how Tacky Howell earned his keep, "but I should add, Mr. Davitt, that there are witnesses. Dated meeting minutes. Computer files. By the way Pentathlon Production's working title, which I can prove goes back over six months, is *Out of Print,* rather apropos I must say. Yogi has a completed outline and his screenplay is now up to 20 pages of polished dialog. The proof's a perfect sandwich, Mr. Davitt."

"Your proof's a barfed bratwurst, Tacky!" I was out of control and fit to be launched, but at least Robbins' face had also turned beet red. "We'll see how it plays with everybody under oath."

"Yes," Tacky Howell smiled and looked like he knew something I didn't, "we'll certainly see."

"You're nothing but an overdressed hoodlum, Oliver, and when I get done you'll be as big a household name as Al Capone—a dime store version." I stared at Robbins, his hands now visibly trembling. I glanced around the room. "I can't wait until after the lawsuit so I can remodel this dump."

Finally, Robbins' volcano erupted in sensurround, "You wanna sue me, fuckeater!" Robbins suddenly stood, his momentum sending his chair backwards against his credenza. He clenched onto his coffee mug and for a long second and I prepared to dive out of his line of fire. "Sue me? Fine! Grab a goddamn number!" He slammed the mug onto his glass desktop, shattering it. "Davitt, you two-buck whore wordsmiths are a dime a dozen. You hear me? A dime a fucking dozen! No one comes into my office and talks to me this way! No one! I will crush everything about you, Davitt—I'll use your nuts for badminton and your skull for an ashtray."

"I'll quote you on that should this ever go to jury," I replied.

Pentathlon Security, three mouth-breathing musketeers, followed us out, all the way to Frances' car in the Universal City parking lot, then the three musketeers stood there watching to be sure we drove away. I now knew why Robbins seemed so distracted in our first meeting, he was plotting exactly which angle he would use to stick the knife in our backs.

"I'm going to sue fatboy into debtor's prison!" I shouted at the dashboard.

"Have you got an attorney?" Frances asked.

"I'm hoping Carlos Tapia can schedule me in," I looked over at her in the passenger seat. "And why didn't you chime in? Robbins set us up, he con jobs a cover story to steal our script idea right out from under us, and you don't say boo."

"You looked like you were booing pretty well all by yourself, Guy."

"Did you get a load of that lying dweeb of a writer? God knows how many generations of intermarriage it took to birth that critter."

"Guy?"

"I know we can smack Robbins down, we can bite that bastard back with bad PR, and sell *Vanity Fair* a series about this experience, Pentathlon'll settle to keep this out of the media."

"Guy?"

"What already?!"

"Why are you so angry? It was our cover story, that's all. We weren't ever really going to get in bed with Robbins. *Our cover story.* And you want to start World War Three over it."

I slowly brought my eyes back to the road.

"Besides, Guy, Oliver produces mush, remember?"

That's why Frances didn't see red. She kept in mind we were there on a scam and Oliver's theft didn't matter. But I still burned and boiled, knowing Robbins had tap-danced the Tinseltown Two-Step right across my face.

"Plus, Guy, did you notice what almost happened?"

"What?"

"Robbins has an almost uncontrollable temper. For a second there I thought your tombstone would read 'Death via Coffee Mug.' And another important thing to note," Frances held an echoing silence until I turned back to face her, "he certainly has no love for wordsmiths."

Chapter 30

Lieutenant Neff led us into a vacant conference room and quietly shut the door behind us. Frances and I sat on one side of a table and Maddie pulled the chair out on the other, but remained standing. She'd called us less than a half hour earlier as we were in Frances' Lexus returning from Universal City. Maddie had asked if we could drop everything and come by.

"Frances, I owe you an apology."

"What's up, Maddie?" Frances asked.

"Masloski called me an hour ago with the DNA results," Maddie sat down. "It was Pizzaro. On your boat."

"I knew it!" Frances beamed directly at me, "I told you so, Guy."

"I never said it absolutely wasn't him," I came to my own defense, "but the odds were infinitesimal…"

"You tried to make me out as crazy."

"I didn't make you out as anything."

"Quit bickering, kids," Maddie cut us off. "This requires some gray matter."

"Pizzaro is Scythe?" Frances asked.

"I've churned this over in my mind since I got the results and I came up with three scenarios," Maddie flipped open her notepad, glanced down quickly and then looked back up at us. "The first scenario is that Pizzaro has absolutely nothing to do with Scythe, but he ventured into Florida and figured what the hell, as long as I'm here soaking up the sun, why don't I croak a random lady writer on her yacht."

"And the sun orbits the earth," I derided.

"I know. Next scenario—Pizzaro is secretly Scythe—he had a quantum higher IQ than anyone knew, but still managed to get himself butchered by unrelated perps from his long and tattered criminal career."

"Far too coincidental for my likes," Frances observed.

"I know," Maddie replied. "If you two think I'm shocked by this connection, you should have heard Masloski on the phone…he's stunned…he's gonna shake some of Pizzaro's known associates and see if there's a Florida connection somewhere in the haystack. Plus I gave him the dates of the *accidental deaths* of those other authors, told him to timeline Pizzaro's movements."

"Go to scenario three," Frances requested.

"Scenario three is that the real Scythe subcontracted Pizzaro for help with the murders. When Pizzaro failed in Florida, and Frances had disfigured him, Pizzaro became an enormous liability so Scythe killed him."

"If we allow that Pizzaro is a piece in the puzzle," Frances said, "then, if we find Pizzaro's killer, we find Scythe."

"Exactly my thought," Maddie flipped her notepad shut. "But what scares me down to my bone marrow is this scenario raises the possibility Scythe's running a unit. Even with Pizzaro dead, Scythe and his other hired help could be more than one person."

"This thing's getting less penetrable every day." I shook my head in frustration. "We completely strike out with Thornton Senior. We get totally screwed at our meetings with Robbins."

"That's truly rotten luck. Scythe would have needed big bucks to jerk Pizzaro's chain, money that would be chump change to Robbins. Or to Thornton Senior for that matter," Maddie reasoned.

"Thornton Senior did not kill his son." I was adamant on this point. Frances and I had confirmed Jax's scribbled signature was indeed on several documents in the photographed Tapia files.

"Bottom line, Lieutenant, what will LAPD do?" Frances asked.

"We've got a murdered L.A. thug that we're investigating with vigor," Maddie stared at Frances. "Don't underestimate Detective Masloski, if there's something findable about Pizzaro there, he'll find it. And then we'll nail Scythe."

"But what about the dead writers?" Frances asked. "I know they were all murdered just as well as I knew that it was Pizzaro on my boat."

"I've reread all of the reports, Frances. Twice over. The damned things have accident stamped all over them. And only Jax Thornton III falls under my jurisdiction. I've got nothing to break the log jam besides our conjecture. I plan to bring it to Captain Vasquez, set up a meeting between him, Masloski, and myself for tomorrow morning."

"Realistically?" I demanded.

"Realistically?" Maddie looked down at her sinewy hands and shrugged, "I'm sorry."

Chapter 31

Frances went up to her room at the Star Motel announcing she wanted to bag her laundry for room service, have a long soak, and a nap. We agreed to meet at The Harthrop—a white linen eatery down the block—for a late dinner. I, on the other hand, took the car to a nearby Borders bookstore, ransacked the shelves, and returned with a couple of Frances Whiting mysteries. I returned to my room, plopped on the bed, and began.

The Harthrop was about half full. For starters, we ordered crab cakes with a bottle of German wine that rhymed with "Sangfroid" but only Frances could pronounce.

"I finally got around to reading some of your work," I announced, by unspoken agreement steering clear of our dismal sequence of dead ends.

"Oh? Which book?"

"*The Bowsprit Alibi.*"

"Don't trust the tour guide."

"He did seem a little slippery. Thanks for the ruin."

"Just messing with you, Guy. So what do you think so far?"

"Logically plotted, rich characterizations," I fought my wicked impulses but lost, "much reminiscent of Nancy Drew."

"Long pause," she stared narrowly over her glass of red at me, "and most un-Nancy-Drew-like the offended author seethingly declared, 'Up yours, Davitt.'"

"Just messing with you, Frances. I'm only at page 70 and it's pulling me right along." I closed my menu, had already decided on the almond crusted salmon. "Your Sally Kerentine reminds me a lot of you."

"I get that all the time."

"Really?"

She shrugged, "There is one difference."

"What's that?"

"Can't tell you. An inside joke an old college sorority sister came up with some years back."

"Wait a minute. You can't toss something like that out there and let it hang in the air. It's unconstitutional. What's the inside joke?"

"After another glass of wine, perhaps," she blinked coquettishly.

"How 'bout another glass of wine?"

"I've only started this one."

The waiter took our orders, then Frances graciously let me steal the last crab cake. I was hungry, likely due to the lateness of the hour and my general frustration over the case. I glanced about the room, did my best to keep my eyes from settling on Frances' luminous beauty for too long at a spell, figured she got plenty of that. Besides, beautiful women still make me slightly nervous...on edge...a car wreck actually. If you add brains to the mix, I become 13 again and revert to the pubescent nerd. My reserve stash of witty banter had already been exhausted and I could feel my inner geek preparing to seize control. Then, from God knows where but thank Him anyway, it dawned on me.

"Occam's Razor." I took a big mouthful of wine.

"What about it?" Frances asked.

"I've been thinking zebras instead of horses."

"What on earth are you rambling about, Guy?"

"We got derailed, Frances. As a result we've been chasing our tails. Thornton Senior. Pizzaro. That dungbag Robbins. I can't tell you what fits what anymore. It's time to walk back the cat. You know, start at the beginning."

"Grasping at more straws?"

I ignored that, "Do you remember how I told you about my going through all of Jax's writing materials?"

"Yes yes, Mirabella's the mistress and not a hurricane."

"Jax left other odds and ends besides that. In fact I picked up my box of his materials this morning and re-sifted through everything again. Not much to go on, but Jax had this one sheet of paper with a bunch of chicken scratchings on it that's been nagging at the back of my mind. They're authors' initials I figure." I took the yellow sheet out of the breast pocket of my sport jacket, unfolded it on the table and studied it to build suspense.

"Hand it over, Guy. Let the pro have a peek."

"Sure thing, Doctor Watson," I slid it to her across the table. "See the letters T.G.D., Jax put a question mark next to them...I'm fairly sure those are my initials...as though Jax was wondering if or how I fit in. I think A.M. stands for Angus MacDougall. Pretty obvious. And if that scribble on the left is a B and not an D, it's likely B.Q. for Beck Quinn—looks as though Jax had made the Beck Quinn connection before his death."

Frances smoothed the page flat in front of her, absorbed in study. After a minute's silence, I reached over and refilled her glass with wine. After another lengthy silence, the waiter brought our salads but Frances quickly shoved hers aside, clearing a place for Jax's notes, ignoring her food. She kept concentrating on the page. Between peeks at Frances, I inhaled my salad.

"Of course!" she said, finally looking up.

"Huh?"

"L.M.L. *Lady Mesmer's List*." Frances looked down at her salad as though first noticing its arrival. "There's an arrow from L.M.L. to A.M. *Lady M's List* to Angus MacDougall."

"So that's an L.M.L. and not an I.M.I.?" I pointed at Jax's scribblings.

"It must be terribly difficult writing your stories, Guy, what with not knowing the English alphabet and all." Frances said, smiling at me. "And we both know how Angus died."

"Alcohol poisoning."

"Yes," Frances forked absently at her lettuce. "My villainess in *Lady Mesmer* used hypnotism for her alcohol poisoning of a known lush who'd tripped over her true identity."

"So the unidentified initials aren't necessarily all authors?"

"Evidently some of the initials represent book titles. Books from which our killer is plagiarizing."

"Plagiarizing?" I asked.

"Figure of speech…plagiarizing the M.O. of the murders."

I saw her point. "Plagiarizing to death in a sense. Lifting fictional M.O.s to actually murder writers such as Angus."

"Bingo. *Lady Mesmer's List* became a prescription for murder."

I felt like a deep-sea diver coming up for air. "So what novels do these other initials—the T.W. or the C.S.—stand for?"

"A doozy of a question, Guy."

"Serials are often so…so complex to decipher."

"The deranged psyche is very complex."

"I don't mean the Freudian voodoo jargon. More their patterns. I once researched that homicidal Oxford student that Scotland Yard caught. You know about that one, Frances?"

"Vaguely…something to do with numbers?" she asked.

"This kid—Copeland was his name—strangled people seemingly at random. Impossible case, until one of the Yard's brainiest detectives figured the pattern was based on a mathematical progression formula. Copeland began by taking the square root of the date Princess Di was killed in that Paris car crash, then reduced it to prime numbers and used corresponding numbers in the Oxford phone book to…well, anyway, he picked his victims by numbers as revealed in the phone directory using this bizarre logarithm he'd constructed."

"So?" she asked.

"So, for all we know, this list could merely be the tip of an iceberg."

"Terrifying thought, Guy. I say we hit the public library as soon as it opens and try to crack these connections."

The food came and I think the salmon was good but I ate on autopilot, my mind focused on Jax's diagram. I knew most of the authors in my genre, and I knew the titles of the more popular mystery novels, but voracious reader that I am, still the search seemed needles and haystacks. Say we find additional authors, who've died in apparent accidents. Okay, how do we cull through four thousand books to find from where each homicidal premise was stolen? The calculations and permutations could be infinite, unless we got lucky we might need a Copeland-like logarithm to crack the pattern.

I also ate on autopilot because there was something else tugging at the back of my mind. Something I'd not quite put into words, not yet, something that needed a tad more digging.

Finally, I gave up and returned to the here-and-now. "Hey, Frances, before I forget," I tossed my plastic at the waiter and awaited his return, "now that you've had a couple glasses of wine, that inside sorority sister joke? What's the only difference between you and Sally Kerentine?"

"The inside joke is," Frances folded her napkin on the table and looked me evenly in the eyes, "I've got bigger knockers."

I dumbed out, at a loss for words. I felt myself blush. My inner geek temporarily resumed the reins of control. I groped for words but none were at hand.

"What, Guy," she was clearly enjoying this, "no fast quip?"

"Sure," I mumble-feigned a recovery, "I was just musing over a similar issue between me and Connor Alba."

After dinner I walked Frances back to her room, both of us adrift in quiet thought. We knew we'd latched onto something tangible—a clue that we could finally sink our teeth into—could feel it churn in our guts, no more pin-wheeling, no more redherring trails. Jax had given us a roadmap and we could follow it wherever it led.

"The Agathas are being held in Scottsdale this year," Frances said absently.

"Oh, right...I'd forgotten they'll be in Arizona."

"I'll need to head out next Thursday."

"You're going to The Agathas?"

"I won an award last year, so they want me to be a presenter this year," Frances responded. "You know how it works."

"I won the Egg Spoon race at my Third Grade Field Day. I still have the blue ribbon if you'd like to see it."

"And you didn't get any on your face?" Frances asked.

"Egg?"

"Mmhmm. I wish you'd attend The Agathas this year...we could go together. It's at the Four Seasons, Guy, just one state away."

I lied, "Before everything got turned on its head, I toyed with driving out for the main dinner, but I'd probably blow off most of the other events as usual."

"C'mon, Guy, it'll be a hoot to see some of the gang. I'll drive."

"The notion deserves some serious thought," I replied, realizing I'd just committed to going.

"I doubt I'll be able to sleep tonight," Frances said while unlocking the door to her room. "Sure wish they'd invent the all night library."

"You know, Frances," the wine swirled in my veins, I couldn't let the WatChat boys down, "if we were characters in a novel, it's right about here that you and I would..."

"Have a nice night, Guy," Frances said closing the door.

Chapter 32

The main library was not crowded. Frances and I set up shop in the mystery section. She grabbed a copy of *Lady Mesmer's List*. She softly read aloud the key passage containing the premise that our killer had used to O.D. Angus MacDougall's brain with alcohol. I already knew how the accidental death Jax and I had concocted for one of his *Corpse* books—the ladder fall gambit—had finished Beck Quinn. Beck's ladder had been kicked sideways and a forty-foot tumble to the unforgiving rock bed below. That explained Jax's logic in the arrow from his own initials to B.Q.—obviously Beck Quinn. Another set of initials on Jax's chart was T.W., which included an incoming arrow from C.S. as well as an outgoing line to A.C. We assumed A.C. indicated Alexandra Case, but were at a complete loss regarding the other initials.

We made photocopies of Jax's scratchings and each of us headed to different fiction rows.

"Funny," Frances called softly from several racks away, "I don't seem to see any of your books here, Guy."

"That's cause they're all checked out, Watson," I whispered back.

I couldn't find a mystery author with the initials "C.S.," and C.S. Lewis died in the sixties. I was approaching Frances, her nose in the Ws as she exclaimed, "That's it."

"That's what?"

"Tim Willi."

"Who?"

"I think T.W. stands for Tim Willi." Frances handed me a paperback called *Entitlement Cuts* by the author Tim Willi. A connection flashed through my mental synapses—this was what I'd been trying to remember, the mystery containing some rather interesting scenes of faked fires, a wrestler's sleeper hold, and a particularly unpleasant intruder sporting a gas mask. Willi's mystery *Entitlement Cuts* was the missing link to Alexandra Case's demise. I'd read the novel in the mid 1990s—its overall plot, fairly ingenious, had something to do with the elderly being bumped off by a secret government organization.

The smoke inhalation death was just one of many utilized by the book's villain. The killer had set everything up, even worn a gas mask, and held the victim—some frail, elderly female—locked tight in a cushioned half-Nelson until she'd succumbed to the smoke. Then he slid her body to the floor, slipped out the back, and escaped Scot free—

until unmasked by Willi's heroic protagonist in the final denouement, of course.

"It says Tim Willi lives with his two dogs outside Embarrass, Minnesota."

After *Entitlement Cuts* Willi had published a couple follow up books, none Frances or I had ever heard of. We bee-lined over to one of the library's Internet-access terminals, signed on, and Googled Tim Willi. There were about a dozen items, mostly regarding *Entitlement Cuts* but the most recent, the one that jumped out and grabbed us by the throat, was an article from the Embarrass Minnesota Pioneer, a rural weekly newspaper. The florid writer for the Pioneer issue, dated February 6 of last winter, graphically detailed how the local novelist died from exposure less than a mile from his home. Tim Willi froze to death it was assumed, because his aging Blazer had broken down alongside the county road, the SUV found with its hood up and bent backwards on its hinges from the fierce February winds. Tim Willi's frozen carcass was found in the gravel road a few hundred yards away, curled into a fetal position, his dead marble eyes staring vacantly across the windswept tundra. Officials figured his remains had lain out there for a day and a half before the police found him. Talk about a stiff stiff. The article went on to say he was frozen so solid the medics broke off two of Willi's fingers while hauling his remains into the medi-van. The Sheriff speculated Willi, a lifelong bachelor and avid outdoorsman, had decided to drive into town in the middle of a howling artic freeze, windchills reaching 85 below. Probably his car had stalled. Being an amateur mechanic, Willi had seemingly popped the hood and tried to start it. Not dressed for such horrendous conditions, Willi had evidently given up on the repair attempt and decided to try and run back to the warmth of his house and must have lost his bearings in the whiteout. Eventually, he'd simply curled up on a snow bank and died from exposure.

"Good God," Frances sat up, "freezing to death! Guy, I remember reading some book where that was used as part of a murder conspiracy."

"I remember something, too. Years back, a real obvious title."

"Maybe Gifford's *The Wind Chill Factor*?" she suggested.

"Nada. But, um…oh damn, I can't quite…"

"*Cold Snap!*"

"That's it!"

"The author?!" My fingers flew across the library's computer keyboard.

After a lengthy e-tussle, the great god Google revealed the author's name—Blake Cornell. We rushed back to the bookshelves.

Fate smiled on us as two copies of *Cold Snap* sat on the rack. Simultaneously, both of us began skimming the book.

Blake Cornell's killer in *Cold Snap*, a deputy sheriff named Tate, had used a mid-western blizzard to do away with certain human pockets of corruption in his small rural county. The gang's crooked accountant had been tossed, nearly naked, outside his country home to face a 60 below wind chill in his boxer shorts and slippers, flopping about like a fish tossed onshore, as he died from the hostile elements. Deputy Tate had taken out one of the main mobsters, the fence, by pulling him over on the outskirts of town, yanking him out from his car and, at gunpoint, pitching him down into a deep gravel pit, its banks of swirling snow becoming the criminal's cold white tomb.

I brought out Jax's list. Once more I began at the top. More tumblers began clicking into place. The easy one, A.M., being Angus MacDougall, its connecting arrow leading to L.M.L., meaning *Lady Mesmer's List*. The arrowed line from Jax's own initials led to "B.Q." meaning Jax had realized Beck Quinn's fatal fall came in a manner detailed in one of his books.

"So far," I summarized. "We have B.Q.—Beck Quinn—zapped as in Jax's book. And..."

"Angus MacDougall offed as in my *Lady Mesmer's List*. And..."

"Tim Willi's done in courtesy of Blake Cornell's *Cold Snap*," I cut in.

"And then Alexandra Case—A.C.—ala Tim Willi. Which brings us back around to Blake Cornell's *Cold Snap*, thus the arrow from C.S. to Tim Willi—T.W. I suspect each author will prove to be a homicide M.O. as well as a victim. Why else was I attacked on my boat?"

"Maybe. But we don't have a complete picture yet, Frances. We know only that many on Jax's chart died in mysterious accidents that had been chronicled in another mystery writer's fiction. And, Jesus, that means our killer has created a geometry of death, a homicidal Rubik's Cube."

I looked at Jax's initials "P.J.T." on Jax's doodle sheet, followed by question marks. I saw a connection, a far more tragic umbilicus than the one Jax's mother had mentioned. I stared down the sheet at my own initials. The hair on the back of my neck rose as I took out my pen and drew an arrow from my own initials T.G.D. straight over to P.J.T.

The cracked piece of mirror I'd found at Jax's death site had bothered me, burrowing away in my thoughts. I'd just not been able to put a voice to it as though that'd give it some authenticity, somehow tip it over into the realm of daylight.

"What does the new line mean?" Frances asked from over my shoulder.

And I told her. "There was a short story once, a mystery of course, where the killers knew their victim would be heading along a deserted mountain road late at night. They stole one of those short trucks people rent for moving, like a U-Haul. Then fastened a plate glass mirror to its side, and parked it sideways on a hairpin turn. Positioned it exactly right. The victim took the curve, saw his own reflected headlights coming straight at him, and panic-jerked the wheel to avoid a collision, swerved his car off the side of the mountain and into the never-ending statistics of accidental highway deaths. The killers popped the mirror back into the U-Haul truck, and escaped into the night. The hack author of the piece had actually lifted the ploy."

"He did?"

"He stole the concept from a comic book he'd read once as a kid."

"How do you know the author..." Frances began to ask, but figured it out in mid question.

I was lost in silent deliberation. I tend to know quite a bit about this particular author because, well...he happens to be me. The short story had appeared two decades ago, I was still at UCLA, got it published in my first collected volume called *Per Diem*, a couple dozen of my early Connor Alba shorts. A pretty good effort, I must admit, for someone only a few hiccups out of high school.

And now it broke my heart.

"Guy," Frances tugged gently at my arm. "We *must* find Blake Cornell."

Chapter 33

It'd taken us two days to track down Blake Cornell's whereabouts. To start with, Frances and I had each left urgent e-mail messages for Cornell telling him to contact us immediately. We weren't able to get a phone number on him from any of the mystery writers' lists Frances or I had access to. Finally we went through Maddie, who made us swear on our grandparents' graves we'd never admit she was our source in obtaining Cornell's unlisted number.

Using the number, Frances made the call from her room at the Star Motel safehouse and wound up talking to Cornell's wife for most of an hour. Women. By the time she joined me in the bar, she had a smile on her face indicating victory.

"Cornell's wife is great—a bubbly Spanish lady named Teresa—she told me he's holed up in their cabin where he does all of his writing. He goes Howard Hughes for two, three months at a stretch when he's in what Teresa calls 'Blake's Muse Zone.' Drove his family zonkers whenever he gets in his writing moods—his Muse Zone—guess that's why they got the cabin in the first place. And he generally comes back with the first draft of a bestseller."

"Cornell sounds even odder than you, Frances."

"Remind me to show you my Edgar someday, Guy…I'll even let you polish it if you're a very good boy."

"You'd trust me with a blunt object? I'm touched." I took another swig of Guinness, "So, did his wife give the phone number for Cornell's cabin?"

"I got the number, but Teresa said that he never answers the phone—actually pulls out the jack—while he's in the Muse Zone. So calls won't break his flow. She said we could leave him a message with her, but don't count on him calling back for a week or two. Dutiful but distracted husband, she said, and he only calls home randomly now and again, and then only while he takes a 'potty break' Teresa said. But even when he does phone home she can tell his mind isn't really on her. She said she'll let him know we're trying to get in touch with him on his next 'potty break' call, which could be soon since she hasn't heard from him for over a week."

"Just great, we're dealing with Mr. Incommunicado himself."

"For sure. Teresa said there could be a nuclear war and he'd work through it and then drive to his publisher and wonder why the elevator wasn't there. However…"

"Do tell."

"I got detailed directions—are you up for a road trip in the morning?"

Blake Cornell's mountain cabin turned out to be a two-story house overlooking secluded Little Gorgonio Lake in the San Bernardino Range west of Snow Summit—a good half hour drive on gravel beyond tiny Fawnskin, California. The narrow road that wound about the lake was a picture postcard setting—far too quaint for me to get anything done if I'd dwelt there—but Blake Cornell had become a very prolific writer in this wilderness. Different strokes.

I drove Frances' Lexus slowly as the gravel road curved and doubled back, climbing steadily upward to the lane of Cornell's lake cottage. At last I pulled to a stop in a circular turnabout in front of his garage. It had been a three-hour drive, including a couple wrong turns I'd made after we'd left County 18.

"I hope we don't piss him off just dropping in—committing Muse Interruptus," I worried aloud, strongly empathizing with a hatred of anyone who'd yank me out of my own, far too rare, writing moods.

"Not to worry, Guy. We left that message saying we were coming. And after all, we're here to alert him about possible mortal danger—I think messing up his Muse Zone should be the least of Cornell's concerns."

We climbed the squeaky wooden steps onto the front porch and pressed the doorbell. Waited. Pressed it again. Waited more. I put my ear against the door and rang the doorbell a third time. I could hear that it was working—a chime chip played the opening phrase of a Paul McCartney number. Frances leaned across me and began rapping politely on the oak door. We waited more, hoping for footsteps. No response. She rapped louder. Still no answer.

I pounded with a closed fist and hollered, "Cornell? Blake Cornell?"

"Maybe he went into town, Guy."

"Or took a long walk to blow out the cobwebs."

Frances grabbed hold of the doorknob and twisted. Firmly locked. "Damn."

"I'll peek in the garage, see if his car's there." I hopped down the porch steps and began loping across the driveway, calling over my shoulder, "You keep trying the doorbell. It's ten o'clock, but possibly he's sleeping or in the shower."

I grabbed the knob on the side door of the big garage. Locked tight. I tried to lift the double door. Also locked. I pressed against the tiny side window to peer in. The glare from the sun made it difficult, but I could see what looked to be a white Range Rover parked in one of the stalls. The other stall lay empty. Obviously Cornell would only bring one car, unless he also kept a junker parked up here. As my eyes adjusted I made out a hanging mountain bike, a rider lawn mower in the corner, a couple of aged rakes, a dust-covered snow blower, not a heck of a lot else. A loud car horn erupted, honked steadily. I jumped back as though pulled on a wire, and then realized it was the alarm horn from Frances' Lexus.

"What in hell are you doing?" I called from the garage. Frances was still at Cornell's front door, but her arm extended toward the Lexus. The honking ceased.

"I don't intend to wait out here for 40 minutes trying to get him to come to the door. Is there a car in the garage?"

"Yeah," I nodded, "a ritzy SUV. Hey, Frances, can you smell that?"

"Smell what?" she asked.

"I just got a strong whiff of something. From the rear of the place."

"There's probably no trash service this far out. I bet Cornell has to haul it to a landfill near town, or maybe he burns it. What's it smell like?"

"Rotten food. Could be rotting fish—the lake's just down the hill."

Frances joined me. "Whew! That is powerful."

"I think it's coming from over there." I began walking toward Cornell's back door, made it across the yard before I veered right. I raced to the wooden steps that ran down the steep bank to the lake, knelt over the edge, barely in time, and dry heaved. Loudly.

I like to think I have a highly disciplined gag reflex. I grabbed my handkerchief to cover my nose and mouth. Then wiped the streaming tears out of my eyes with my sleeve. I glanced back, saw Frances, who was approaching behind me, her chrome-plated Kahr P45 in hand. And a face that looked as though she'd bitten off half of a rotted lemon.

"Damn, you're quick with that weapon," I stammered between coughs.

"You okay, Guy?"

I straightened up. "The stench would gag a maggot. It even sears my eyes."

"I think we both know that smell's not rotting garbage or fish."

"Rotting Blake?"

"Let's move into the tree line, Guy. Fast."

"What's up?"

"I'll tell you when we're in the trees." We quick-footed it out of the open until we were in the shade of a thick stand of yellowing Aspen, out of view of anyone from the house.

"What's the deal, Frances?"

154

"I saw some movement in the upstairs' window. The windows are all open, there's a breeze and it's probably just the curtain fluttering, but it got me worried." Frances touched my arm, "Scythe might be inside, Guy. Or perhaps Blake Cornell isn't the victim here."

"Oh shit!" what she was suggesting came through loud and clear. "Out here alone in the middle of nowhere, no neighbors, no one can reach him—or turn him in—and he feeds his wife some silly crap about needing to be alone in his Muse Zone in order to write." I looked at Frances, "Cornell could be Scythe and that smell a victim." I reached into my pocket and wrapped my palm around Lady Smith.

"Only a working theory. The window…there it goes again!"

We both focused on the rear upstairs' window. What looked like a white towel hovered and floated along the side, coinciding with the breeze off the lake. After a minute I decided to take a breath.

"I think you're right about it being a curtain. But what if someone in there needs our help?"

"Whoever's in there, Guy, doesn't need our help. Needs an embalmer."

"Let's call the police."

"Yes," Frances agreed, "we should call the police immediately."

We stood still for several seconds, not opening our cellulars.

As my eyes cleared I studied the house. "Like to get in there…without upchucking this morning's burrito omelet."

"The back door doesn't look fully closed. From here I'd guess a *person* would only have to open the screen door to gain entry." Frances assumed a reflective tone of clinical objectivity as if she wasn't itching to go inside.

"At most, people hook screen doors to keep them shut," I thought aloud. "A *person* might want to open it with a small stick so as not to mess up any potential prints."

"And if both *persons* were to go inside, they'd want to be sure not to touch anything," Frances added.

"I guess both *persons'd* probably want to cover their noses with one hand while keeping their gun hand free."

"I'm not sure about that. It could prove awfully hard to maneuver if both *persons* wound up in a life-or-death struggle with Norman Bates and his mommy dearest. Now what if the brainy one kept, say, a box of Kleenex, in her car—they might be able to stuff wads up their nostrils to reduce the awful smell."

I nodded in agreement.

"And they'd certainly have to hit it hard and fast, just in case he's working on someone with his Ed Gein Crafts Kit in there."

"I know everybody needs a hobby," I observed, "but speaking for myself I'd make a very despondent armchair."

I refused to let Frances go in first. Told her she was better with a pistol than I was and could therefore provide better cover. I stuck a twig the size of a Popsicle stick inside the slot handle of the screen door and pulled hard. Unlocked and popped it open. As Frances had thought, the rear door itself was ajar. I kicked it hard and bolted straight across the Dutch-style kitchen, spun at the fridge. I leveled my gun on the kitchen hallway while Frances darted inside.

We made quick eye contact, then she covered the hallway while I used the twig to pull open the refrigerator. Gourmet foods by my standard—bread, beer, curdled milk, butter, half a dried chocolate cake—nothing bizarre.

The Kleenex sort of worked and although I did my best to gulp down small amounts of air through my mouth, I felt my eyes begin to tear up again. I did the same procedure with the stick to open the upper freezer. Pizzas, burgers, big carton of butter pecan ice cream, and the suspicious absence of the human body parts I'd half expected.

In fragmented sentences, Frances and I worked out the details on how we'd sort through Cornell's house of stink.

"Guy," Frances whispered, "hallway."

"Yeah," I nodded back.

She pointed with her pistol, and then we both cornered the hallway simultaneously. There was a wide staircase on the right. Straight ahead was a door to what was likely the dining room. Frances motioned us forward. My eyes burning, Frances and I chicken-peeked high and low around the dining room doorframe. We'd found the source of the god-awful smell.

The cadaver, male, its back on the floor at the foot of the table, was missing the upper left side of its face. An armada of flies were buzzing about the gaping crater and the dried gore puddle on the floor. There was a halo of brain tissue on the wallpaper. Blake Cornell's burly black hair and matching beard, which I'd memorized from his Web site, was recognizable through the decaying, crimson mess. A pistol lay in the dried puddle nearest his right hand.

"Long pause," Frances gasped for air. "I don't think Blake's in his Muse Zone."

"Time to call Maddie. And the local cops."

"Wait, his laptop may still be on," Frances stared at me. "See the red light on the D.C. converter?"

"Let's not."

"Look, Guy, it's on this side of the room. I can see the console light blinking—the laptop's in sleep mode, not off—and there may be something there."

"So after he got his head blown off, he left a note about his killer? C'mon, Frances, don't touch."

"Just a few taps of the mouse," she said.

"Supremely bad idea."

"Look, Guy, just ask your nose if Blake hasn't been dead for several days, so the killer's long gone. If you want to you can wait out in the car."

"Aww fuck it, in for a penny. Just don't step in anything."

We cautiously advanced toward the long table. This was obviously Cornell's writing area, nearest the kitchen and the beer. Stacks of books and notepads. A coffee mug, detective magazines, and a battered *Rogets' Thesaurus* were spread across the tabletop. The laptop sat in front of us, plugged into a wall socket. With the nose of the Lady Smith I gently touched the mouse and the screen sprang to life. Revealing Blake Cornell's final message. The cursor blinked as though in amusement at the end of three short sentences.

Fear no more the heat of the sun. Thou thy worldly task hast done. Forgive me, Teresa.

Chapter 34

"**Butchering Shakespeare does not a suicide make**," I grumbled at Maddie when she finally exited Blake Cornell's lake house, the latest dead writer site. The grim day had become a grimmer early evening and, except for a quick run to town for aspirin and soda around four, Frances and I had been hanging there all day.

"I agree," Maddie said, "this was no suicide. Forensics workup will tear that notion to shreds. It was clear two seconds into my walkthrough. Angles, blood splatter, nothing lined up." Lieutenant Maddie Neff stared at the front door to the cottage, "Clearly Scythe's no longer hiding in the shadows…feigning accidents. The bastard has gone public. Big time."

"Appears so," I replied. A pale, lip-biting Frances just nodded.

"Goddammit, I should've taken you two seriously from the get go, then maybe what's left of Blake Cornell wouldn't be fly fodder."

"But you have been taking us seriously—helping us check out Thornton Senior and Oliver Robbins."

"For the entirely wrong reasons. Daddy Thornton only because of an alky-mom's mumblings. I figured Daddy Thornton could have done in Junior over the trust fund. Classic homicide motive, a family feud over money. And then Robbins, or someone connected to Robbins, electronically threatened your life, Davitt. However half-assed, I take threats to my friends very seriously."

I tried to lighten the moment, "You're saying I'm your friend? That's progress!"

"Don't let it go to your head, Davitt, you're my if-no-one-else-is-around kind of friend."

"I'd have it no other way."

"Here's the deal," she continued, "I was on the phone to Captain Vasquez. He's decided to contact the FBI's L.A. rep. About twelve minutes after Vasquez's phone conversation the Bureau's going to storm into this case like wasps on clover."

"That's a good thing, right?" Frances asked.

"Yes on the surface, no in my world. Yes because this sort of serial killing—interstate crimes, international if you include Toronto—falls under FBI purview. And in theory they have the expertise and manpower to taskforce something like this. The Feebs'll be able to coordinate reopening the individual cases, pore over files, scour for commonalities. And this is very good because Alexandra Case, Beck Quinn, and the others were all written off as accidents by various local authorities. By looking at things with a broader view, the Bureau may find overlooked items. That's the upside."

"What's the downside?" I asked.

"The downside is a bit more personal, something I'll just have to get over." Maddie turned from squinting into the sunset and looked squarely at Frances and myself, "Captain Vasquez says that as of now we're out of it. The Bureau'll take over the investigation and we'll only get to cheer from the sidelines."

"They might need us."

"Sure, for half an hour. To suck out background data for their files. Then things will sink into the shitswamp of Bureau politics, with the usual pricks in expensive suits vying for photo-ops." Maddie's gaze settled back on Cornell's entryway and her jaw became tense. "Christ, Davitt, I'd give anything to nail this Scythe fucker."

"Look," I tried to cut the tension, "I for one will never be able to eat again, but what say we all go grab a drink somewhere? I'm buying."

"Rain check, Davitt." Maddie left us and strode toward her car. "There's one last thing I need to do."

"What one last thing?" I called after her.

"You don't want to know."

Chapter 35

By its tenth ring the bedside phone in my Star Motel room cut into my deep REM dreamscape. Before finally drifting off I'd tossed and turned most of the night haunted by images of Blake Cornell, the searing stench that clung to my olfactory nerve, the knowledge that the whole nightmarish business of Scythe and my dead colleagues had become surreally graphic, like we all were trapped alive inside the deepest, most putrefying circle of *Dante's Inferno*.

By its twentieth ring I groped for the bedside phone.

"Brrrrsnugggler," I mumbled into the mouthpiece.

"Guy," it was Frances, "turn on your TV immediately."

"Huh?"

"Turn on your TV."

"What channel?"

"Any news channel, idiot. I'm coming over." Frances hung up.

"Idiot?" I muttered resentfully, and then proved it by wasting several minutes searching vainly for the clicker only to discover it in its cradle, Velcro-ed to the top of the television set. I turned to Fox Cable News in time to see a photo of Beck Quinn before it changed to Angus MacDougall and that shifted to Jax and then to Blake Cornell. There was a loud banging at my door. Chilly, I gathered the bedspread about me and stumbled to the door, looked through the peek hole. Frances, already dressed and coiffed for the day, wore a tormented look.

"They're calling him the 'Sleuth Slayer'—the LA TIMES." Frances marched past me, dropped the morning paper on my bed and began prepping the room's Mister Coffee.

"No shit?"

"No caffeine, no sugar, no trans fats, and no shit, Guy." Frances flicked the coffee maker switch and observed with amusement, "Technically, the *Times*' headline is misleading...the victims are authors, not detectives."

I picked up the paper and began to read. Above the fold, the entire front page of the *Times* shouted in giant bold type.

SLEUTH SLAYER STRIKES AGAIN!
Publishing World Steels Itself as More Murders Hinted
At Hollywood & TV World Stunned
FBI Task Force Refuses Comment
Exclusive Warning
by Leo Castello, LOS ANGELES TIMES
       Staff Writer

The entertainment world was shocked to its core yesterday by news of the gunshot death of award-winning author Blake Cornell at his mountain hideaway. The *Times* has learned that the publishing world must steel itself for what's coming next. A source very close to the investigation has informed the *Los Angeles Times* that Cornell's death, staged like a suicide was definitely murder, his body discovered only yesterday. And Cornell's murder is but the tip of the iceberg. The source went on to explain that noted mystery writers across the United States as well as Canada appear to have fallen recent victim to a serial killer.

The *Times'* source confirmed that the FBI has begun an inquiry into the peculiar deaths of numerous authors stretching back over the past 18 months. Writers that have died over this period include, but are likely not limited to, such notables as Edgar Award Winner Angus MacDougall of Toronto whose death of alcohol poisoning was initially deemed accidental by the Royal Canadian Mounted Police (RCMP), but now foul play is suspected.

Our source revealed that questions now shroud the recent death of the popular and revered Alexandra Case, the aged author who seemingly died of accidental smoke inhalation in her San Francisco home. The *Times'* source says that the Case death is being re-opened by the FBI. Alexandra Case was widely regarded as the Grande Dame of Gay Detective fiction after nearly five decades of her beloved sleuth, Simone Pointer, cleverly solving San Francisco homicide after homicide through a total of more than three-dozen novels.

Less well-known but critically respected master of what is regarded in the industry as the "hard-boiled P.I.," writer Timothy Willi of Northern Minnesota was at first viewed as the victim of accidental hypothermia. His death was originally attributed to a flukish overexposure to the elements but is now undergoing reassessment.

And in rural Connecticut the celebrated Beck Quinn, many of whose atmospheric mystery yarns have found their way to film and TV, died at her home in rural Connecticut following what appeared at the time to be an accidental plunge from a tall ladder into her rock garden. The *Times'* source says there is new evidence that Quinn did not die in that fashion but her death may have been staged. And authorities are also looking into the death two weeks ago of novice writer Jax Thornton. Thornton's life was lost in an unexplained single car accident near his mountainside home above Santa Monica. Thornton was apparent heir to the Thornton Swimming Pool fortune amassed by his late grandfather and namesake, colorful California business tycoon Jax Thornton I.

Our source indicates that recent threats and attempted homicides have been reported by noted crime writers Frances Whiting of Florida and Guy Davitt of Los Angeles. The source cautions that it is too early to tell at this point in the investigation, but "there's a good chance that all these deaths were part of a pattern of homicide." Our source also reports that authorities suspect there may be more, both past and future victims.

To make matters more complex for authorities, each death was taken from the pages of a mystery novel. For example, Timothy Willi froze to death in a blizzard, which is a premise that appeared in a Blake Cornell story. Beck Quinn's fall from a ladder was depicted in a Jax Thornton novel. It appears a killer is using the plot devices depicted in various mystery novels to murder mystery writers in real life.

Our informed source close to the investigation repeatedly refers to the serial murderer as "The Sleuth Slayer." The source, who spoke on an agreement of anonymity, only agreed to speak to the *Times* on the specified condition that an urgent warning be published. The specified language of the source's warning:

"Mystery writers, do not underestimate the very real danger you are in. The Sleuth Slayer is a resourceful serial murderer. All authors everywhere in the U.S. and Canada must be alerted. Mystery writers are methodically being targeted, stalked, and executed by this Sleuth Slayer. I urge all of you, as potential victims, to take immediate precautions and do everything possible to ensure your personal safety."

The bedside phone jangled again. It was clear this day there'd be no rest for the weary.

"Hello."

It was Lieutenant Neff, sounding very grim. "You and Frances need to be here at 8:00 a.m. for a debriefing by the FBI."

"That's only half an hour from now."

"Actually 25 minutes. There'll be a feeb waiting at headquarters' main desk to bring you up. Don't be late." Maddie clicked off.

"What's happening?"

"Bring the car around." I trudged into the bathroom. "I'll tell you on the way."

Chapter 36

"Special Agent Lance Hartwick," we were greeted at the Sergeant's desk by an immaculately groomed man of about 35 in an immaculately pressed black suit and spit-shined black wingtips. "The Task Force is meeting in 9 South. I'm here to escort you there."

We trudged after Agent Hartwick to the elevator bank. He seemed grimly aloof, but in the elevator he looked over at me and said noncommittally, "I've read one of your Connor Alba books."

"Thank you." A few seconds of awkward silence passed before I added, "You read any of those Sally Kerentine yachting mysteries?"

"Yachting mysteries...?" Agent Hartwick's eyes became heavy lidded and he squinched his mouth, the message being he'd rather chew off his own toe.

"I'm sure you'd love them," I enthused, "the heroine battles shoplifters, rescues kitties from trees, that sort of tomfoolery."

Frances cut in, "Just ignore the misogynist, Agent Hartwick, he's still upset because I had to show him how to use Spellcheck."

The unsmiling Agent sullenly stared at his black wingtips.

Frances and I were ushered into a large conference room, four tables pushed together with about 20 chairs, half of them filled with serious looking suits, each as crisply pressed as Agent Wingtips. I didn't spot Maddie Neff, but I escorted Frances over and introduced her to LAPD's Captain Tony Vasquez, who'd isolated himself in a corner of the room. Tony Vasquez was one of those fortunate guys whose flesh defies gravity after age 17 so they get to look the same for decades on end.

Maddie had often expressed her utmost respect for Vasquez, told me nothing gets past the boyish-seeming Captain, though she did confess resisting an impulse to burp him every now and again. I'd met Captain Vasquez a year or two back when I'd stopped by to pick Lieutenant Neff's brain over a police procedural item that Connor Alba and I had butted up against. Vasquez had been nothing but graciously political, shook my hand, pretended to know about my books, asked a few questions about the publishing industry, and then joked about how he hoped I didn't portray police officers as lunkbrains in my novels.

If my radar hadn't picked up that there was something heatedly amiss by the brisk manner in which Agent Wingtips had escorted us up, I caught it immediately from Captain Vasquez. He shook Frances' hand, mumbled a terse hello, and then turned back to staring icily out the window. Frances and I stood awkwardly silent for a several seconds before deciding to grab a couple of lonesome chairs near the door.

A gentleman of about 50, short gray hair neatly trimmed, pricey dark suit, walked in and shook Vasquez's hand. "Captain Vasquez, I'm Special Agent in Charge Alan Mayer. We spoke on the phone yesterday evening. Nice to meet you in person. I'll be running the Task Force."

"Pleasure's all mine," Vasquez flatly responded with a forced smile. "Wish it were under different circumstances."

"We're going to work hard on changing those circumstances, Captain," said Special Agent Alan Mayer. "Captain, have you been introduced around the table?"

"No sir."

"Of course you know Special Agent Eunice Lehman from the Los Angeles Field Office," Mayer pointed toward a 40-something brunette several chairs away from Frances. "I believe you two touched base quite a bit yesterday."

Vasquez gave a grimly polite nod in her direction.

"Right next to Agent Lehman is Special Agent Susan Rees, the Bureau's ace in Behavioral Sciences at Quantico. Agent Rees flew in late last night and burned the midnight oil to present us with her preliminary profile. Next is Special Agent Lance Hartwick from Washington's Serial Crimes Unit."

Rees and the wingtipped Hartwick smiled and nodded at Captain Vasquez in sync. I looked at my hands just to verify I hadn't become invisible as Special Agent in Charge Alan Mayer jumped over Frances and me.

"Across the table is Special Agent Ted Moss, the Bureau's foremost forensics specialist. Ted works magic, Captain, but you'll need a translator to talk to him."

"Thanks, Alan," Agent Ted Moss saluted Vasquez with his Styrofoam coffee cup. "I think there's a compliment in there somewhere."

"Agent Moss is the lab magician who tied half a hair strand to the Kennel Land Killer last year, you may have read about it, Captain. One sick veterinarian, that puppy." Mayer finished introducing the circle, "And that crusty looking fellow over there is Assistant Special Agent in Charge Pete Gillespie. Case like this we're certainly going to run Agent Gillespie ragged. Pete'll manage all logistics and local liaison. And I'll personally run the Crit Sits."

"Crit Sits?" Vasquez asked.

"Priority one critical situations," Special Agent Mayer replied, "which is a fifty dollar term for coordinating high impact information, High Imps as we now call them. In fact, Captain, we've already got

165

field offices working the POIs—points of interest that is—we're working to reopen the prior cases as potential homicides in each of the POIs." Mayer looked at the speaker box positioned precisely in the middle of the table, "Minneapolis, it's Alan Mayer, are you there?"

"Good morning, sir. Agent Emily Houseman here. One of my team is en route to Embarrass, Minnesota to review the Timothy Willi death. Unfortunately, it was assumed an accident, so no autopsy was performed. Ordinarily we'd exhume the body but Willi was cremated and his ashes scattered."

Special Agent Alan Mayer said, "Wouldn't have been terribly difficult to force Willi at gunpoint to go for a drive, in Willi's own vehicle in the middle of a blizzard, then force him out of the car and put up the hood. But I wonder how the killer got back to Willi's house where, I assume, he'd left his own vehicle?"

"Our killer was undoubtedly bundled in winter gear and made the hike back," the voice from Minneapolis chirped through the box. "Of course even with a snowmobile suit on, that mile walk would be agony—it was 30 below with a wind chill of minus 60. I'm thinking our unknown subject parked at a spot near where he'd picked as the murder site, say a half mile from Willi's house, and walked to Willi's place. Then spun him a yarn while he warmed up, then coerced or begged a ride back to his own car. He likely pulled a gun and kicked Willi out of Willi's car wearing nothing but a sweatshirt, jeans and boots. Probably drains Willi by making him pop the hood, stand around in the minus 60 until he turns blue, then tells Willi to get moving. Probably sits in Willi's vehicle long enough to make sure the victim doesn't double back. Ten minutes in that white hell would about do it. He makes sure Willi's down for the count, then our bundled up killer hikes back to his own car. I don't even want to think about the other alternative, sir."

"Which is?"

"Two killers."

"Yes, we'd touched on that in regards to Blake Cornell being killed following Pizzaro's death." For the first time Agent Mayer looked in our direction, "Pizzaro being the perpetrator that attacked the author Frances Whiting in Florida. Susan, what's your profiler's take on the question of two killers?"

"Please understand the time constraints and the limited data access I have at this point," Agent Rees smoothly hedged her bets, "but as a general principle it's highly unlikely. We chart our unsub," Agent Rees glanced at Frances and myself, "that is our unknown subject, as a soloist. A single white male between the ages of 25 and 50. Above average intelligence, at least moderately affluent, obviously literate, arrogant, and obsessive. Remember, this is quite preliminary. I hope to have him more fleshed out by this time tomorrow."

Frances leaned into my ear and whispered, "That description fits you."

"And most of the guys in this room," I whispered a reply. Agent Rees smoothly presented the obvious as though it were something profound. "Profiling 101." A sideways look at Frances told me she had picked up on this as well.

Captain Vasquez cut to the heart of things, "The question I'd like an answer to, Agent Rees, is what are the odds of our serial killer contracting out work? You know, to a chump like Pizzaro?"

"Virtually unknown in cases of psychotic serials," Rees continued smoothly, "we'll have to dramatically rethink motivation if there's a conspiracy involved. Naturally, Pizzaro is a factor to be considered."

Special Agent Mayer shrugged, "The relationship, if any, with Pizzaro would certainly be a twisted one. But Pizzaro himself was quickly eliminated once he was of no more further value." Mayer looked at the telephone speakers on the table, "San Francisco?"

"Hello, Alan, this is Agent Mike Servantes from the San Francisco Field Office. Let me start by saying Alexandra Case didn't make that fire. At least I don't believe it. Here's an aged, increasingly arthritic woman who's in her seventies. She recently listed her house for sale with an agent precisely because of all the stairs involved. She could barely use her downstairs. Plus, she has modern natural gas fireplaces in both the upstairs living room and dining room. I hate to be blunt, but I just don't see this elderly woman hauling firewood downstairs and then playing with matches."

"Seems odd, indeed," said Special Agent Mayer.

San Francisco continued, "Two main possibilities at this point. Our unsub could use nylons to tie Case to a chair, get the smoke going, go upstairs then run back down later, remove the nylons, shove her unconscious body to the floor, toss things around a bit to set up a scenario about Case's feeble struggle against the fire. Second, and my favorite, our guy would probably wear a gas mask, you know, like a fireman's. Hell, he could even wear one of those and hold her in a full Nelson next to the fumes—three minutes and she'd be unconscious. Five or six, she'd be dead."

Special Agent Alan Mayer interjected, "I tend to agree with you, Mike, because your scenario fits into the pattern. In fact, it's used in one of the referenced novels that LAPD turned over to us—see page three of the findings report. You each have a copy of the report in front of you."

"Say, Alan," San Francisco continued, "are the two literary types there? Our pair of leakers?"

"What in hell?" Frances mumbled in my ear. I looked at her tense white face, not quite sure what she'd picked up on.

"They're both sitting right across the table from me, Mike," Agent Wingtips said with great disdain, staring daggers directly at me.

San Francisco's voice came from the speaker, "Alan, I do not understand why you're allowing the two leakers to be in present at this meeting."

I was jarred. My mind raced. Leakers? Frances and me? What the hell were they talking about?

"I'm miffed too, Lance, but we need to draw together all we can glean from them," Special Agent Mayer explained. "So like it or not, they're our principal fount of information at this juncture."

"But Alan, everything they hear will wind up in this evening's paper," Agent Wingtips protested.

"Lance is absolutely right, Alan, they've already compromised our investigation," Minneapolis piped in from the speakerphone.

"Leakers?" I asked aloud, my indignation over the false accusation temporarily had me tongue-tied.

"I certainly have not talked to anyone in the press," Frances objected.

All eyes in the room suddenly turned to me.

"You people are nuts!" I barked at the table. "I didn't leak a damn thing to anyone."

"Right," Agent Wingtips frisbee'd a copy of the *Los Angeles Times* across the table at me, "eight minutes into the investigation and the *Times* already says there's a serial killer and mentions our code name 'Sleuth Slayer.'"

"For one thing, Agent, that name doesn't make sense technically, because all the victims are authors, not detectives," I repeated Frances' earlier observation.

"Oh for the love of God, Alan," came the voice from San Francisco, "you may as well have invited CNN to this meeting." A plum-faced Special Agent in Charge Alan Mayer glared at Agent Wingtips who spread his hands in front of him.

Wingtips said, "We've got a killer out there who's making Ted Bundy look like Mister Rogers and these two enema-mouths are giving everything away to the Dead Tree Society."

"That's complete bullshit, Pal!" rising, I hurled his newspaper back at Wingtips with force.

"Hold it!" Lieutenant Maddie Neff was standing in the doorway. "These two enema-mouths didn't give a goddamned thing to the media. I did."

There followed a stunned silence.

"You're the leaker?" Special Agent in Charge Alan Mayer's mouth had dropped so far open you could shove in a tennis ball.

"Maddie," Captain Vasquez arose and strode over to her, "You leaked everything to the *Times*?"

"Correct."

"You reckless bitch!" yells a fuming Agent Wingtips.

"You have no idea," Maddie snapped back.

"What the hell for?!" Agent Wingtips asked. Amazingly, he and I were wondering the same thing.

"Jesus!" proclaimed Agents Lehman and Moss in unison.

"Let her talk," Tony Vasquez continued staring at Maddie as he walked to the door and closed it behind her. Special Agent Mayer began to say something, but Vasquez stuck his open palm out toward the table to hush the cadre of FBI agents. "Why did you do it, Maddie?"

"Someone had to start thinking about the potential victim pool— there's scores of authors out there," Maddie said directly to Agent Mayer.

"But going to the *Times* violates orders."

"I was never instructed *not* to talk to the press."

"Because that's a fucking given, you stupid bitch!" Wingtips leapt to his feet, tipping over his chair.

"Sit down and keep your mouth shut, asshole, or you and I'll take it to the parking lot!" Captain Vasquez shot a murderous look at Wingtips.

"Anytime, Babyface!"

"Shut up!" Special Agent in Charge Mayer suddenly remembered that he was supposed to be Ringmaster of this circus, "Everybody, just shut up!"

The room fell silent. I felt taut, like piano wire. The hair on the back of my neck crawled. Mayer's face had turned cherry-apple red. All eyes focused on Maddie Neff.

Special Agent Mayer shot, "Now, Lieutenant Neff, if it wouldn't be too much trouble, could you possibly explain to me why I shouldn't have you tossed in a federal cell?"

"Aside from the Bill of Rights you mean?" Maddie shot back.

"Don't smartmouth me, Lieutenant. This time tomorrow I'll have the legal groundwork set to boil you in oil." I could feel the heat rising off the flushed Alan Mayer whose pounding neck veins had become thick as bell ropes. I seriously hoped LAPD had a defibrillator somewhere nearby. "Answer up or get the hell out of my sight."

"What was your thinking, Maddie?" Captain Vasquez asked quietly. "Please explain."

"It was the smartest thing to do, sir." Maddie motioned toward Frances, "Ms. Whiting here was almost killed two weeks back. Mr. Davitt's life has been threatened. Five others killed in prior weeks. Blake Cornell was shot and killed a few days ago. The perp's accelerating the body count while we're doing these dog and pony shows. Someone needed to warn the writers so each could take necessary precautions."

"You never gave us an opportunity to discuss these concerns in private." Special Agent Mayer turned to Captain Vasquez, "You can believe I plan to follow up on this."

"Her badge stays with us," Wingtips called out.

"I sure would hate to hold a press conference, Agent Mayer," Maddie said very calmly, "to inform the public how Special Agent in Charge Alan Mayer had personally decided the FBI was proceeding to use America's mystery writers as bait. I can't imagine the Bureau will be delighted by their portrayal in books, films and TV for the next generation or two. Once the heat builds I expect the White House would send your smug ass to Anchorage—assuming the Bureau has an igloo there!"

The odor of blackmail hung in the air.

In a shaky but determined voice, Frances added her two cents, "I heard reports on the radio that Mary Higgins Clark and her daughter are leaving for France. Others are putting on special security or going into hiding. As one grateful citizen, I've been very pleased Lieutenant Neff and the LAPD has acted maturely, has kept me safe and in the loop since the first possibility arose of serial homicides."

I spoke up and was pleased how calm and resonant I sounded as I poured it on, "LAPD and Lieutenant Neff have played this thing exactly right. In the interest of protecting human life LAPD has warned my colleagues all across the country. Thank God this concern for humanity trumped the Fibbies' bureaucratic procedures. If need be, the moment I leave here I'll say that and plenty more to my friends at the *New York* and *LA Times*, plus my contacts at CNN and Fox."

During the ensuing silence, I noticed a white-knuckled Frances gripping the hand rests on her armchair.

"Lieutenant Neff, you compromised an investigation," Captain Vasquez quietly resumed, staring intently at Maddie. "The killer now knows we're onto him."

"Look, Tony, the killer is one very brainy SOB. If Blake Cornell's death were anymore staged, it'd be opening Off Broadway. It was never going to cut it as a suicide, not in a million years, and we both know why. Our guy purposely saw to that and he obviously knows we're aware of him. He's light-years from being retarded so he also knows the Feds would be called in. Hell, the bastard wouldn't have it any other way. He was never going to stay in the shadows into perpetuity. Scythe wants to come out and dance in the spotlight."

"You broke protocol," Mayer muttered mainly to himself as he slumped far back in his chair, the redness beginning to seep from his face.

"I repeat, nobody told me not to," Maddie insisted.

"Save it for the attorneys, Lieutenant, you knew the protocol," Captain Vasquez summed up.

"I can't let you use people as killer-bait, Tony." Maddie's face wrenched in regret at having burned a bridge, a bridge she cared deeply about. "Honestly, Captain, we're talking about more than a hundred people scattered from coast to coast. We simply mustn't use them as bait."

The two LAPD cops stared unbudgingly at each other.

"My hand is forced, Maddie." Suddenly the baby-faced Vasquez looked a lifetime older as he sadly declared, "I have no choice but to suspend you."

"I know, Tony. I put my badge and gun on your desk before I came in here." Maddie Neff left the room, closing the door behind her as she departed.

During the stillness that followed I realized I no longer wanted to be in the conference room with these people. Not anymore. I jumped up and went out the door myself. I caught up to Maddie by the vending machines near the elevator.

"It took my dollar," she banged on the side of a vending machine, "but it won't give me a Snickers. Crissakes, I need some chocolate."

I jammed the Coin Return button and four quarters fell out. I pressed them back into the machine and punched the Snickers button. The bar plunked to the tray.

"Sorry, Guy," Maddie grabbed her candy bar, "I guess my calling the *Times* really screwed the pooch. Royally."

"I don't think so, Maddie. I think it was the right thing."

"I appreciate what you said in there. I never meant for them to drag you into the shit."

"Not to worry. Besides," I Jerry Maguired, "you had me at 'enema-mouth.'"

171

"Hello there, Goldenboy." Sandra Kearns' voice burbled happily from my cell phone sounding like a kid with cotton candy on her first Ferris wheel ride.

"Goldenboy?" I asked.

"You've got the Midas touch, Guy Davitt. I've been on the phone all morning...just wait'll you hear Barnstorm's latest offer."

"I'm confused. Barnstorm fired me. Come to think of it, so did you Sandra."

"A silly misunderstanding, Guy, let's put all that ugliness behind us. Barnstorm's moved on. So have I."

"What are you talking about...?"

Bubbling with excitement she rushed on, "Guy, you rascal, you should've told us you were tracking the biggest serial killer since John Wayne Gacy. Barnstorm and I figured you were jerking our chain."

In a flash everything became clear. Opportunity was kicking down my front door. I relaxed and adopted an intimately confiding tone, "As you can imagine, Sandra, this thing's been totally hush-hush. Very intricate, very involved. The case didn't break until we found Blake Cornell at his cabin."

"Hush-hush works for us, Guy. Get this for a marketing grabber—'a first hand look at evil from the popular mystery writer who helped nail the Sleuth Slayer, Timothy 'Guy' Davitt.' Has that certain *ka-ching* ring to it, huh?"

I played coy. "I don't know, Sandra, these events have kind of shaken me."

"Look, Guy, I know it's been a rough year for you, so here's my line of thought. Just talk it all into a cassette tape. Everything from square one. Get all the details down while they're still fresh in your mind. Easy as pie. Then give us the tapes and we'll have a typist take care of the rest."

"But there's no ending yet, Sandra. It's only Act Two. The son of a bitch is still out there."

"Doesn't matter, Goldenboy. But stay involved in the investigation, at least as much as you're allowed."

"What about *Return of the B-T-M Killer*?"

"The *B-T*-what...?"

"My Connor Alba novel. Barnstorm wants the advance back or their lawyers will piss in my Starbucks."

"All is forgiven, Guy, and forgotten. Don't give it a second thought."

"But when's my next Connor Alba due?"

"Next year…the year after…whenever. Just don't lose focus on this golden opportunity."

At that we clicked off. A great sense of relief washed over me, as though a colossal weight had evaporated off my shoulders. Perhaps I wouldn't end up scrubbing out urinals at UCLA.

After all, I was Goldenboy.

Chapter 37

"You dug through the guy's trash?!" I cried out.

"F'crissakes, Davitt," Maddie Neff hushed hoarsely, glancing nervously toward a suppertime crowd at Burbank's packed Macaroni Grill, "this is a family restaurant, keep it down—people are eating."

"You actually dug through Oliver Robbins' trash?" Frances reiterated.

"What is it with you two? Perhaps you can use the PA system and share things with the drunks in the bar."

"Is digging through someone's garbage even legal?" I whispered.

"Once it hits curbside it's fair game," Maddie defended. "How do you suppose *National Enquirer* gets half its stories?"

I leaned forward, "You rifled through Robbins' bags of trash at the end of his driveway? In Bellaire?"

"Dear God, Davitt, were your mommy and daddy blood kin?" Maddie realized she'd said that louder than intended and took it down several decibels. "I borrowed my brother's beater Ford pickup, pulled up at curbside, tossed the bags in the back, and zipped off. It took all of four seconds."

"Did you find anything really juicy?" wide-eyed, Frances asked in a conspiratorial tone.

"Apart from fatty's used Pampers," I softly added.

"First off, whatever AA group Robbins attends ain't cuttin' the mustard. His trash overflowed with empty gin bottles. He must like his martinis pounded, not stirred."

"Maybe he had company…or tossed a party."

"Nope to both."

"How could you know that?" I asked.

Maddie Neff stared at me across the table and gave me a guilty-but-so-what shrug.

"You're running a stakeout on his place? Jesus, Maddie, aren't you already in enough trouble with LAPD?"

"Not a real stakeout and drive bys ain't a crime, Davitt. Being suspended, I suddenly found myself with lottsa free time."

"So what's Robbins up to lately?" Frances probed.

"Gotta say he's one hardworking SOB. He puts in 16-hour days at his office. But every night he hermits up with his martini shaker."

"After 16 hours fucking people over, who wouldn't?" I closed my eyes for a second, "Robbins is definitely an asshole, but I must admit…"

"I believe you pegged him as, a quote, 'one totally creepy asshole' after your last meeting with him," Maddie corrected.

"He certainly has an abundance of creep about him," Frances answered for me.

"Is the FBI doing anything about the computer threat to me from Robbins offices? The Scythe message?"

"I talked to Captain Vasquez yesterday," Maddie waived off the Macaroni Grill's opera singer who was yodeling his way distractingly close to our table. "Special Agent in Charge Mayer sent a star-struck sycophant over to talk to Robbins's head of security. Captain said star boy came back with one of those eight by tens of Sharon Stone bearing a stamped autograph. Anyway, the chat room threat was pretty flimsy to begin with. Far as LAPD's concerned, WatChat's regarded no more'n a jerk off room for unemployed mystery writers."

"I told you so," Frances beamed at me in triumph.

"I've read some WatChat transcripts and quite frankly, Davitt, the P.C. Police oughtta arrest your ass for a lot of the comments you yourself made in there."

Frances continued staring at me with arch superiority. I looked down in defeat at my undercooked mushroom ravioli.

"Find anything else in Robbins' garbage bags?" Frances asked, after the waitress had refilled our ice teas.

"Well, some damned things must be eating up his flowerbeds. There were several empty boxes of Insecta-Gon smushed in with the gin bottles, rotting veggies, and coffee grounds. Yup, I'm having a barrel of fun during my suspension."

Frances commented, "You'd expect he'd hire a landscape company to care for his flowers."

"He does," Maddie affirmed. "I 'spose they toss their empty containers in his trash, saves the landscapers from hauling them away."

"Find anything else?" Frances persisted.

"The oddest thing, Frances. He had shredded road maps. Lots of them."

"Shredded maps?"

"Yup. Damp, too. Like maybe he tried flushing them, but they clogged up his crapper."

"Maddie, Shhh," I brought my finger to my lips. She'd unconsciously raised the decibels and I noticed a stare or two coming our way.

Neff glanced around, nodding awkward smiles at surrounding tables, "Sorry."

"That's pretty neurotic...I mean, who on earth shreds their road maps and flushes them?" Frances asked.

175

"Oliver Robbins it appears," Maddie replied.

"Did you piece any of the maps together?"

"Yeah right, Davitt—I've got an extra 4,000 hours to play fucking jig-saw puzzle with a million tiny strips of wet pulp."

I beckoned for the check.

"Sweet dreams, Frances." I turned to head back to my room at the Star Motel.

"Wait a second, Guy."

I turned back.

"Any interest in stopping in for a minute?"

"Your room?"

Frances nodded her head. Rather bashfully.

"For a minute?"

"Long pause," she whispered, then added, "maybe longer."

"You do have bigger knockers," I murmured under my breath.

"Say what?"

"I said I'd love to, Frances, love to."

Chapter 38

The next couple days passed quietly. Uneventfully.

At her insistence, Frances met with Special Agent in Charge Alan Mayer and his FBI teams on two more occasions. She pressed the Pizzaro angle, which SAC Mayer promised to look into, but nothing new had developed. I was called in for a brief meeting with Mayer—you could just feel the love—and Mayer swiftly palmed me off on Agent Rees, the psychological profiler, with whom I walked through all of the events that had occurred since Jax had banged on my door late that dark night. Which now seemed ages ago.

I kept mum about my Lady Smithing without a permit as well as how Frances and I had illegally gone about obtaining some lawyer files in Miami. Frances and I were in agreement that such items were on a need-to-know basis, to wit, no one needs to know. In my mind's eye I could visualize both Agents Mayer and Wingtips salivating like the creatures in those *Alien* flicks should news of any of my transgressions, however minor, reach their ears.

Remote pickup showed both of our home phone answering services were stuffed full of inquiries and requests for interviews from a seemingly endless array of media outlets. Call it a minor difference in style, but I deleted mine *en masse*, took me about one minute, while Frances took the time to ferret through each message individually. We followed similar approaches in sorting through the avalanche of e-mail clogging up our Web sites.

Frances desperately needed to get back to work. She had meetings with her publisher in New York the next week. She needed to set up a safe place in Florida to live until they captured the Sleuth Slayer. And she'd grown tired of Star Moteling it in L.A. As for hoteling, it'd grown infinitely more pleasant, not to mention the economic factors, now that Frances and I had begun sharing a suite.

I finally agreed to go with her to The Agathas. I pretended I only wanted to go in order to spend more time with Frances, but she easily saw through that pretense. We both knew what would be on the tip of everyone's tongue at the event. The Convention would be a nonstop Sleuth Slayer gabfest, 24x7, and here we were, Frances and myself, smack in the middle of the action. Hell, we'd both be seen as the subject matter experts. Something told me I needn't worry about buying any of my own drinks over the long weekend.

Frances needed to be in Scottsdale a day early for the presenters and speakers to meet and sort out whatever it is that presenters and speakers need to sort out. I talked her into leaving even sooner so we could get in some golf, but mostly I wanted to get the hell out of L.A.

A couple nights before leaving The Judge had us over for dinner. A barbeque. A meat and potatoes man, The Judge grilled us some brats and chicken to go with beans, coleslaw, chips and beer. Frances and The Judge hit it off famously. Within half an hour they were both taking great delight at my expense. The Judge shared with her every embarrassing thing I'd ever said or done since birth. Frances snickered noisily and requested repeats of the particularly humiliating episodes. During a trip to the bathroom I wondered how much effort it would take to pop the screen and make my escape.

"Your father is an absolute sweetheart," Frances said on the ride back to the Star Motel. "So very charming."

"That's what they say." I concentrated on driving the car. I could feel her eyes hovering on my profile and knew there was more to come.

"You must have had such a wonderful childhood...Timothy."

I wondered silently if I was too old to be put up for adoption.

Chapter 39

"What the hell's in Scottsdale?" Maddie Neff shouted at me, our cell connection being very bad.

"The Agathas are this weekend."

"What in hell's an Agatha?" Maddie responded.

"Mystery awards. Named for Agatha Christie. Best novel, best short story, best newcomer, that kind of stuff. Frances is presenting, so she needs to be there a day early. I talked her into two days early so we could golf."

"So 'we could golf,'" Maddie chuckled, "Cupid aimed bad, hit you in the ass, Davitt?"

"Funny you should ask. Frances and I, well, our friendship has...how shall I put it...evolved."

"Evolved? Be sure Frances tosses the bouquet in my direction," Maddie grunted. "So did you win one of those bowling trophies, or whatever it is they give away?"

"Frances won an *Agatha* last year, that's why she's presenting this year. She's in Mesdammes trying on a dress. I'm at the food court trying on a Cinnabon. Where are you calling from, Maddie?"

"I'm just pulling up outside Oliver Robbins' Bellaire house."

"Say again, not sure I caught that." Half a battery bar remained on my cell and I blamed that for what I thought she'd said. "You didn't say you're outside Robbins' house?"

"Yup. I think it's time that Mr. Robbins and I have a little heart to heart."

"That's nuts, Maddie, you're in enough hot water already."

"Let me tell you what's nuts, Davitt. I've followed Robbins to three garden stores today, and two yesterday."

"So, he's a secret gardener—that's not a crime. The fat prick's so full of himself, he probably saves on fertilizer."

"I followed him around in one store. And used binocs to watch him pack his Mercedes at another. Robbins is loading up on more Insecta-Gon. Pounds and pounds of the stuff. Now that's nuts."

"I thought he had gardeners?"

"He has a team of gardeners. They come Monday afternoons and Thursday mornings. Rain or shine."

"Robbins could have an infestation of some kind. This is California, Maddie, all sorts of creepy-crawlies."

"So he buys enough Insecta-Gon to de-louse the Amazon rainforest? I don't think so. Ever read one of the labels, Davitt? The stuff's chock full of lethals."

"Jesus." I tried to collect my thoughts. How many mystery stories utilized some type of poison as a plot device? A hundred? A thousand? "Maddie, you need some back up."

"Ergo, I'm calling you, Davitt. You don't hear from me in 30 minutes, get in touch with Captain Vasquez. Tell him everything I told you."

"Look, Frances has Robbins' home address from our investigation. We can be there in under an hour to back you up."

"Can't wait, Davitt. I want to confront the son of a bitch while he's unloading the boxes of insecticide. And see how high he jumps?"

"But you're suspended, you got no badge, Maddie, you can't do this."

"Get a clue, Davitt. I ain't fired, not yet. I can introduce myself as Lieutenant Neff. I'm just there to pick his brain on the Sleuth Slayer case, a friendly chit-chat is all. Just to see if he has any insights I can glean. Start off innocently—'Hey Mr. Robbins, why don't you let me help you put some of that stuff away? Wow, what a lot of pesticide ya got here.'"

"Don't do this, Maddie."

"Lighten up, Davitt. I'll call you back in a half hour and let you know how things went."

"Maddie! Wait!" But she was no longer on the line.

I tore Frances out of Mesdammes, leaving an unhappy sales clerk in our wake. By the time we were in the Lexus, racing toward Bellaire, Frances grew as pale as I felt. I ran two red lights, broke speed limits by double digits, and passed some pokie drivers on the shoulder. The Lady Smith felt a dead weight in my breast pocket.

"Use your cell, Frances, mine's shot." I flipped my phone onto the backseat to focus on driving.

"It's been a half hour, since her call?"

"Longer, but Maddie could be calling me. I don't want to go 9-1-1 and screw her with Captain Vasquez just cause my phone is dead. Ring her cell."

Frances pressed redial. I continued driving, tensely, much like a 10-year old boy in the death throes of a video game. Great speed. Increasingly reckless.

"No answer."

"Keep trying. Goddammit! I gotta get to the right lane to exit." I gunned the engine to pass a Mazda3 and swerved in. I'd cut it paper thin and heard the horn and saw the driver's flying finger salute in my rearview. The Lexus flew down the off ramp like the famed bat from hell.

"I'm calling Captain Vasquez," Frances was determined.

"Yeah, okay." My heart was pounding, "Do it—go go go!"

Out of the corner of my eye I saw Frances frantically raking through her purse, in search of Tony Vasquez's card. "Found it," she punched in his number. After some moments of bureaucracy, Frances's call was rolled over to his cell phone.

"Captain Vasquez, this is Frances Whiting. Lieutenant Neff wanted us to call you to…"

She listened for several seconds. I heard a distant siren, checked the rearview in case my remaining luck had just run out, and then realized the noise was from Frances' cell.

"That's right, we're heading there now."

More listening.

"Dear God." Frances' lip quivered.

"What's going on?" I slowed slightly for an upcoming turn.

"We'll meet you there." Frances flipped her phone shut.

"What in hell's going on, Frances?" I repeated, fearing the answer.

"Vasquez's already on his way to Robbins' house. Someone phoned a 9-1-1 from there, Guy." Frances choked up, "There's an officer down."

I jerked the wheel sideways, narrowly avoiding a head-on with the ambulance screeching out of Robbins' long drive. Three police cars sat on the scene, lights flashing, and a squad of unmarks at the curb. I jammed the Lexus's brakes, stopped with the right front tire several feet onto the lawn, threw her into park, and popped out. Frances and I sprinted up the driveway only to be stopped by a pair of uniforms.

I barked the name "Captain Tony Vasquez" into their faces a half dozen times before one left to go into Robbins' house. Minutes later Vasquez and two uniforms came out and hiked across the lawn toward us. The years were now seriously catching up with the captain's baby face.

He took us over to the side and told us what little he knew. Maddie Neff had been knocked about, stabbed, and slashed, but she was going to make it. That was her in the ambulance being rushed to the hospital.

On the other hand, Oliver Robbins was D.O.A.

Chapter 40

"**Good Christ, Maddie.**" I crossed the hospital room and stood beside her. Lieutenant Neff lay on her stomach on the hospital bed watching the national weather report on a muted CNN. Her left hand was heavily wrapped in bandages. Through a rear gap in her hospital gown I could see her hand wasn't all that was heavily bandaged.

"Dammit Davitt," Maddie twisted her face upward to see me, revealing yellow-orange bruising all across the left side of her face, "the crazy son of a bitch stabbed me in the ass."

"I'm so sorry, Maddie," I whispered in sympathy. "How's your hand?"

"Full of stitches and pounding like a bongo drum. Some tendon damage. The Doc says I'll never play the cello again, but what the hell, my cello playing sucked anyway. Good news is my pistol hand was untouched." Maddie shot me that stoic but world-weary snaggly grin of hers and my anxiety over her battered condition dissolved.

"Captain Vasquez told us you were cut up, but not how badly. I had visions of you hemorrhaging out and I broke every speed limit getting here only to sit in the hall for five hours."

"Relax, Davitt. If I'd been a little quicker, I would've dodged the knife."

"Jesus, Maddie, Robbins damn near killed you. You should've waited for us."

"If I hadn't been suspended, I could have nailed his ass on the up and up. As it is howeverrr...." She shrugged her brow and eyelids at me.

"What in hell happened? I hear from a couple uniforms in the waiting room the place is full of souvenirs."

"Yeah, the whackjob had a treasure trove that'd make Son of Sam envious. Robbins'd pinned Sleuth Slayer news clippings thick as wallpaper alongside his hot tub. And had mementos he'd taken from the different murders cubby-holed around his house."

"No shit?"

"Trophy taking's textbook classic by such kind." Maddie's eyes grew wide, "Hey, will you apologize to Frances again for me?"

"What for?"

"They found a .357—serial number filed off—stuffed under a mattress in one of the guest rooms."

"The gun used when he did Pizzaro?" I asked.

"Probably. They'll run tests to be sure, but my thinking is that Robbins walked the pony—that is, Pizzaro—who was his hired helper in several of the killings. But after Pizzaro screwed up in Florida, and Frances disfigured him, he became a liability. Had to be dealt with."

"I always felt Scythe needed assistance with some of the killings, no matter what that profiler said. Too much was involved for a one man job."

"Robbins was a classic *meshugana*. He kept MacDougall's pocket watch in his nightstand drawer. Alexandra Case's hairclips were in a little packet of tissue paper under his bed. Earrings they believe to be Beck Quinn's were under the handkerchiefs in his bedroom bureau. Even as we speak, the CSI folks are finding more trophies stashed around Robbins' place. Vasquez is phoning me every fifteen minutes with an update. Get this, Davitt, Einerssen, you remember our PC guru, says the nutball's hard drive was stuffed with digital images—'a cornucopia of virtual porn' is what he called it—LAPD might ream my ass, likely fire me, but fuck it, nailing Robbins was my grand slam."

"Just feel lucky to be alive, Maddie."

"Don't I know, pal," she nodded. Her subdued tone finally acknowledging the seriousness of what had gone down. In a hush she said, "The bastard was going for my throat with a butcher knife, Davitt, but by then I was stumbling backwards and got my hand up in time."

"What exactly happened there?" I asked.

"After our phone call, I parked down the street from his place. Walked straight into his garage where he was stacking the Insecta-Gon. He was leaned over the trunk of his Mercedes, and when I introduced myself Robbins looked like I'd zapped him in the armpit with a cattle prod.   So he slams down the lid, Davitt…could he be any more obvious?…but he recovers fast, pushes a couple of bags of Insecta-Gon against the wall with his foot. Then peels off his gloves and shakes my hand. All very civilized."

"He'd been wearing gloves?"

"MmHmm."

"So then what?"

"He invites me into his kitchen through the garage walkway, into a mudroom larger than my house. At first, he seems fine. Blustery and arrogantly prick-like, as you had told me he was, but not behaving like some rubber-room loony. I'm even starting to think I may've misread him. As we're talking I walk around the kitchen and notice he's got some more garden bags of Insecta-Gon on the countertop. I ask him a few questions and he goes off about you and Frances."

"Me and Frances?"

"He tells me how the basis of your movie proposal is suddenly on the front pages of every newspaper. Said he told the FBI about all this, but they said that even though you two were involved in the investigation, you weren't actual suspects. And I tell you, at that point he starts ranting."

"Ranting?"

"Oliver Robbins obviously hated your guts, Davitt, down in his bone marrow he truly despised you. Figured I'd give it a little push and told him that you were telling anyone who'd listen that he was the killer. That you begged LAPD to focus on him like a laser. I laughed and told him ain't-that-Davitt-daft, I was all full of apologetic smiles and dismissive tones. But Robbins continues raving about you. Suddenly he realizes that he's setting off my shit detector and tries to reel it all back in. Sweating like a 300-pound Arkansas hog now, he asks me if I'd like some wine or perhaps something to eat. No thanks. So then he asks if I'd mind if he makes his dinner? Of course not, Mr. Robbins, go right ahead. He starts getting out some utensils and opens the fridge. I meander over to the Insecta-Gon, and see he's watching me. I glance into the living room and notice a couple more garden store bags, all the time I pretend not to notice that he's watching me like a cat. So I pick up a box of Insecta-Gon. Very purposefully I'm reading the label, and then I ask him point blank just what the hell he's doing with all these boxes of poison. Robbins goes bi-polar on me. Right then in the kitchen, he makes all these Dahmer noises."

"Dahmer noises?"

"Remember those reports back when Jeffrey Dahmer was arrested? He makes this bloodcurdling moan when he realizes the police have found the body parts and that his goose is completely and forever cooked. Anyway, I hear this moan coming outta Robbins, real guttural low, like from down in his nuts. The fucker's three bus stops past legal sanity…he slams shut the refrigerator and he's staring at me, all bug-eyed like that Edvard Munch painting. Immense beads of oily sweat running down his face, he yanks the butcher knife from the countertop and lunges at me. At this point I unfreeze, stumble backwards, knocking over a chair as I go, and get my hand out in front of me. I stopped the blade with it or he'd have sliced me in the jugular."

"Good Lord."

"I know. I turn and bolt off running out of his kitchen. And I begin matching his moan with my own shouts and screams. The guy was fat but fast, Davitt. What a fucking pair we made, the whole bit must've looked like something out of Laurel and Hardy Meet Freddy Krueger. I'm struggling to get my gun out of my shoulder holster while trying to stay several steps ahead of this agile hippo brandishing a knife. Fortunately, his living room circles around toward the front hall. I jump up the main staircase. That's when he shoves the butcher knife into my rump roast.

"I swivel, go down hard, hit my head and hip on the marble stairs," Maddie points toward the bruising on her face. "But my pistol's finally out of the holster and I tap him. Four rounds in the chest, close range. He drops the knife, stops shouting like a screech owl, and stares up at me. With this look of confused inquiry...sort of like asking what the hell's gone wrong?...finally goes to his knees, stares at me open-mouthed drooling until his eyes roll up. Finally he slumps over. Bye-bye Hollywood's homicidal nutcake."

"A life-or-death struggle in the monster's home lair—Jodie Foster eat your heart out!—I love your guts, Maddie, but still, you should've waited for us."

"You knew where I was, so even if he'd done me, LAPD'd have gotten him in half an hour."

"That wouldn't be much consolation to you and your friends."

"Do me a favor and just shut the hell up with that stuff, Davitt. It's not like I haven't gone over it in my mind a thousand times already."

"I wonder what warped shit made Robbins do all this?"

"Way beyond my pay grade, Davitt," Maddie responded, "I don't believe in shrinks, but I imagine they'll mumble jumble about how he had some deep-seated jealousy complex over the artists he had to work with day in day out. My guess Robbins absolutely detested truly creative talent, hated you people's guts, at least on a subconscious level, probably more. Most saw the arrogant asshole on the surface, but that covered up a raging monster lurking beneath. Vasquez told me they found, as it turns out, Robbins was on a pharmacy full of prescriptive anti-depressants. Sounds like he was popping psych meds by the fistful."

"Obviously not a high enough dose," I observed. "By reputation he was in constant lawsuits, probably from screwing people over. He tried doing that with Frances and me."

"Maybe writers were the tipping point," Maddie said back. "He really fixated on you writers, likely laid awake at night concocting scheme after twisted scheme until he came up with this whopper. And you've got to admit, Davitt, it makes a certain amount of sense, using the writers' own artwork against them. Robbins's ultimate *Fuck-You-and-Your-Thesaurus-Too*, if you get what I mean."

"But why fixate on mystery writers?" I asked. "We're all certified saints. Why not actors? Hell, if he'd been bumping off actors, I'd have helped the son of a bitch."

"Stop making me laugh—it hurts my ass." Eventually Maddie's giggling subsided, "I imagine he had some warped hierarchy of skillsets. Robbins hated writers maybe...because maybe to him actors were only underwear models that talk. But his intense jealousy of truly creative people set him off."

"Interesting theory. But how would Robbins suck Pizzaro into his madness? Only money?"

"It wouldn't be terribly hard to walk that pony…maybe Robbins had the fartskull believing he'd make him the next Brad Pitt."

"Or Karloff. Christ on a crutch, Maddie, you just nailed Jack the Fucking Ripper. What a story," I grinned. "You write the book, Maddie—or I will."

"I told you laughing hurts my ass, Davitt. Look, can you make yourself useful for a change? Since I'm gonna be dry-docked here for a few days, score me a crossword puzzle book and this week's PEOPLE from the gift shop. And Davitt Honey," Maddie gazed up at me, "don't even dream of buying me one of your mysteries."

I stopped at the door and looked back. "How was Robbins going to use all that Insecta-Gon?"

"Captain Vasquez said the lab boys told him something about a cook and mix. Apparently, there's some kind of formula out there that can turn it into an almost tasteless paste, which can then be mixed into food or drink. He certainly had enough to do in a couple hundred."

"Jesus."

I was almost through the door when she called, "Hey, Davitt, what was that silly ass happy dance you and Frances were going to?"

"Happy dance?"

"Y'know, Davitt, that awards show in Arizona?"

I stiffened as though slapped in the face and stared back at Maddie. "The Agathas."

186

Chapter 41

Six Months Later
Brentano's Bookstore, San Francisco

"Who truly understands the workings of Oliver Robbins' warped and lethal mind? Surely not the thousand so-called psychiatric experts whose arrogant public natterings have blared from the media since the very afternoon I faced him in his lair and brought him down..."

Former LAPD Homicide officer, Lieutenant Madeleine Forbes Neff, recently retired due to her injuries, had hit this audience like a cruise missile. I watched her totally wow the upscale San Franciscans, jam-packed into the new Brentano's on Market Street, the first book-signing stop in her 20-city promotional appearance for her just-released true crime account titled *Sleuth Slayer*.

"That yammering army of forensic mind-mappers will speculate on-and-on about Oliver Robbins' dysfunctional childhood. Or his inherited megalomania. His jealousies, sexual inadequacies. His fantasies. His dreamlife. Cutting through the voodoo, here's what we law enforcers truly know for sure: Robbins' scheme was a ghoul's nightmare, a scheme for creating death and terror on a massive scale. While I was recovering in the hospital from his knife wounds, the FBI found boxes of the deadly pesticide Insecta-Gon hidden in the crawl space in his home as well as..."

Maddie was already midway through her spiel and I'd missed the first part. I listened in fascination to her windup from my belated niche at the rear of the room. Belated thanks to The Judge, typically marching to his own beat and other drummers be damned. He was supposed to have called me half an hour earlier, so I wouldn't miss much of Maddie Neff's reading. Once I finally got him off the line, I flipped my cell phone to vibrate. Then wedged my way into a position in the rear, in the shadow of a tall shelf at the crowded Brentano's and studied the S.R.O. crowd.

Clemson House had just dispatched their newest star author on a 20-city signing tour...five-star accommodations all the way. A first printing of 500,000—numbers reserved for the *Bible* and *Playboy Calendar's 50th Anniversary*—with inside word that was just for starters. Clemson House expects second and third printings just as big. With numbers that huge, why go shabby for their newest literati, the cop who shoved Oliver Robbins into a vase at Forest Lawn.

I've done okay myself. I'd be a bald-faced liar if I didn't admit that there's been a noticeable—and much-desired—bump in my personal cash flow. Meetings with my publisher had never before been so laid back and pleasant. I can do no wrong in their eyes. But I'd also be remiss if I didn't mention the pangs of guilt I'd been struggling with these past few months, having personally profited from such a horrific series of events. I don't know, perhaps that's why God invented Vodka.

Maddie, Frances and I had gone on *Oprah* a short time after the dust had settled. I'd mumbled what I thought was a serious, albeit nervously tongue-tied, comment regarding Robbins' perverted psychosis in the first segment of her program only to have the audience laugh and clap uproariously. During the commercial break I turned around and brushed both nostrils with my thumb in case something might be hanging there, and then pretend smiled for the remainder of the talk show. However, Maddie and Frances were sufficiently bubbly and personable enough to carry the day. What the hell, at least they served free donuts in the green room.

In recent weeks Maddie appears on *Greta* nearly every other night, one of those regular experts they cut to for analyzing the crime-du-jour. She's got that certain knack for TV banter. I even heard a rumor that Court Channel plans to offer Maddie her own show.

Her Brentano's presentation was even being broadcast live on Booknotes, nationwide to C-SPAN's audience, thousands of book-buyers hungrily salivating to get their copy of—as the book jacket blurb put it—'The Inside Story by the Woman Homicide Detective Who Single-handedly Brought Justice to the Sleuth Slayer and Saved a Hundred Famous Writers!' For my money, Maddie's success couldn't have happened to a more calculating master of the criminal mind.

Racing faster, Maddie was now extemporizing, no longer reading.

"In their post-mortem searches, the FBI located boxes of Insecta-Gon hidden in Oliver Robbins' crawlspace along with a printout of instructions on how to distill the active ingredient from the pesticide into a highly lethal concentrate, a water-soluble paste. From my hospital room I heard one of the talking twits on CNN call it 'Robbins' Recipe for Writer-cide.' And the FBI found everything you could ever possibly want to know about the Agatha Awards on Robbins' hard drive. And a MapQuest from his place in Bel Air to the Scottsdale Four Seasons. And layouts of the Four Seasons' conference rooms. According to the final crime scene inventory, the twisted movie producer even had a Starbuck's apron, visor, and nametag hidden in his crawlspace. Every indication that Robbins planned on turning The Agathas into Jonestown."

I knew she'd borrowed that 'Jonestown' quip from *Newsweek*, whose cover story immediately after Maddie shot Robbins, had done a frighteningly graphic job of walking readers through the deadly scenario. Oliver Robbins sets up at the convention center at 6:45 a.m. Nobody's going to question some fat guy in a Starbucks apron setting up several vats of free Java and scones—not even if there's another table nearby with the usual hotel coffee and Danish. Nothing says "Good Morning" quite like a steaming cup of Almond Cappuccino laced with poly-Octachloro-dene—or whatever the hell the toxin is. And even if you could slightly taste the poly-Octa-whatever…when it comes to that first morning cup of Joe, the bitterer the better.

Thus, *Newsweek* had surmised, a French Vanilla or Hazelnut flavor would cover the mildly unusual odor, the slightly offish taste, half an hour later—fatal convulsions everywhere. By the time my writing colleagues came swarming into the morning's deathtrap, Robbins would already be 20 miles down the interstate. Or perhaps, the reporters speculated, a twist-o like Robbins would have hung around a bit, off in a dark corner, to watch the fun. Most authors thinking that first poor sod collapsed over there on the floor with the medics working on him, must be having a seizure or a heart attack and, by God, that certainly calls for a strong cup of Jamaica Morning. Then sick people rushing into the johns or hurrying back to their hotel rooms for the Pepto-Bismol. Who knows how much would've been guzzled before anyone realized it was in the coffee?

Maddie had autographed and FedExed me an advance copy of *Sleuth Slayer* a couple weeks back. But, having lived the harrowing thing, I put off actually reading her tale until a few days ago. Maybe I delayed because it was her first book and knowing I was one of the central figures, I feared she may not have captured all of my depth and complexity, you know, my dogged pursuit of truth. My being tough, sensitive, and brilliant in equal measures. That kind of stuff. Maddie had also handwritten something terribly sappy about me on the inside front page:

Davs,
I could never have done it without you.
Love,
Maddie

The speed and intensity of her voice signaled she was nearing the finish of her remarks.

"*…and into Robbins' nest of depravity. In retrospect it's easy to see how his inner reality had snapped some years earlier, his addictions, his incessant bizarre sexual experiences, the booze, and the anti-depressants aggravating an already bad chemical mixture in his*

189

brain. Or, in layman's term—my terms—Oliver Robbins had become flat-out evil."

I dislike attending book readings, especially my own, which, by the way, never draw a crowd remotely close to this Brentano's throng. And when I spoke I'd always noticed my clumsy wording and would self edit in mid-sentence. I'd all but whip out my red pen to correct myself as I mumbled into the microphone. While at readings by others I constantly had to stave off a Tourettes-like urge to make fish faces at the author and shout four-letter homonyms. But not today. Not at Maddie Neff's red-carpet maiden voyage. No, today would be far different. I'd see to that.

"...his jealousy flowed deep within Robbins' veins, haunted him through sleepless nights. Surrounded on all sides by the true talent he despised, he hid his secret cauldron of self-loathing that finally frothed into hatred and a bloody, homicidal thirst which demanded quenching."

Sure, her writing was over the top, but, hell, it was an over the top story. In the first days of release, advance sales for Lieutenant Madeleine Neff's *Sleuth Slayer,* subtitled *My Lethal Battle of Wits and Brawn with Scythe, the Serial Murderer* had flown off the store shelves. For a True Crime hit of this magnitude you'd have to go back to Capote's *In Cold Blood* or Bugliosi's Charles Manson piece *Helter Skelter.*

Frances, sitting beside the aisle in the middle row glanced anxiously about her, spotted me, and silently mouthed something disapproving, something suspiciously like 'It's about time, Dorkface!' Although I hoped I was mistaken about the sobriquet. I'd invited Thornton Senior to Maddie's book reading, but he had business pending in Europe. Life goes on.

"...thus Robbins' warped mind birthed a plan, a plan cultivated in the dark madness of his twisted psyche, a plan of vengeance on those who were his creative betters. Robbins was going to beat them at their own chosen game. Robbins had thought it brilliant, deliciously ironic, as—he proved he was more creative about their deaths than the writers had ever been in their lifework. No, this time Robbins would not use paper, film, canvass or clay. He'd write his epic in blood."

Maddie Neff gazed up from the podium, caught me standing in the back. I winked.

She winked back at me as she said, "Well, ladies and gentlemen, if you want to know more, you'll just have to pony up twenty odd bucks and buy the damn book. The video crew from 'Booknotes' asked me to leave plenty of time for a Q&A. But first we have a very rare treat today. I see in the audience famed mystery writer Guy Davitt, my longtime friend—and by a twist of fate, now one of my peers as a writer—and those of you who've already read an advance copy of *Sleuth Slayer*, you know Mr. Davitt was among Oliver Robbins' targeted victims."

There was a smattering of applause and a PBS techie in beard and Bermuda shorts crowded in near me and shoved a pole mike into my face.

"Good afternoon, Maddie." I showed my best Colgate smile, momentarily uneasy with all eyes zeroing in on me. "Great speech. You're a natural at this, I was sweating so hard before my first reading, I sprayed Right Guard on my face."

"The Margarita or three I had for lunch kicked in," Maddie deadpanned as laughter filled the room.

"Did you notice that Frances Whiting flew in for your reading?"

"Yes, Davs," Maddie scowled playfully at me, "some of my friends made it for this event on time."

The audience chuckled more and I hung my head in contrition until it subsided.

"Nice to have seen you again, Davs. Now if any members of the audience..."

"I enjoyed your book, Maddie...so much, in fact, that I read it three times in as many days."

"That is so nice of you to say, Davs," Maddie beamed. "Quite frankly, I was all braced for one of your acerbic quips. I did want you to write an advance quote, but the publisher felt that that wouldn't be appropriate as you factor so heavily in the book."

"That's too bad, Maddie. I'd have given you a quote that'd have done you proud."

"I'm definitely going to hunt you down for the second printing." Maddie glanced about the room, "Now, if anyone has a question for me please raise..."

"I discovered one minor puzzlement in your book," I interrupted, steadily grasping the pole mike.

Maddie looked at me quizzically. "And what would that be, Davs?"

"In that very gripping passage about Scythe's first break-in to my home...page 144 to be exact...I found your account of how Scythe achieved it riveting."

"Thank you very much for the praise, Davs. As a first time author I worked extremely hard for perfect accuracy." She smiled and turned to look at the other side of the crowd, "Now, any comments or questions from you ladies and gentlemen?"

I held tight to the PBS pole mike so the techie couldn't move it away from my voice, "On page 144 you wrote something perplexing.

191

You wrote 'while seated at Davitt's computer, Oliver Robbins—Scythe—stared out the big bay window. There, in the light of the full moon, in the rear yard, flowering with its enormous bouquet of red and gold energy, stood the tall bloom of a magnificent Century Plant, its towering stalk bulging with a thousand blue yucca spikes. After a long moment's distraction while studying this rarest of sights, Scythe returned to the business of hacking into Guy Davitt's desktop....' The plant is a beautiful plant, by the way, but how did you turn those facts up?"

"I've been to your house, Guy. Although I was careful not to write about your sinkful of dirty dishes." Maddie giggled along with the audience. "Now are there any other..."

"But at the time my landlord's Century Plant was in bloom the floor space in front of the bay window was wide open. Purposely. Just a throw rug. I loved to...as did my various houseguests during all of last May and June...loved to stand for hours in the bay window and look at the magnificent blooming plant. Which was lit, by the way, on moonless nights by an outdoor spotlight my landlord had mounted on the eaves."

"Moonlight, spotlight? You say tomahto, I say tomayto," Maddie laughed, "now do any others..."

"My computer table was not in that room, not by the bay window. I had my computer set up far away in another room. Not until September when the Century Plant stopped blooming did I put it in front of the bay window. How do you account for that bit of perfect accuracy, Maddie?"

"Well, the computer table stood exactly there by the bay window when LAPD removed your desktop to investigate the hard drive."

"Which was many weeks after the Century Plant stopped its bloom, Maddie. It was also weeks after the Century Plant had bloomed when Scythe first appeared at the WatChat room."

"Irrelevant trivia, Davs. I really must insist we move on to questions from others in the aud..."

"Meaning the *real* Scythe first broke into my place long before Jax was killed, long before the WatChat events. Meaning the *real* Scythe stood in that bay window months earlier at night, and was as captivated by the sight of the Century Plant as everybody else was. It was impossible not to be."

Maddie Neff's smile showed definite stress. "What do you mean, Davs, the *real* Scythe? The *real* Scythe was Oliver Robbins of Pentathlon Productions."

"Maybe you should've checked Oliver Robbins' travel schedule and compared that to the blooming of the Century Plant. And those few nights when there was visible moonlight in the L.A. Basin, for that matter," I persisted. "If you had, Lieutenant Neff, you'd find the things you described on page 144 were not physically possible. Not if Oliver Robbins was really Scythe."

"Look, Davs, I'm sorry, but this just isn't the place for such quibbling." Maddie looked solicitous, trying for humor but now her nervousness poked through, "I know it hurt your feelings when I turned you down as my co-author for *Sleuth Slayer*—I know how terribly disappointed that made you—but I really needed to write this on my own. It worked as catharsis during my healing."

"Co-author?" The nasty looks from the audience didn't keep me from bursting out in laughter. "I love a girl who can think on her feet, Maddie, and this entire scam of yours has been a case study in manipulation." I bowed in her direction. "My sincere compliments, your choice of a fall guy to frame was inspired—when Homicide's Greatest Heroine emptied half her clip into him the damn town was too busy singing 'Ding-Dong, the Witch is Dead' to take a cold, hard look. Until now."

"Fall guy? Frame?" Neff shook her head. "I have absolutely no idea what you're going on about."

The crowd had grown weary of me. A wave of disgruntled voices rippled across the room. The woman in front of me turned around and told me, in no uncertain terms, to *shut up*! I felt some firm nudges against my back and from both sides.

"Let him speak," a nervously smiling Frances stood and held her palms out to quiet the audience. "Please. Please, I'd like to hear what Mr. Davitt has to say."

"Hell, Lieutenant, your scenario was a Masters' thesis in misdirection. You spun everyone every which way but toward the truth. You placed the spotlight on the Thornton dynasty...had us pry up that fresh scab...and blunder our way through a Shakespearean tragedy. Then you red-herringed the focus onto the quintessential Hollywood gasbag that was Oliver Robbins." I ignored the scattered hisses rumbling from the crowd and clung tightly to the C-SPAN microphone, "The things you described were possible only to the real Scythe, not the late Oliver Robbins. The real Scythe whose cash borrowings from her LAPD retirement account, it seems, coincide exactly with certain deposits by one Charlie Upchucks Pizzaro, Scythe's junior employee and all around patsy, later found in the Los Angeles reservoir with numerous bullets through his skull."

193

Maddie's eyes burned through me. I looked about the room and saw surprise and confusion. Some muttered in protest at my dominating the microphone—but I also saw the C-SPAN crew whispering together, saw the director's gesture, then felt the techies' grip relax and leave the microphone to me. *Booknotes* had never before captured such live drama.

A second pole mike angled toward me, the local ABC affiliate had now materialized…thank you, Judge.

Now my voice was sure and forceful, "I had a long talk with Frances Whiting, and then with my father. And yesterday we all had a pow-wow with LAPD's Captain Vasquez. You were right about the captain, Maddie, he misses nothing. Initially he wanted to toss us out on our ears—to put it nicely—but then he started to track the time sequences, when you'd taken off this past year. He expected to quickly prove us wrong. Can you guess what he found instead?"

The room was hushed. Maddie Neff stood silent at the podium.

"I'm late today because I had to wait for a call, get the results from a search warrant. It turns out Maddie Neff wasn't listed on any flight itineraries to Minnesota or Connecticut or Canada at the time of those murders, but I wonder what the names on those fake IDs Vasquez found inside that carton of frozen chicken in your freezer will turn up? Hmm. Vasquez thinks you traveled as the anonymous 'Carol Brown,' but my money's on the one named 'Laura Leigh.'"

I locked eyes with Frances. She nodded for me to continue, to end this travesty once and for all.

"I doubt you ever spent your vacation time on any singles' cruise, did you Maddie? And what do you suppose those make-believe vacations of yours could possibly align with?"

"Fuck you, Davitt."

"What's wrong, Lieutenant?" I looked about at the now still, edge-of-their-seats crowd and then back at Neff—the bona fide Sleuth Slayer, and asked, "Are you not enjoying your Perry Mason moment?"

Maddie Neff started left from the podium to exit. She saw her way was blocked by a deadly serious Captain Vasquez and another plainclothesman, badges exhibited and coats open to reveal calm hands resting on their weapons. She turned right hoping to leave that way, only to find herself facing several Federal Marshals led by The Judge, who was grinning so much like the Cheshire cat I half expected him to belch feathers.

I continued speaking into the microphone. "Demonically clever, Maddie—investigating murders that you yourself had planned. Setting up suspects. Using Pizzaro for thug work. And disposing of your fall guy, Oliver Robbins, in your thrilling personal confrontation with pure evil, right out of a grade-B film script. Your slip-ups were never in the murders themselves, but in your writing. For a long time you pulled my strings, but once you committed it to paper, Lieutenant Neff, you entered my world."

"You're a lying prick!" she shot back at me.

"You'd never have had Pizzaro at your house, but, Dear God Maddie, was he ever in your car? How'd he get to the aqueduct? And now that they're fascinated," I motioned toward a solemn Captain Vasquez, "I wonder what other interesting tidbits LAPD's full procto scan will reveal."

"You goddamned bastard, Davitt, I should have...." realizing the less said for the TV cameras the better, Maddie suddenly bit her lips together. Tightly. But her green eyes flared into me with burning, murderous hate.

"I have a newsflash, Lieutenant Neff." I wish I felt triumphant, but my thoughts leapt back to that picture of Jax and myself, the one that hung above his computer everyday as he wrote his books. "You just went out of print."

They cuffed her. Led her down the aisle as she mumbled something about "Johnny Cochran this...Goddamn Joke... laughed out of court." But her lethal, barbwire gaze never strayed from mine.

Captain Vasquez, the consummate politician, took control of the microphone and turned the arrest into an impromptu press conference. Instead of staying, I chose to follow Maddie as they perp-walked her out the door. I watched as a police car, siren blaring, did an abrupt u-turn and squealed to curbside. The officer leading Maddie opened the rear door, put his hand on her head, pressed her down into a different part of the squad car than she was normally accustomed to and slammed the door. Our eyes stayed glued together as the car sped from the curb.

Five minutes later a couple of kitchen employees found two unconscious uniformed cops, both had been anesthetized. They'd been stuffed into a food dumpster in the alley at the rear of the Kaplan Brothers Deli across from the book store. The officer's hands and feet were flex cuffed, duct tape expertly wound across their mouths and eyes but leaving their nostrils clear for breathing.

And if these were the officers that Captain Vasquez had at the ready to transport Madeleine Neff downtown, exactly who were the imposter blues that had spirited her away?

Epilogue

"What you do in this world is a matter of no consequence. The question is, what can you make people believe that you have done?"
-Sir Arthur Conan Doyle

I'm asked all the time why Maddie Neff did it. Fame? Fortune? Vengeance? Childhood trauma? Bad Karma? Take your pick. Here's mine.

Bitter from endless acknowledgments, finished with being the bridesmaid…an idea had taken root in Lieutenant Neff's psyche. Deep root. Imagine if Jodi Foster's FBI agent had mocked up the homicides in *Silence of the Lambs* in order to reap the whirlwind of superstardom in a media-crazed culture. That's exactly what Lieutenant Madeleine Neff did. She knew the book and movie deals would pour in, along with guest spots on *Oprah*, *Geraldo*, *Larry King*, and *Greta*.

Yes, Lieutenant Maddie Neff had positioned herself so she controlled the harvest of all the evidence—everything visible was the fruit of her poison tree. She was puppet master to a dozen dupes, the foremost dupe bearing my name.

Wish I could paint myself the hero of this train wreck. But I'm only the guy who stumbled into knowing where the marbles are. My everlasting regret is that I was thoughtless and didn't jump in when my young friend and fellow writer Jax Thornton needed me most. Needed my belief in him. A cruel mistake that shall haunt me the rest of my life.

The police have not found hide nor hair of Lieutenant Maddie Neff. It certainly turned out not to be the career-boosting publicity plug Captain Vasquez was looking for, but he strikes me as the type who always lands on his feet. Of course the conspiracy theories abound. Some cops say there must have been more Charlie "Upchucks" Pizarros in the woodwork that sprung her for their own reasons. Others think some of Maddie's pals at LAPD engineered her escape. Frances even sent me a link to a rival hack's web site where my envious colleague pins the entire elaborate kit and kaboodle on little ol' moi.

As for little ol' moi, I have a wild theory that nobody will ever prove but allows me to close my eyes at night. I'd always wondered why Thornton Senior couldn't put off his European business trip when I'd called him about Maddie's upcoming book signing. I didn't directly tell him about the fireworks in store, but strongly urged that he make every effort to attend.

I did get a postcard from Thornton Senior awhile later from somewhere in the South of France, near Cannes, judging from the blurred postmark. The picture is a sweeping panorama of the Mediterranean. On the back a jotted note, not terribly long, very inexplicit, but the words hit me like a shot to my solar plexus nevertheless. It was the kind of message that might make a guy feel a bit paranoid, make him start thinking his phone's been bugged…he's been followed…closely monitored.

Thornton Senior's tantalizing message: "Dear Guy, Thanks for being the big brother my boy never had. I had an inkling you'd ferret out the truth and you certainly didn't let me down." Then, after his scrawled initials, he wrote a two- sentence postscript: "It's a small world, Guy, you'd be utterly astounded who I bumped into over here. I doubt she'll be coming back anytime soon."

It looks like Maddie finally got her chance to see Europe, albeit a truncated stay…

As for the pound of paper you're holding in your hands—well, this book is for my diminutive pal, Jax Thornton III—the true hero of this train wreck of betrayal, murder, and intrigue.

Dedication from *The True Sleuth Slayer*
A True-crime Bestseller by mystery writer
Timothy "Guy" Davitt
Published by Barnstorm Press

ABOUT THE AUTHORS

The lies of Jeffrey B. Burton have appeared in dozens of mystery, horror, and science fiction magazines. His collection of horror stories, *Shadow Play*, was published in the dead of winter, 2005. Jeff is a member of the Horror Writers Association. Visit Jeff's website at: www.SomeHack.com

Bruce W. Burton has published dozens of law articles and books, but *Sleuth Slayer* is his first work of fiction.

www.ingramcontent.com/pod-product-compliance
Lightning Source LLC
Chambersburg PA
CBHW051653260626
47170CB00004B/1477